Kingdom of Thorns

A Sleeping Beauty Retelling

Katherine Macdonald

Cover design by: GermanCreative
Title page, dividers, chapter headings etc: Elisha Bugg (Inkwolf Designs)
Rose Motif: Katherine Meyrick
Edited by: Jess Lawrence

Contents

"Within a quarter of an hour there grew up all round the park so vast a quantity of trees big and small, with interlacing brambles and thorns, that neither man nor beast could penetrate them."

LES CONTES DE PERRAULT, AN EDITION OF CHARLES PERRAULT'S FAIRY TALES ILLUSTRATED BY GUSTAVE DORÉ, ORIGINALLY PUBLISHED IN 1862.

Prologue

She should not have gone to the wishing well.

It was a thought that would haunt her for years afterwards, a regret that stung every moment she felt a twinge of happiness. But she did not know then, what true misery was like. She did not know true fear. She was not yet a mother.

Eleanora couldn't remember not wanting to be one. There must have been some time in her childhood where such a thing hadn't really mattered, but those days were as dull as a rusted blade. Her desire had nothing to do with her duties as queen; the longing went deeper than that, the emptiness of each barren year swelling into a cavern inside her. Her grief for something she had not even lost carved out riverlets where a child should have been.

She had dreamed of having several. Now she thought she could be content with only one.

So when she heard that there was a well nearby that could grant wishes, how could she resist? It did not matter that the locals warned her the well had a way of twisting those wishes, distorting them until you regretted ever asking. It did not matter.

Anything for a child. Anything at all.

How could she ever regret holding a healthy babe in her

arms? That was all she needed, all she craved. She would have been willing to pay with her life, the emptiness consumed her so.

She dithered a little, her fingers shaking over the darkness of the pool, as if that blackness were a tangible thing she could feel on her skin. A cold, creeping sensation spread up her arm.

Don't do it.

She dropped the coin.

It broke the surface of the water far below, sharp and sudden and endless. That moment went on forever.

"What did you wish for?" asked a voice.

Queen Eleanora startled. At the edge of the glade was a beautiful woman in a gown the colour of night. Her white skin shone iridescently, making her violet eyes glow. Thick chestnut hair fell around her shoulders. She flashed the queen a radiant smile, filled with flawless teeth. She was not human. A fairy. There were a few still living within their realm. Eleanora had been tutored by one herself. But there was something... different about this one. A chill that her smile couldn't mask.

"I... I..." Eleanora's words fell away from her.

"I hear there's some myth around the human folk that if you tell someone a wish, it won't come true," said the fairy, "but I assure you, that is not the case. You made a wish. I might be the answer. If you tell me."

Eleanora saw no harm in it. She had made the wish already. Surely that meant it would come true regardless of her next actions?

She swallowed. "A child," she said. "My husband and I have been married for many years now, but we have never been able to conceive. I... I *must* have one. I must."

The fairy tilted her head. "For your kingdom?" she asked softly.

Eleanora bristled. She was not wearing a crown. Her clothes were fine, but not ostentatious. There might have been a Verona royal crest somewhere–

"Do not worry yourself, Your Majesty. The face of a queen is not one easily forgotten. But please do answer; do you seek a child for yourself, or your kingdom?"

She should have lied. Perhaps things might have been different. Perhaps not. "For myself," she admitted.

"And what would you give for such a blessing?"

"Anything," said the queen, without hesitation. "I would give you anything you wanted."

The fairy smiled. "I can cure your infertility. But in return, I will hold you to that."

The queen glanced back at the well.

"You made a wish," said the fairy. "I have an answer. Your fertility. Any one thing. Do we have a deal?"

The emptiness inside her swelled. "Yes," she said. "We have a deal."

A year later, Eleanora sat in the throne room, the gleaming halls bedecked in banners, the guests flocking in to welcome the new little princess. Briar-Rose lay in her cradle, gurgling and babbling, blue-eyed and rosy-cheeked. She was the most perfect creation Eleanora had ever seen, a view echoed by her husband, who promptly declared a feast in her honour and invited every fairy in the land to attend.

A quiet dread padded inside her. She had not heard from the one who met her at the well. She had not demanded her payment.

She glanced back at her daughter.

Whatever it is, it was worth it, she convinced herself. *As long as I have her.*

Twelve fairies pooled into the hall and made their way towards the cradle to coo over the princess and bless her with their gifts. The thirteenth was not amongst them.

"Strength," said the first fairy, as the infant wrapped her fist around her long, elegant finger. "She can work out for herself what that means."

A small, green-haired fairy, half the size of the others, crept up to the crib. "Song," she said, "so that she may find joy even in the dark."

A stately, eagle-eyed fairy placed a hand on her shoulder, nodding approvingly. "Intelligence."

"Resourcefulness."

"Courage."

"Determination."

"Sass–"

"Ariel!" snapped the stately fairy. "You can't gift a princess with *sass!*"

"Why not?"

"It's unbecoming!"

The yellow-haired fairy pouted, her gold wings flickering. "Fine. Wit, then. Be funny, human child. Find laughter when there is little to be laughed at."

The stately fairy seemed to approve, and backed down to let the remaining five impart theirs. 'Resilience', 'kindness', 'practicality', and 'beauty' followed, the last receiving a tut from some of the other fairies, who considered it to be an outdated gift. The eleventh fairy huffed and said all the good ones had been taken. The twelfth fairy, now looking very nervous, stepped up to take her place.

A cool and sudden wind seized the throne room. The sun slid behind a cloud. The other lights grew dim, and a woman, cold as she was beautiful, appeared in the centre of the room.

The queen stifled a cry. The Thirteenth Fairy. The one from the well.

"Good day, Your Majesties," said the dark fairy, stooping into a low bow. Her shimmering purple robes brushed against the flagstones, like liquid smoke. "My, my, my. What a happy day we see before us. The queen has finally birthed a child. You must all be so *thrilled.*"

The queen let out a slight whimper, inching towards the crib.

"You have not forgotten then, I see," said the dark fairy. "Do you remember what you promised me, Eleanora, if I could cure your infertility?"

The queen shuddered. "I promised you... anything you

wanted."

"*Anything I wanted...*" The fairy smiled. "Anything. That was our bargain. You said you would do anything, give anything. At the time, I believed you meant it. Do you still, I wonder?"

The king snapped his fingers. A dozen guards pointed their lancets.

"Be gone, sorceress. You were not invited."

"By the laws of fairy, by which the queen is bound, I will have my payment. I demand your firstborn child."

"No!" wailed the queen. "Please! Anything but her!"

"You can have another now, you know. You won't have to wait long. My kind... well, that's a different matter. You could have a dozen, if you wished. We are not so fortunate. My exchange is more than fair."

"You will not have my daughter!" said the king. "She is not my wife's alone to bargain with. She is ours, not yours. She will never be yours."

The fairy's eyes darkened. "We shall see. Very well, Your Majesties. You may keep your child. She will be yours for seventeen years. But hear this: on the day of her seventeenth birthday, the princess will prick her finger on a spinning wheel, and fall down *dead*."

"No!" The queen clutched the baby to her chest, who squirmed and wriggled, oblivious to the curse that had just been thrown upon her.

The fairy smiled. "Seventeen years you will have to love her, to watch your affection for her multiply by the day. And when that day comes... when you see your beloved child lying dead at your feet... ask yourself if it was worth it. If you wouldn't have much rather given her to me seventeen years ago."

She vanished in a flash of darkness.

The king turned to the remaining fairies. "Help us," he said. "Take away the curse, I beg you!"

The fairies looked amongst themselves.

"We cannot," said the stately one. "You cannot undo a curse, only break it. But all curses can be broken."

"How will we break this one?"

"True love always works," said one fairy. "But that is a rare thing. Why, you could wait a hundred years for that to happen…"

The final fairy sighed. "I have an idea," she said. "I can soften the curse, though not undo it. If… if I may?"

The king and queen nodded vehemently, and the final fairy crept towards the princess, still held tightly in her mother's arms.

"Little princess, you shall not die as the curse commands, but fall into a sleep like death, to be awakened by the kiss of one with a noble heart. In this slumber you shall remain for one hundred years, and awake as if no time has passed at all."

She sealed the protection with a kiss of her own.

"A hundred years?" said the queen.

"It is as many as I can manage. It is as much as I can do."

"Will any kiss awaken her?"

The fairy shook her head. "Would that it were that easy. No, it will have to be a special kiss, something pure… else anyone, including yourselves, could break it. Dark magic is seldom easy to break."

"A hundred years," wept the queen. "We may never see her awaken."

The stately one sighed, and placed a gentle hand on the queen's arm. "In seventeen years, we shall return. We shall place the kingdom in a similar slumber, to awaken when the princess does. You shall never be without your child."

"Thank you," said the king. "A thousand thanks and more."

"Do not thank us yet," returned the fairy, "but let us pray that you may one day have cause to rejoice. Call on us if ever you have need. Until that day, farewell."

Part 1

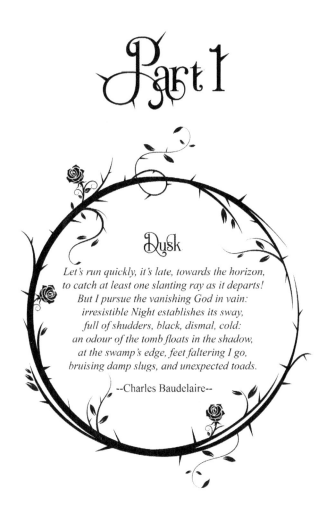

Dusk

Let's run quickly, it's late, towards the horizon,
to catch at least one slanting ray as it departs!
But I pursue the vanishing God in vain:
irresistible Night establishes its sway,
full of shudders, black, dismal, cold:
an odour of the tomb floats in the shadow,
at the swamp's edge, feet faltering I go,
bruising damp slugs, and unexpected toads.

--Charles Baudelaire--

1

The Quest Begins

A hundred and seventeen years later, minus a few weeks, Prince Leopold of Germaine and his entourage reached the village on the edge of the forest that now divided what remained of the Kingdom of Verona from the rest of the world. The story of its downfall was legendary, how the Princess Briar-Rose had been cursed from birth to prick her finger on a spinning wheel and fall into a death-like slumber, and how the entire kingdom slept behind a forest of thorns, waiting for her to be awakened with a kiss. By royal decree, whoever rescued her would win her hand, a binding agreement, a prize worth the danger that lurked within the forest.

Over the years, hundreds had braved the place. Many had perished. Those that returned spoke of untold horrors, of an evil that inhabited every shadow. It was said that the wicked fairy who cast the curse still resided within, preventing it from ever being lifted.

Stories told that when the time was up, not only would the inhabitants finally succumb to the ravages of time, but that the evil fairy would be freed to wreak havoc on the world.

King Albert, Leopold's father, was keen to avoid such an occurrence. Germaine sat right on the borders of the Kingdom of Thorns. They would be the first to fall. For years, knights had been sent into the dark, but none prevailed. Finally, he consulted a good fairy, who told him to send his son. She could not tell which one.

Everyone expected it to be his eldest, Wilheim. He may have been the crown prince, but he was the bravest and the strongest. If anyone stood a chance of surviving the woods, it was surely him. Wilheim knew this. He heard the fairy's words, nodded, and promised that he would do it for his kingdom.

But waking the princess meant having to marry her. It was binding. It could not be broken. Wilheim was already in love, and Jakob was too young. What kind of brother would Leo be, if he was prepared to jeopardise one brother's happiness, or another's life? And what kind of prince would he be to risk the heir to the throne?

A cowardly one, he thought.

He could see the forest now, behind the village, stretching for miles and miles, the kingdom swallowed by the trees. It looked like a dark shadow on the land, a stain on the fields. What was he thinking? He was not built for this. Yes, he had been trained in combat, but no amount of training could stop the tremor in his legs.

Wilheim would not have been so afraid.

He took a deep breath. "We should stop for the night," he told his party. "One final comfortable sleep. Begin at first light."

No one argued, though there was plenty of light left. They made their way to a nearby inn. It was too early to be busy in the tavern below, but a group of the king's men entering the room sucked any chatter away entirely. The people of the village knew the deadline was looming, and didn't know if they should be elated or horrified by the presence of the young prince in their midst. Was the king truly that desperate?

Leo ordered a round of drinks and something warm to eat. "Have many travelled into the woods of late?" he asked the barkeeper.

The man nodded solemnly. "Many a last-ditch attempt these past few weeks." He pointed to a group of three men, huddled in a corner by the fire, their eyes dark and hollow. "Those three came out a week ago. One's still upstairs recovering. But most of the folk here have tried it at some point."

"I didn't know there were so many survivors."

"There aren't," said the barkeeper darkly. "That group of men by the fire? Ten went in."

Leo swallowed, thanked the man for his intel, and went to speak to the group. "Good afternoon, gentlemen," he said. Only a couple of eyes glanced his way. "I am sorry to disturb your rest, but my companions and I are bound for the forest and–"

"Don't do it," one of them said. "Nothing is worth it. Nothing."

"I'm afraid I have little choice."

One of the men looked at him fully, taking in his immaculate clothes, slim frame, unblemished skin, and judged him eminently unsuitable. "No prize is worth it," he said. "Go home, boy."

Leo did not like calling a living human being a *prize* no matter how much of a stranger she was, but pointing that out was unlikely to gain him any favours. "I do not seek the princess," he said. "I seek to save the kingdom. Perhaps two. We are short on time–"

"No horrors the fairy could bring are equal to the ones that lie inside."

"You should have taken a guide," said another man at another table. "Tried it myself a few years ago. Didn't get far, but stayed safe... mostly." He held up a hand, revealing two missing fingers.

"The guide," said another, not far away. "You should have taken her."

"Talia," said a third. He was as wrinkled as a prune in a pint glass, not an inch of him free from the look of well-beaten leather. "She's as wise as she is old!" he said with a cackle. "What she doesn't know about the forest isn't worth knowing. Why didn't you take her?"

One of the recent adventurers shrugged. "Didn't want to waste our supplies on another person, or our energies protecting her."

The old man snorted. "Talia can look after herself."

"Where do we find her?" Leo asked.

"Ring the bells," said one of the travellers. "By the edge of the forest. Ring the bells, and wait for her. She will come."

He looked back at his own men, a few of whom were listening in. He thanked the gentlemen for their time, and went back to join them. He tried to partake in their revelry and enthusiasm, but his stomach had no appetite, and he wasn't interested in drinking. He wanted his wits about him for the journey tomorrow. His knights had no such reserves, although George looked a little apprehensive.

"How are you, George?"

The knight shrugged. He was one of Wilheim's finest and had been in his service for as long as Leo could remember. He'd never seen him nervous before.

"I'd hear your worries."

"Not worries," the knight assured him. "Only... only just before I left, Clara told me... well, it looks like she's finally expecting."

Leo beamed, clapping his friend on the back. "Well, that's wonderful news! You must be thrilled!"

"Thank you, Your Highness."

George did not look thrilled, even though he and Clara had been married for several years and a child had long been expected. *Of course,* thought Leo, *with all this talk of dangers, he's worried he won't ever meet it.*

"You should have said something, George. There are other knights–"

"There are, but I'm one of the best, and Wilheim was insistent–"

"You didn't tell him, I take it?"

He shook his head.

"If you wanted to back out now..."

"I couldn't, Your Highness. Please don't ask me to. One more request and I'll consider it."

Leo smiled grimly. It was tempting. "Another round, I think." He got up, but George forced him back down and said he'd get it. He'd barely been gone a second before a tankard sloshed in front of Leo.

"Drink up, lad," said the ancient man, slumping into

George's seat. "You'll need the energy for your journey." He grabbed Leo's arm, squeezing tightly. "You've some muscle on you, at least." His face came uncomfortably close. "Good looking, too."

"Why... why would that help me?"

"Never underestimate the charms of a pretty face!" he hooted.

Leo sighed, running a hand through his thick chestnut hair, feeling more and more self-conscious by the minute. At least the growing rowdiness of the tavern meant he stuck out less.

"You're a prince then, I take it?" the old man asked, pointing to the crest on his tunic. Leo had tried to dress down, but his mother was insistent that no son of hers should go gallivanting off into the forests without looking a *little* regal. She didn't mean to sound vain. Her insistence was born out of the desire to control something, *anything* about the situation.

They hadn't spoken a great deal before he left. They had so much and nothing at all to say.

"I'd go in your place, if I thought it would do any good," she said, her jaw tightly clenched. She forced a hard kiss on him, and then swept from the room. He heard her weeping in the corridor. She would have said something else, the next morning, if he'd given her the opportunity. But he couldn't. She might beg him to stay, kingdom be damned and dash the consequences, and few things were harder to say no to than a weeping mother.

"Second prince," he said in answer to the old man's question.

"Not in it for the glory, then? The prize?"

"I hardly think a *person* can be described as a prize," he snapped. "Forgive me, that was rude."

"Was it?" The old man's golden eyes twinkled. "You may be right, lad. But if you're not interested in the princess, why risk it?"

"For my kingdom," he said. "And hers. Small as it may be, I do not want the weight of their deaths if I do nothing at all."

"A noble endeavour," he said.

"Or a cowardly one. I'm only doing it so I don't feel the guilt of *not* doing it later."

The man smiled. "Drink up. Get some rest. Remember the bit about the guide." He got up and hobbled back to the bar, leaving Leo alone while the rest of his men drank themselves into a stupor.

He excused himself early from the revelries, craving silence over distraction, and made his way upstairs to the chambers he had procured for their usage. Halfway there, one of the doors at the end of the corridor opened. He could hear moaning within, and a healer hurried out. She closed the door behind her and nodded to him.

"Another victim of the forest," she said. "I hope his moaning doesn't disturb you."

"What's... what's wrong with him?"

"Went in with a whole mind, came back with half of one. There's more than monsters in those there woods."

Leo prickled. "Can you heal him?"

She gave a non-committal gesture. "I do not know. Sometimes time heals them, sometimes... nothing does."

"We're supposed to be setting off into the woods tomorrow..."

The healer's face paled. "I would advise against it, but if you are set on your path, take–"

"The guide, yes. We've been told."

She nodded. "Good luck, sir. Take care."

She hurried off down the stairs.

The moaning intensified as Leo passed the door, but he dared not look inside. The sound seemed to penetrate the walls, groaning into the wood as Leo lay on his bed. He imagined dark, empty eyes, a hollowness where a soul used to sit.

His men trickled in as the night wore on. Would that be them, in a few days' time?

Or would they be the empty chairs at the adventurers' table?

Leo did not sleep easily. He could not unlatch the empty look in the adventurers' eyes from the back of his mind, nor the missing fingers of the one that proclaimed he was protected, or dissolve the groans of that haunted man. Just what had his men signed up for? Most of them had families to support, families that would struggle without them... or who would share in their suffering if they survived.

And numbers hadn't mattered to that one group.

Would George's child ever know its father?

He pondered on it for hours, and as the watery light rose into the room, he made up his mind. He crawled out of his bed, picked up his pack, left half of the money his father had given him for the journey, and headed downstairs.

He would brave the forests alone, along with this guide. No one else had to die or be hurt because of this. Just him.

He crept downstairs. It was too early for even the barkeeper to be awake. Several of the patrons, including the recent adventurers, were passed out in their places. The room was filled only with the sound of shuffling bodies, snoring, and the soft puff-puff of a pipe.

"Good morning, Your Highness." The old man from last night was wide awake, puffing away silently in the corner.

"Shouldn't you be asleep, old man?" Leo snapped. He was in no mood to converse, and he didn't want to risk rousing the others.

"Oh-ho-ho!" the old man cackled. "And yet you were so polite when everyone else was around!"

Leopold fidgeted with the hem of his sleeve. "Sorry, I get rude when I'm nervous."

"Going off to the woods alone, are we?"

He nodded. "I... I didn't mean to disturb your rest. Or snap at you."

The old man waved his hand. "Ah, at this age, sleeping seems like a waste of my very precious time. Come, I'll walk you to the forest."

"That's not–"

"It could be my dying wish!"

"You're looking fairly spritely to me."

"Good, then you won't have any problem with me walking you to the edge of the forest." He seized his walking stick.

"Come on, it's almost dawn."

They set off at a brisk pace, considering how ancient the man was. The bluish light lifted. Dawn crackled along the horizon, like ribbons of liquid fire. Morning dew coated the ground. Leo tried to enjoy it, but he couldn't shake the growing feeling of dread as the blackness of the forest grew larger. He doubted he would see much sunlight in there. What if this was the last true sunrise he ever knew?

"Nervous?" asked the old man.

"I'm about to enter a deadly forest by myself that has an impressively high mortality rate. Wouldn't you be?"

The old man hooted. "Honest *and* amusing. You'll do well."

"I fail to see how either of those things will help me in there."

"I don't know, humour wards off insanity, or so I hear."

"You're really selling this experience for me."

The old man laughed long and hard. Leo really couldn't see how he could find amusement in such a thing.

"I... I left a letter, for my family, back at the inn," he told him. "Could you... could you make sure my knights find it, just in case?" He'd written it before setting off from the castle, knowing his strength could well fail him before that point, but he hadn't had the courage to leave it then. It was almost like admitting defeat.

The old man nodded, the light in his gold eyes dimming. "Stick close to Talia," he said. "Heed her instructions. *Listen to her.*"

"It is a fool that does not listen to those wiser than himself," Leo said, repeating an old proverb. "And a fool who believes himself wise."

The man agreed, and pointed ahead. They had reached the edge of the forest. A silver bell hung from one of the trees, and someone, a long time ago, had etched 'ring for the forest guide' into the bark. There were signs of it having been re-etched over the years.

"Thank you," said Leo.

"You are welcome, young man. Good luck. You appear to have a good enough head on your shoulders, but at times, you may need to listen to your heart. Farewell."

The old man turned, leaving Leo to stare at the bell and summon the faint remnants of his courage. He could not falter here. This was only the beginning.

He rang the bell.

A breeze whispered through the trees, stirring the branches, twisting the darkness within like a spot of blue in black paint. He tried not to shiver, stamping his feet to gain a fragment of warmth, and stared up at the sky.

"Are you looking for passage?" said a voice from behind.

Leo turned back to the forest. A woman stood there, perhaps a girl. She was far younger than he envisioned. He was expecting a much older woman, someone gnarled and weather-beaten, but he would be surprised if she was much older than he was. There was a grimness to her features, aided by the layers of mud baked onto her clothes and skin, but beneath that... no, she wasn't old, despite the weariness in her eyes. Was this perhaps Talia's assistant, or her daughter?

She was otherwise unremarkable, of average height and build, with mouse-coloured hair and stormy eyes. A locket of some kind, about the size and shape of a walnut, hung around her neck. It was the only thing that distinguished her from the woods behind, a flash of gold amongst the brown, green and grey.

"Are you... Talia?" he asked, his voice catching.

The guide bristled, as if unused to the sound of her own name. "Expecting something else?"

"Which answer would you prefer?"

Talia ignored his question. "Are you alone?"

"Yes."

She admired his clothes for a moment. Her gaze was unnerving, like she was stripping him naked. Her eyes lingered where his armour should have been, and over the crest he bore on his clasps.

"You are no knight," she deduced. "Though you carry yourself well, and your hands are no strangers to some combat, at least. You're a lot younger than most who come here, barely more than a man. A noble?"

Leo gave an awkward bow. "Prince Leopold," he said. "Second prince of Germaine."

"Second prince?" she raised an eyebrow. "Out of how many?"

"Three," he said.

"Are you the fastest and the strongest and the smartest? Is that why they sent you? Or are you just the most... expendable?"

It was a word that frequently trummed, unspoken, in the back of his own mind. It hurt no less coming from a stranger. "Um, well, actually... my older brother, Wilheim, was initially chosen, but..."

"But?"

"He's fallen in love with someone. He was prepared to do his duty, of course, but... I didn't want to see him so unhappy. And Jakob may be much smarter than me, but he's only fifteen. Too young. So I volunteered."

"Volunteered? You make it sound so noble. There's a terrific prize at the end if you succeed, or so I hear."

"I... that's not quite..."

"Go on."

"I mean, I've no grand desire to marry someone I don't know, and I daresay she hasn't either. That's not why I'm doing this."

"Then why are you doing it?"

"No one wants the dark fairy free," he told her. "And time is running out. Germaine will be the first country hit if she escapes, so..."

"So... your parents sent their child out into the forests alone–"

"I had men with me. They're back at the tavern."

"Why did you abandon them?"

"I didn't want any more than was necessary to risk their lives."

"Hmm. Noble. Or foolish."

"From what I hear, numbers don't seem to help much in there."

"We'll see, won't we, Your Highness?"

"You can call me Leo, if you like. I daresay formalities are rather pointless in the forest."

Talia snorted, and then stood up straight. "I daresay... you're probably right." She surveyed him again. "What do you have in that pack of yours? I travel light, as you can see." She had a knife strapped to her side, a few packs on her belt. Nothing else, no bedrolls or bulky equipment.

"Oh, I–"

"Unpack it."

He did as she asked, spreading out his rations, bedroll, cooking utensils, medical kit, a pouch of coins, and weapons. Talia gave them an approving nod.

"Good," she said. "You are decently prepared. Very well, young Leo, I shall escort you into the woods on three further conditions."

"Yes?"

"One, you have to follow my instructions. You run when I say you run, and fight when I say you fight. Two, if I cannot answer a question, you drop it. You do not argue. Clear?"

Leo nodded. "And... third?"

"You don't touch me. Not a handshake, not a pat on the back... nothing."

Leo swallowed. He did not want to think about why she had such an aversion, and he certainly wasn't going to push it. "Of course."

"Good. Then we have a deal."

"How shall I pay you?"

Talia scoffed. "You can pay me when – *if* – we reach our destination."

"And if I die before then?"

"Then I will raid your corpse," she said, her eyes glinting. "Any further questions?"

Into the Woods

Stepping into the forest was like stepping into the shadow of a mountain. A cold darkness hit him like the force of a boulder. Light was sucked away, only slight, sharp tendrils of it slithering through the gaps in the treetops far above. Dawn vanished in an instant. He was conscious of a thousand different sounds and odours, the scuttling of wildlife, the rustling of bushes, the stench of damp earth and rotting leaves, but despite them all there was only a vast, uneasy quiet.

"You get used to it," said Talia, several paces ahead.

"Get used to what?"

"The sounds, the quiet, and the darkness," she said. "Your eyes will adjust quickly, although I should warn you, it gets darker."

Leo groaned. "Wonderful."

"Losing your nerve already, Prince?"

"I'm not entirely sure I had it to begin with..." He tripped on something, regaining his balance seconds before he hit the floor. Talia jumped clean out of his way. "What was that?" he hissed.

"That was a branch, Your Highness. You may encounter a fair few on your journey."

Leo glanced back, spotting the culprit on the ground. "I...

I thought it might be a snake. Or a vine trying to eat me or something."

Talia laughed. "Vines won't *eat* you!"

"Good."

"They will strangle you to death though. Keep that sword close, Prince."

Leo gulped, taking a few quick steps forward. There was a path of sorts, at this point, although he wondered how long that would last. "Are you always so abrasive?" he asked.

She shrugged. "Pretty much."

"Get many customers that way?"

"Oh, I'm sorry, would you like the other guide?"

"Right. Forget I asked." He swallowed again, finding her almost as terrifying as the horrors he imagined lurking further in. There was always something scary about people who had seen such things and now laughed at them. "I'm probably going to regret asking this too, but... what sort of things can I expect to encounter here? I've heard all sorts of stories."

His younger brother had given him a long and very detailed list, which he'd read extensively and really hoped was largely based on myth and rumour.

"Assume they're all true."

"Yup. I regret asking."

Talia laughed. She pointed to a nearby oak. It had an arrow etched into the bark. "Look at the oaks, if you want guidance but are afraid to ask. Arrows pointing up lead to the centre. Arrows down lead back to the edge of the forest. And some offer a warning..." Her finger drifted to a symbol below the arrow, the unmistakable sign of a spider.

Leo shivered.

"Questioning your resolve, Prince?"

"Slightly." He tightened his hand on his sword. "But not enough to turn back. I'd be a coward indeed if I ran away from fear alone."

He waited for her to tease him, or to tell him it was all right to be afraid, but she said nothing. She simply walked on ahead, her tangled braid swaying along her back. He followed her as the path grew narrower, as darkness and silence thickened.

"So... how long have you been a forest guide?" he asked, after an hour or so had passed.

"What feels like a lifetime," she remarked. "You don't have to make conversation, if you don't want to."

"It's to ward off the silence," he admitted. "Unless you have an objection?"

"Suit yourself."

"Where do you live? When you're not serving as a guide?"

"Nowhere," she responded, her voice faint. "The woods are the only home I know, now."

"But... your family?"

"They aren't around anymore."

"I'm sorry," he said. "Your family... were they guides too? Is it a family occupation?"

"Something like that," said Talia, with the ghost of a genuine smile. Some pleasant memory of them must have bubbled up. He would have pressed her about it, but it occurred to him that a great tragedy must have occurred for her to be alone in the world so young. It might be best not to ask. They had only just met, after all.

"What's the best part of your job?" he asked instead.

She stopped for a moment, blinking at him, as if no one had ever asked such a thing. "I suppose the time for self-reflection," she said. "And learning. I am seldom bored or lonely whilst I am learning, and the forest has many secrets, good and bad."

"What about the woods?" he said, leaving no room for silence. "Were they always this way?"

"Well, they've always been enchanted, but the darkness is a result of the evil fairy's magic. She lit up a beacon summoning all manner of evil creatures to the woods before becoming trapped in them herself."

"How did that happen, I wonder?"

"Sorry?"

"Everyone knows that the princess was cursed to slumber for a hundred years, but the evil fairy was never supposed to be tied to her fate. How did she succumb to it as well?"

Talia shrugged. "It was a long time ago," she said. "I couldn't possibly know."

An owl hooted in the distance. Leo startled.

"That's an–"

"An owl, I know," he said shortly. "I'm not a complete idiot. A little late for an owl though, isn't it?"

Talia shrugged. "I think even the creatures forget the difference between night and day, here."

Leo's stomach rumbled loudly.

"You've not eaten?" Talia asked.

"I was up very early..."

"You need to eat to keep your strength up," she said. "There is a clearing up ahead, and water. Come."

A few minutes later, they reached a glade. A shaft of light fell from above, directly into the path of an old well.

"What's that?" Leo asked.

"A well."

"I worked that part out, smart ass. I meant what does it do? I highly doubt it's benign, not in these woods."

"Hmm. You are not a fool, after all. It's a wishing well."

"That sounds surprisingly non-evil."

"It will grant your wish, but... it will twist it. Curse it. So, you could wish for riches, but be murdered for them. Wish for love, only to have it snatched from you."

"So, even if I was super specific, like, 'I wish to rescue the princess and free the kingdom and live happily ever after', I'd regret it?"

Talia did not smile. "It would find a way to ruin it. Don't risk it."

"Have you ever?"

Talia did not reply. "You can drink from it safely," she said instead. "But do not drop a coin, no matter how tempting. I'm going to scout ahead. There's some mushrooms by the foot of that tree you should pick for later. I'll be back soon."

She swept off into the woods.

Leo stared at the bottom of the well, at the unfathomable, swirling darkness beneath, trying not to think about how many coins lay at the bottom, how many wishes had been uttered and regretted. What did they wish for? Safe passage? Prosperity for their loved ones? Riches? Happiness?

How could happiness be twisted? How could 'I wish to live a long and happy life' be made into a regret?

He didn't want to know. He didn't want to risk it.

Instead, he chewed some of his provisions, picked the mushrooms Talia had suggested, and drew a deep drink from the well. It made him nervous, sipping from the depths, as if a wish would be snatched from him, regardless of the lack of an offering. He took a few sips and was done.

Talia returned not long after. "The river has burst its banks," she said. "There's a crossing several miles uphill, or a riskier crossing a mile downhill. Which would you prefer?"

Leo did not want to wear himself out so soon into the journey. He was not used to rough travel, and he didn't want to give Talia any more room to doubt him by watching him wheeze and huff his way uphill.

"How risky are we talking?"

"It's a log over high-speeding rapids."

"Wide log?"

"Wider than you."

"I will take the wide log route."

They proceeded onwards in silence, creeping closer to the river. It was more of a ravine, a deep cut in the rocky earth. Leo waited for it to become shallower, for the distance between bank and riverbed to shrivel. It did not. When they reached the felled tree that was to be their bridge, Leo's stomach churned like the waters below.

He had no fear of heights, but the distance made him dizzy. "You first," he said.

Talia sighed. "So chivalrous..." She flew across with the speed of a squirrel and turned back to face him. "It's best if you don't think about it."

Leo suspected this was true, but wondered what else he could focus on with the water rushing beneath him. He stepped out onto the log, each movement careful and precise.

"I did say *don't* think about it," Talia said.

"I'm trying!"

He inched forward. The trunk was sturdy enough, but the moss was damp and slippery underfoot. It squeaked under his boots.

"The day is waning, prince…"

"You are not helping!"

He'd made it halfway. *All downhill from here,* Wilheim would say. Unfortunately, the tree inclined ever-so-slightly upwards, disrupting his balance by a thin but countable margin. The unsteadiness seemed to ripple up from his toes, turning his knees to jelly.

Another step. Two, three.

His foot slipped on a patch of moss. Talia jolted forward as his legs slid out from underneath him, and he crashed into the river below.

The water sucked him under. He spluttered to the surface, spitting out water, flailing. Talia was calling from above, but he could barely hear her over the rush of the current.

It pulled him downstream. He fought against it before deciding there was little point, and let himself be dragged. He grappled for a nearby rock and clung to it, his pack smacking against his back. His sword dragged along the riverbed. He wondered if he should unbuckle it, if he should dump his equipment entirely. It would be easier to swim, but the loss of the equipment could be just as deadly as the rapids. Wilheim would have known what to do. Wilheim wouldn't have fallen off.

"Leo!"

Talia shouted from the bank. She'd climbed down remarkably quickly.

"I'm all right!" he insisted.

"Can you swim?"

"Yes, quite well, so I'm told, although I've never done it in *so many clothes.* Should I dump–"

Talia ignored him, running on ahead, to where the bank slid into the water. She glanced onwards, her expression grim.

"Huge waterfall?" asked Leo, dreading her answer.

"I'd say 'moderate'."

Leo craned his neck over the rock, but he couldn't see. He glanced at the distance between himself and the bank, trying to guess his trajectory.

Talia seemed to read his thoughts. "Can you make it?"

"Do I have a choice?"

He kicked himself away from the rock, struggling against the current as it tried to drag him under. His lungs burned in his chest with every stroke, every desperate lunge. The bank was slipping away from him. He kicked harder, forcing himself back, seizing fistfuls of earth with his hands.

Talia stood far back, as if the water were lava.

He hauled himself out, collapsing in a sodden heap on the mossy bank, gasping and coughing up water. Talia crept forward, her face very white.

"Are you hurt?" she asked.

Leo struggled into a sitting position, still breathing hard, and checked himself over. A few bruises and grazes, nothing that needed attending to although they hurt like hell. He shook his head, his throat too raw to speak.

"Can you move?"

He nodded.

"Then get up."

"Give me... a minute..."

"No. You're too cold. You need to keep moving. Get up, take off as many layers as you're comfortable with, and *move*. We can't stop to make camp here."

Leo groaned, rolling onto his feet. He took off everything but his long shirt, squeezing the moisture from his garments and tying them to his pack. Talia looked impressed by his swiftness and knot-tying, if nothing else.

It was a long, cold, uncomfortable trek into the woods before Talia finally stopped in a clearing. "Here is safe enough," she said.

Leo sank to his feet.

"Don't stop," she said. "You need to make a fire."

"Can't you–"

"Do. Not. Stop. Moving!"

He sighed, and she slipped away into the trees, presumably to make sure the clearing was as safe as she declared. He set up camp without her, stripping off everything, hanging it from the branches, and wrapping the blanket around his shoulders instead. He'd packed it well enough that it was only damp. His fingers were numb, but the fire had finally started to reach some of him by the time Talia returned.

She sat down on the ground, far from the fire, and said nothing.

"You're angry with me," said Leo eventually.

"Perhaps," she said. "Or myself. I'm trying to work out if either is justified."

"Why would you be angry at yourself?"

"For letting you cross. For not insisting we take the safer route. We are not yet pushed for time. A few hours would have been lost, but now they've been lost anyway; we cannot move until your clothes dry."

Leo nodded. "And... you're angry at me because I slipped?"

She shook her head. "Anyone could have slipped. You were being as careful as you could be. I think I might be angry because you came alone, because it's harder when you don't have help, but..."

"But what?"

She shook her head. "I have decided not to be angry," she said. "So it doesn't matter." She looked up. "It's midday. This clearing is as warm as it can be. Keep turning your clothes, rest. Hopefully we'll get a few more hours to travel before nightfall." She got up again.

"Where are you going?"

"Not far. Shout if you require me."

Leo watched her go, vanishing almost immediately into the trees. She certainly was a strange one. Did she live a life such as this because she disliked company so much? Maybe she was uncomfortable about the fact he was naked underneath the blanket. It wasn't necessarily his preference either, but you couldn't see anything.

Then again, if her aversion to being touched came from a violent act in her past, he couldn't blame her.

He wished she'd come back, if only for someone to talk to. Warming up was a miserable enough affair as it was, and passing the time by himself, trying not to fixate on the sounds of the forest, was no easy task.

Talia reappeared a few hours later. "Are your clothes dry yet?" she asked promptly.

Leo shrugged. "Almost."

"And you have recovered?"

He nodded.

"Good. We have at least three hours of daylight left and the terrain is easy enough. Let's not waste any more time."

Talia turned around while he changed, rolled away his equipment, and stamped out the fire, glancing back only briefly to ensure he was ready. She set off at a brisk pace and did not stop for several hours. She didn't break a sweat, not even as the 'easy terrain' gave way to thick undergrowth, the forest floor dense with ferns and branches that snapped underfoot. It was dispiriting to spend so long clambering through it, only to glance back and realise how little you'd travelled. Talia seemed to glide through, as if the plant life was no more trouble than a breeze.

Three hours later, maybe more, he was soaked through again and panting hard. He was unprepared for this. If he'd had longer to train, if he'd been more active in his youth…

"That… was easy…?" he wheezed.

"Well, nothing came alive, chased you, poisoned you or–"

"All right, yeah, easy. Gods," he stared at the ground, trying to steady his breathing, "how do you live like this?"

Talia did not answer. "There's a stream ahead, if you want to freshen up," she said. "I'll see if I can get a fire started."

Leo did not argue. He dumped his pack, unbuckled anything vaguely loose, and strolled off in the direction she indicated. He shoved his entire face in the water and guzzled greedily, splashing his neck, arms, anything. He'd sweated more in the past few hours than he had in an entire summer back in Germaine. Just how easy had his life been before?

He knew he was privileged. He knew that other people had it much harder. But he hadn't even begun to understand just how that felt until now, until he'd felt a fragment of their exhaustion.

He stumbled back to camp, sodden and fresh, slumping down beside the fire and groaning as he rubbed his aching muscles.

"Missing your comfortable castle?" Talia smirked.

"Who wouldn't miss that?"

"Fair point."

She'd set up a fire and was cooking mushrooms over it. She'd added a bit of his smoked meat and tossed some herbs in. Rosemary? Simple a dish as it was, it smelled delicious, although there wasn't much for two of them.

"I'm going to, er, freshen up," she said. "I've already eaten, so don't hold back."

She couldn't have eaten much, but he wasn't going to push the issue. She hardly seemed like the type to go hungry on his account.

"Thank you," he said.

She shrugged, as if ashamed of the praise. "It's nothing," she insisted, as she slipped away.

He tucked into his meal alone, once more aware of the pressing silence. Talia wasn't gone for too long, this time, although she didn't look much fresher when she returned. She was still streaked with mud. She sat down opposite, straight as an arrow. He'd never seen someone so stiff beside a fire before.

"Tell me about yourself," he said.

Talia bristled. "There's... little to tell."

"How old are you?"

She opened her mouth quickly, as if to spit out the answer, but then closed it momentarily. "I've lost count," she admitted finally. "About your age, I assume."

"I'm nineteen," said Leo. "Is that about right?"

"About. I think. Like I said, I lost count, when there was no one..."

When there was no one to count it with her.

"Favourite colour?"

"Blue."

"Favourite food?"

At this, Talia let out a soft moan. "Apple pie. But it's been so long I can barely remember the taste, or the smell..." She sighed longingly.

Leo smiled. "I like that, too. We have a version in Germaine with dates and raisins and–" He stopped, suddenly aware that Talia had probably never experienced such luxuries. "Tell me a story," he said. "One of your favourites."

"I am no storyteller–"

"Then tell me why it is your favourite."

Talia chewed her lip. "Have you ever heard the Ballad of Cecilia Brightsmoke?"

Leo nodded. It was a very old tale of a young noblewoman who escapes an arranged marriage by running away to the woods, where she befriends a group of mercenaries, learns the way of the sword, and ends up saving a kingdom from an oncoming invasion. "One of my favourites. Why is it yours?"

"She never has to be rescued by anyone. Why is it yours?"

"The mercenaries told a lot of rude jokes. So did Cecilia."

Talia laughed. "I... I am not one for conversation," she said. "But... if you wanted to tell me some of your stories, I should be glad to hear them."

The Curse Discovered

Briar was ten years old when she found out about the curse. As a princess, her birthday was always celebrated with great aplomb, and her tenth was no exception. Afterwards, when she learned the truth, she wondered whether everyone always went out of their way to be jolly on the day deliberately, to cover up the ticking bomb, the elephant in the room, the unspoken secret.

One of the courtiers set her off, stroking her hair affectionately and sighing, "Only seven years left..." absent-mindedly.

Briar frowned, but said nothing when she saw how distressed the woman became. She comforted her, continued with the party, and cornered her parents at the end of the day, demanding to know what the courtier meant.

Her parents looked at each other, their eyes bright with fear that even a child could recognise, and in that moment Briar knew that whatever the courtier had half-confessed to was serious indeed.

"I'm... I'm sure the courtier was just confused, darling," her father began.

"Don't lie to me," she snapped. "If you do not tell me the truth, I will go back to her, and if she doesn't tell me, I'll ask someone else. I will ask everyone in the castle, if necessary. Someone will eventually give me a clear answer if you won't."

Her father sighed. "Cursed be the fairy who gave you intelligence," he said, with faint affection in his voice.

Her mother looked like she was about to cry.

Then it all came out, how she'd been cursed by an evil fairy at her christening, how she was destined to prick her finger on a spinning wheel on her seventeenth birthday and plunge the kingdom into a hundred-year-long slumber. Only a kiss could awaken her.

"Any kiss?" she asked.

They shook their heads. "A special kind," her mother explained. "Most likely true love's kiss."

"But how can it be true love if I don't know him?"

Her mother smiled sadly, taking her by the shoulders. "Fate? Faith? Hope? I do not know. But you will be saved, my darling, I swear it."

"And... if no one comes after that time?"

Her parents' faces blanched.

"I see," she said. "Just me? Or the rest of you?"

"The good fairies who cast the counter-curse were not entirely sure."

"And... and what have you done so far, to avoid it? Other than the counter-curse?"

"Well, there are no spinning wheels in the castle," said the king.

"That's it?"

"We're still quite far off..."

"We thought about... maybe... when you were older..." started the queen, "trying to find you a suitor to break the curse the minute it was cast."

"But what if I don't like him?"

"It's a long way off, darling–"

"I'd like to learn to wield a blade," she requested, "because I am *not* touching a spinning needle of my own accord. So I would need to be forced. I want to learn how to protect myself."

The king, after a moment's hesitation, agreed.

"And find a good fairy or a sorcerer or someone who can teach me how to withstand mental attacks, in case I'm hypnotised or something."

"Any... anything else?"

She paused for a moment, coming up empty. "I shall let you know."

Few things sounded worse to Briar than sitting back and letting someone else rescue her. She was not about to give up. She was not about to let this dark fairy win, risk letting her kingdom fall to ruin and disgrace.

She would fight her fate until her last breath.

She had no idea how true her resolve would be.

For the next two years, Briar trained with the best swordmaster her parents could procure. His name was Hakido, a true master of the blade, and she, his ever-diligent pupil, barely missed a day.

At the same time, she trained with a strict, matronly fairy named Margaret, and although the lessons only happened every few weeks while Margaret was visiting, she set her a mountain of tasks to complete in-between.

Margaret was one of the fairies that had been at her christening, gifting her with intelligence. She was initially reluctant to train the young princess, – "There's a limit to the magics humans are capable of." – but she had been persuaded by Briar's resolve and a desire to try and side-step the curse as well. "We can't have *her* win, can we? Sets a bad example for the rest of us."

Training her mind was much, much harder than learning how to wield a blade. Briar could see and track her progress with a weapon, commit herself to clear, logical exercises that promoted strength or endurance. Mental agility was far harder and required far more patience, not a trait that Briar boasted amongst her repertoire.

Hours were devoted to meditating, breathing exercises, and focusing, all tasks that felt like they were for naught when Margaret visited and slipped as easily into her mind as a knife through butter. She would make her dance around the room, sing on demand, even draw a bow or swing a sword. Briar could not believe the power that fairies had, how easily they could bend humans to their will.

"This is impossible!" she cried out at one point.

"All right," said Margaret flatly, "then desist. Give up. No one would blame you."

Briar tightened her jaw. "No," she said. "I won't give up. *I* would blame me."

Margaret nodded approvingly. "Then try again."

"I can't practise enough without you. Come and stay here for a while. Or let me come back with you–"

"A human, in the fairy court?" Margaret gasped. "I will never see the day! I suppose, as there are no children at home at present, making my visits more frequent wouldn't deny any fairy child of their tutor. Very well."

Margaret adjusted her visits so she could be with Briar several weeks at a time, then left for longer periods to ensure her pupil didn't grow lax in her absence. Slowly, Briar began to improve, resisting Margaret's attacks for a few moments at first, and finally being able to block her altogether.

The court was somewhat alarmed by the permanent presence of a fairy in their midst. The story of Briar's christening was legendary, and it had tarnished all magical creatures with a similar brush. The servants were silent in her presence, as if the slightest word would cause her to snap and transform them all into frogs. Margaret, Briar could tell, found the whole thing incredibly tiresome, and occasionally performed complicated hand gestures at dinner time just to spook them.

Only one person found it as entertaining as Briar did; one of the young maids about her own age.

When helping Briar dress one day, she asked her if Margaret could really turn people into frogs.

"Oh, no doubt, but whyever would she?"

"I would *love* to see someone get turned into a frog," the maid gushed. "But... only someone who deserved it. Karina, maybe. Michelangelo." She narrowed her gaze. "Promise me, Princess, if she ever teaches you how to do it, you'll let me watch?"

Briar laughed. "Humans can't turn people into frogs," she said. "I could teach you how to fence, if you like? Then you could stab Karina and Michelangelo if they bother you again."

"You... you would teach me how to fence?"

"Of course," she said. "But you must promise me you'll put up a good fight!"

By the time she was thirteen, Margaret declared that there was nothing more she could teach her. Not because she was necessarily a master, but because "There is a limit to what humans can learn when it comes to fairy magic."

Briar was not hurt by these words. She knew Margaret meant them as a compliment.

She was better than most humans.

The only thing that hurt was the fact that Margaret would now be leaving. She hugged her fiercely before she went, which caught the old fairy slightly off-guard. She patted her head.

"I'll be back for your next birthday."

"A year is too long!"

Margaret laughed. "Barely a blink of an eye for me, little princess. What will you have accomplished in that time, I wonder? What is your next challenge?"

Briar had an idea, something other than teaching the maid how to fight, something she'd been thinking of for a while. It was about learning to fight. Not just with a sword, not in a neat and knightly way.

"Something my parents won't like," she said.

Margaret's gold eyes glinted. "I look forward to it."

4

Shadows AND Spiders

After the good fairy's proclamation about Germaine sending one of its princes into the forest, King Albert called Wilheim into his study. Leo paced outside the door the entire time. Eventually, Wil stormed out, saying nothing to Leo at all, but striding towards Ingrid. He pulled her into his arms, and for a moment Leo thought he was going to cry. He hadn't seen his brother tear up since his favourite horse had died as a boy. Ingrid looked stronger, but only just.

"I'll do it," said Leo in an instant.

Wilheim wheeled round, as if surprised to notice him. "No," he said.

"You can't," Ingrid whispered. "You'll–"

"Die?" Leo responded, folding his arms to disguise any trembling. "Oh ye of little faith, Ingrid."

"I don't want you to do this," Wilheim continued.

"Yes, you do. Unless you'd rather send Jakob?"

Jakob appeared from behind a nearby statue. "I'd prefer *not* to go, if it's all the same to you," he said, pushing his glasses up his nose. He held out the book in his hand. "I've been doing some research. Did you know there's supposed to be a basilisk in there? It's a giant serpent that can–"

"I'll speak with Father," Leo said, "before Jakob puts me off altogether."

"Leo–" Wilheim put out his arm.

"What?"

"Thank you."

Leo swallowed, and summoned a smile. "Thank me later. I get to be the favourite uncle."

It did not take long to convince his father to let him go in Wilheim's stead. In fact, he looked almost relieved. The looming threat of the wicked fairy had sucked the colour from his skin, making him look older than his fifty years. Leo's decision was the first time he'd seen Father's eyes – bright green like his – light up in months. He called to him as he turned to leave.

"Leo."

His father's voice stopped him in his tracks. He rarely called him that.

"Yes, Father?"

"Thank you, for doing this for your brother. And your kingdom."

"It's the right thing to do."

"Right isn't always easy."

"The kingdom needs Wilheim more than it needs me. *I* need him more than he needs me. It would not be easy to watch him suffer, or..."

"Son–"

"I'm less valuable."

"You still have great value," his father insisted. "To the kingdom, to your family... and to me."

Leo's throat tightened. Father never spoke like this. Not ever. "I should... I should go and prepare," he said. "There's plenty to do."

"Leo?"

"Yes?"

"Take care."

Leo stepped out into the corridor, but the floor vanished beneath his feet, and he fell into utter darkness.

Leo woke hot, feeling like a weight was crushing against his chest. He'd been dreaming, although the conscious memory of it slithered away the second the sunlight hit him, vanishing into shapelessness and shadow. Only the hot weight of it remained, pounding against his ribcage.

He looked about him. "Talia?"

She was nowhere to be seen, not hair nor hide of her remained. Not a dent in the ground. She'd vanished as surely as the dream–

"Talia!"

"What is it?"

He snapped his head round. Talia was standing behind him, awake and still covered in mud.

"I... er... I thought–"

"That I had abandoned you in the night? I'm not sick of you yet, Prince."

"Er... I was more thinking maybe you'd been eaten by a troll or something."

Talia snorted. "I've survived this long! And trolls don't generally eat humans."

"Er... generally?"

"I mean, if they get hungry enough..."

Leo suppressed a shudder. "Where did you go?"

"I fetched breakfast," Talia said, gesturing to a cloth filled with eggs sat beside the fire. He hadn't noticed them there a minute ago. "I take it you can cook them yourself? I've been up for hours. Already eaten."

Leo glimpsed upwards, trying to gauge the hour. It could not have been long past dawn. She kept strange hours. He supposed she was used to it, and there was hardly any point in lingering in bed when you didn't have one.

"Thank you," he said, leaning forward to inspect the eggs.

"Don't dawdle too long," she said. "We should get an early start. We've a lot to cover before nightfall."

They walked for several hours, through thick undergrowth and smooth slopes, uphill and down, past streams and rocky ground. Some parts of the forest were oddly beautiful. Leo hadn't been expecting this. He assumed all of it was as dark and gloomy as the entrance had been, but stopping beside a river for lunch, he felt a sense of peace. Talia had disappeared somewhere again – she had the stamina of a plough horse – and he amused himself by chatting to a squirrel who was gathering nuts nearby.

"I've heard that talking to yourself is one of the first signs of madness," said Talia, appearing behind him.

Leo suppressed a startle. "I was not talking to myself," he said calmly, "I was talking to my friend, Sir Squirrel, here."

"*Sir* Squirrel?"

"He has a knightly countenance."

Talia bit her lip, reining back a smile.

"You must get lonely sometimes," Leo continued. "Do you never talk to yourself or the creatures around you?"

"Oh, of course. But I'm way past the first sign of madness." Her eyes glinted. "You're a little early in your journey."

Leo swallowed. "I think I'm well-rested enough," he declared. "Shall we head on?"

Talia nodded. He gathered his equipment, shouldered his pack, and followed her trail. While the terrain was still easy, he tried to engage her in conversation. He could get little out of her about her past, or any details about her at all really, but she was happy enough to listen to him and stories of his homeland. He even got her asking questions, once or twice. She was incredibly guarded, spooked by the sound of her own questions. It was odd; that part of her didn't fit at all with the confident forest guide she wore so well. What had happened to her?

He dared not ask, but he knew his curiosity was only going to increase, the deeper into the woods they went.

Late afternoon, they stepped into a darker part of the wood. The forest floor was coated in white.

"Is that... frost?" Leo sniffed the air. "It doesn't feel like frost..."

"It's not frost," Talia said. "It's cobwebs."

"Good. Wait– what?" A cold dread rose from the pit of his stomach.

"Come on, you aren't afraid of a few little spiders, are you?"

"Afraid isn't the word I would use. Terrified might be better. Or... petrified. Yes. Petrified is good."

"Do you always complain this much?"

"Only when I'm way out of my depth and panicking," he said. "So quite a lot, actually."

She sighed, but a laugh twitched in the corner of that sigh. "Well, if it helps, these ones aren't little."

"That doesn't help! That is the opposite of helpful!"

"Draw your sword," said Talia. "And stay alert. They're very good at sneaking up..."

"I know," Leo shivered. "That's one of the reasons I hate them so much."

Talia laughed, shaking her head. "Imagine a prince being scared of spiders."

"Only a fool says he's scared of nothing," Leo said. "And I'd rather it be something like this than something big. There must be something you're scared of?"

Talia paused. "I have conquered most of my fears."

"Most?"

"The small ones. I suppose you're right. The big ones are worse." Talia stepped on ahead of him. "Are you coming?"

Leo tried not to tremble. "Spiders," he sighed, "why did it have to be spiders?"

The forest floor was thick with cobwebs, and he fancied he could see some of them moving. Sweat beaded his brow. Why was this the first true test? He wasn't sure he could move even if he wanted to. He gripped the hilt of his sword, hoping the courage of the heroes who'd wielded it before him would rub off on him.

Talia's face softened, only a fraction. She did not tease him.

"It might help if you don't look at the webs," she said. "Focus on my back."

"There's... there's no way of going around?"

She shook her head. "They often stretch for miles, and the terrain is very difficult." She pointed ahead. Rocky ridges rose out of the trees. "The pass there is the only real route. Otherwise we're looking at climbing forty feet."

Leo was no climber, not up something like that. He nodded gravely. "All right."

Talia swung round, taking the lead. He fixed his eyes on the end of her braid and stepped forward. He kept a count in his head, too. Anything to stay focused. He was annoyed at his cowardice, but at least she hadn't teased him.

"I used to be afraid of very deep water," she told him, sweeping down the path.

"You're not anymore?"

"I waded a little deeper into a pool that terrified me every day for a month."

"That worked?"

"It helped."

Leo sighed. "Wilheim thought a similar tactic might work with me. He kept hiding dead spiders in my clothes to try and help me 'get used to them'."

Talia glanced back, just for a second. "And this is the brother you loved enough to take the place of?"

Leo laughed. "It was not one of his finer moments. I just don't think he understood. I don't think he's ever been afraid of anything."

"No?" Talia sounded surprised. "What did he say when you told him you were going instead?"

Leo put one foot in front of the other, and tried to keep moving. "He said, 'no'. But then, pretty much everyone said that!"

"Why?"

"I imagine they all thought I was a lost cause... hence, the party of knights."

"Which you dismissed." She went silent for a moment. "Tell me, prince, since everyone seems to doubt you... do you believe you can do it?"

Leo swallowed. "I believe – I *know* – I'm going to try my hardest."

He waited for her to tell him that the way was littered with the bodies of others with similar intentions, but she did not. "You think I'm a fool, don't you?"

"I didn't say that."

"I... I had to take my brother's place. I couldn't let him be miserable for the rest of his life. But I know I acted in haste dismissing the guards. I didn't really think it through. Or maybe... the night before I left, I was speaking to this old man at the tavern. He told me about you. I just... I thought I'd be fine, if I listened to you."

Talia smiled. "Old man, eh?"

"Do you know him?"

"Your description isn't exactly specific, but I suppose he must know me. Maybe I guided him through these woods, long ago."

"He was really ancient. And you're... not. It couldn't have been that long ago."

"I suppose not."

They had reached the rocky enclave. Something scuttled ahead.

"What was that?" Leo whispered.

She turned back to face him, raising an eyebrow. "You're in a field of cobwebs," she said. "You can work it out."

"But that... that was the size of..." *A small dog.*

"I told you they weren't little."

Leo gulped. His fear felt like it was choking him. He tried to push it away, but the harder he pushed, the more it seemed to rise.

"They aren't venomous, if it helps," she said.

"It does not."

They marched onwards, through the rocky path, ducking under sheets of webbing, thick as wool. The scuttling intensified. Movement clawed at his peripheral vision, and it took all his self-control to keep his gaze fixed on Talia. If he stopped to look, the fear would paralyse him.

"I take it they don't eat humans?" he asked.

Talia paused, just a fraction. "Umm…" Her gaze drifted, unconsciously, at some of the ledges above them. Piles of bones. "Generally not," she continued. "They don't tend to bother with things bigger than them."

They turned a corner and were met with a wall of white. It was impossible to see through or duck under.

"Let me," said Leo, inching forwards. He raised his blade to cut through the webbing.

Eight eyes the size of his fists, black and shiny as gemstones, rose out of the white. A hairy, pale, monstrous body followed. Its legs were thicker than Leo's arms, its body the size of a horse. Pincers snapped, oozing colourless liquid onto the rocky floor.

Leo's chest pounded. His lungs began to panic, great, shuddering breaths tripping over one another. He could have choked on his heart. He couldn't breathe. He was drowning in fear.

"Leo…" said Talia, "you need to move back."

But Leo couldn't move. Even her voice seemed distorted and far away.

The spider crept closer.

Move, said a voice in the back of his head. *Move!*

The spider was a foot away from him, maybe less.

"Leo!" Talia raced across the spider's path, leaping onto the ledge above with expert agility. "Here!" she yelled at the spider. "Come and get me!"

The spider turned, deciding he preferred the chase. It scuttled up the mountainside, but Talia was quicker. Leo had never seen anyone move like that. It was almost like she was flying.

"*Run!*" she hissed.

The path clear, Leo found his mobility returning. He moved blindly through the passage, trying not to look up, but the massive body was never quite out of sight.

Talia was. He couldn't see her anymore.

He reached the end of the pass. The cobwebs dribbled away, replaced by ferns and woodlands. He was almost out.

"Talia?"

He turned back. She was nowhere to be seen.

Liquid fire replaced the ice-cold dread that had occupied his veins mere seconds ago. He raced back into the cliffs. She was not hard to locate; every spider in the vicinity was crawling towards her. The giant had her in his sights and her back was almost pressed against the rock.

He screamed her name. She shot him a look of pure venom.

The spider did not turn. Leo was glad of that, certain any remnant of courage would have disintegrated under its gargantuan stare. He skidded towards it, blade extended, ducking underneath its huge body and plunging his sword into its belly, hilt deep.

The spider reared, scrambling backwards, sliding off his blade with a gush of green blood. It did not go far, tumbling onto its back, its colossal legs twitching inward.

The other, smaller spiders abandoned any interest they had in the two humans. They scurried towards their fallen brethren... and started to feast.

The dark, cold fear returned in full. Leo sank to his knees, caked in the monster's blood, his lungs assaulted by another hundred, vicious breaths.

"Get up!" Talia snarled. "Move!"

She started to run, and somehow he found the strength to follow her. They hurtled down the mountain path, putting as much distance as they could between themselves and the webbed wasteland.

They stopped beside a stream and Talia turned to face him, her eyes blazing.

"Don't do that," she snapped. "Ever again. Don't put your life on the line to save mine. You wouldn't be doing me any favours."

Leo blinked, baffled. "Of course I'd be doing you a favour," he said. "You'd be alive."

Talia's eyes burned, and he got the distinct impression she wanted to slap him, but instead she clenched her fists. "Don't try to save me again."

Leo was more than a little put-out. He had just saved her

life, after all. Admittedly, after she'd saved his. It wasn't that he expected her to be grateful, but the anger was unwarranted.

"Why not?" he asked shortly.

"You're the one that needs to make it through. Not me. You're the last hope we have of ending this." She turned her back and marched on ahead.

"Talia?"

She did not stop.

"Why– why do you want the curse lifted so badly?"

"Who says I do?"

"It's like... this is your life. Guiding heroes through the forest. Why do you do it? There are easier ways to make a living."

She shrugged. "This is all I know. There's nothing else I can do."

He wasn't sure he believed her. *You're the last hope we have of ending this.* Who was 'we'? And she hadn't answered his question. She *did* want the curse lifted. She'd risked her life to give him a chance of getting through, was mad at him for risking his life – and therefore the final shot – of the curse being broken. Surely, if the enchantment of the forest was broken, and the woods returned to normal, she'd be out of a job?

It didn't make sense.

"Talia–"

"Don't ask questions!" she snapped. "Rule number two."

He groaned, swallowing his frustration, and followed her into the dark.

It is difficult for anger to dissipate when you're fatigued, uncomfortable and still feeling the lingering effects of extreme fear. As it was, Leo was still furious with Talia when they made camp, still furious when he scrubbed the clotted arachnid blood from his clothes, and still furious when he was swallowing down his dinner.

Dark descended on their little camp. Talia's eyes gazed

upwards at the stars, her expression blank. She didn't look at all tired, and despite his aching muscles, he didn't feel ready for sleep yet, either. He was still too angry. He really shouldn't have come alone. Not just for his own safety, but for moments like this, too. He needed other voices around him, a mallet to the tension.

"What do you fear?" said Talia abruptly, cutting through the silence.

He startled. He hadn't expected her to speak at all, and her voice was soft and foreign.

"Apart from, you know, spiders," she continued. "What are you most afraid of?"

It didn't sound like she was trying to taunt him, or even trying to evaluate him. She sounded genuine, like she was making conversation.

Leo thought for a moment. "Failure," he said. "I don't mind not being the fastest or strongest, but if I'm not strong enough to protect those I care about... that would be the worst thing. You?"

"Once upon a time, the same thing," she said.

"Why did it change?"

For a moment, Talia did not reply. "I failed."

Leo paled. "And now?"

Again, she paused. "Powerlessness," she said faintly. "Having no choice." Her voice fell to a whisper. "Losing myself."

"What do you mean?"

"I... I know I can be rather... hard, and abrasive," she said. "Amongst other things. But I am the way I am because of my past. If something happened to erase a part of me... it would be like a lingering death."

Leo frowned. "What could happen that would erase a part of you?"

Talia stared into the dark. "There are a lot of dangers in these woods."

Something howled in the distance.

"All right, you have to follow that with something jolly now," he said, trying not to shiver, "or I'll never sleep."

Talia gave a slight snort. "I'm afraid being 'jolly' isn't

amongst my skillset."

"Hmm, let me try. *There was an old man from Shirringham, who used to live on a boat, not a care had he, when he left for sea, with nothing but him and a goat.*"

Talia blinked at him. "He's going to eat that goat," she said shortly.

"The goat's his friend!"

"He is out at sea, that goat is getting eaten at some point."

"He'll eat fish!"

"You seem very attached to this goat."

Leo shrugged. "It's just a silly nursery rhyme my wetnurse used to tell me."

"I don't think I know anything like that..." She glanced to the side, seemingly lost in thought. When she opened her mouth, it was to pour out a song into the glowing thicket.

"Even in the darkness stars will colour up your skies,
hold on for another night and wish away the lies.
Darkness comes before the dawn, a stranger once told me,
somewhere under shadow a ray of sun waits to be free."

She carried on for some time, uttering shimmering verses of hope and light. The firelight seemed to dance for her.

"You have a lovely voice," said Leo, after the song had closed.

"Thank you," she said. "It offers company from time to time."

Leo yawned, rolling back his taut shoulders. The muscles felt like they'd been branded.

"You're tired," said Talia. Her eyes lit up, a smile playing in the corner of her mouth. "Should I switch to a lullaby?"

Leo would not have been averse to hearing more of her sweet song, but he was not going to invite more ridicule. He scowled at her instead, rolling into his blanket. "Good night, Talia."

A whisper of wind. A pause. Then, "Goodnight, Leo."

Bandits and Bargains

About a month after Margaret's departure, Briar heard reports of bandits in the woods.

Perfect, she thought, with a hunger in her eyes not typically ascribed to princesses.

About a year into her training with Master Hikado, it occurred to her that learning how to fight with a sword made you really good at one thing only: fighting with a sword. Nothing Master Hikado could teach her told her anything about how to fight without a blade. On top of everything, her training partners were terrible. She had no doubt that they were all excellent warriors and brilliant knights, but none of them were ever willing to give it their all when facing a princess. Their reservedness was murder on her plans. How was she ever to learn how to defend herself against a real threat?

Besides which, was the dark fairy going to come at her with a sword? It seemed unlikely. No. She was going to have to find another way to defend herself.

Telling Master Hikado that there was nothing more he could teach her would have been rude, and it never *hurt* to learn how to use a blade. Certainly their daily practise was good for building strength if nothing else. But if she was to stand a chance against the evil fairy, she needed to learn more. She needed another teacher.

This was where the bandits came in.

By all reports, this group had been causing some trouble in the forests for a long time, stealing from the wealthy travellers and then vanishing into the woods like the benign spirits that inhabited the trees. They had bested several of the finest knights. They also tended to leave their victims alive, which Briar approved of. She had no problem cavorting with thieves but figured it was probably unwise to go in search of murderers.

Because who better to teach her how to truly fight than men of the forest, liars and tricksters with loose morals, almost certain not to go easy on a princess? And those sorts of men could be *bought.*

Naturally, telling her parents was completely out of the question. She had to wait until a party of knights was sent to dispatch them, sneaking out of the castle to follow their trail.

Unfortunately, getting past the gate was no simple feat. She was recognised half a dozen times before she even reached the stables.

"May I be of assistance, Your Highness?" asked a small, clear voice.

Briar turned and found the young maid who she'd agreed to give fencing lessons to. They had not yet found an opportunity to begin them.

"I'm trying to sneak into the woods in search of bandits."

"Whatever for?"

"So they can teach me how to fight."

The maid's eyes gleamed. "Oh, Princess! How delightful!" She glanced down at Briar's gown. She'd chosen a plain one, but it still reeked of nobility. "Trouble getting through the gate?"

She nodded.

"Come with me."

The maid dragged her to the servants' courts, lent her some of her own clothes and a particularly filthy cloak, and took her to the stables to procure a donkey rather than her usual fine pony.

"There," the maid declared, "you look quite the part. No one shall ever stop you now."

"Thank you," Briar said with a smile. "I haven't forgotten about our lessons, by the way."

"If this works, you can teach me all the bandit tricks too!"

It worked perfectly. No one so much as raised an eyebrow as she drifted through the gates, picking up the knights' trail quickly.

Briar had ridden into the forests before, but never alone. There were some dangers deep within. A few ogres near the mountainous regions, some giant spiders... but mostly the creatures that called the forests their home were benign. She knew about the centaurs, and not to insult their pride. She knew to cover her ears if she drifted too close to the lake where the sirens dwelled. The dryads and the wood spirits were no threat, and she had a map with her to avoid all the truly dangerous areas.

She hoped the bandits' lair wasn't too close to any of them. She was armed, and confident, but she was not foolish. She could easily be outnumbered.

Despite her fears, the forest was oddly beautiful. She had never been able to admire it quite so perfectly before, with others by her side, as if their presence snatched a fragment of the experience from her, their noises draining the sounds of the birds, the breeze, the trickling stream. Shafts of light illuminated the path, casting dappled shadows across the earth. Briar watched as the shadows danced with the sway of the trees, and felt like swaying too. The forest played a song that only she could hear.

I could spend an eternity in this place, she thought, *and never grow bored.*

Something rustled in the undergrowth. It did not alarm her, at first. It could be any number of creatures. A deer, a squirrel, a sparrow. Nothing amiss.

The mule stiffened beneath her. She patted her neck. "It's all right, girl. Don't be afraid."

A boy appeared on the path ahead. A scrawny, dirty child, no more than seven. He could almost be mistaken as part of the forest itself, the amount of leaves and twigs tangled in his ruddy hair.

"Hello," said Briar gingerly. "Are you lost?"

The boy shook his head.

"Are you... alone here?"'

The boy shook his head again.

Briar realised her mistake seconds before the bandits appeared, rising out of the undergrowth, crossbows pointed towards her. The donkey bolted, knocking Briar clean off the saddle, but the boy and one of the other bandits blocked her path and grabbed her reins.

"Don't hurt her!" Briar yelled.

The man who had raced to grab her rolled his eyes, and soothed the mule with a gentle voice. He was as slim as a reed, with long black hair, tied surprisingly neatly for a man of the woods.

A blade appeared at Briar's chin. She looked up into the face of a haggard, weather-beaten man. His skin looked like crusted leather. "Worried about your mount, girlie? You should be more worried about yourself."

The slim man was taking apart her saddle, admiring the jewelled hilt of her sword. "Pretty blade," he said. "Do you know how to use it?"

"When it's in my hand," said Briar pointedly.

A short, red-haired, bearded fellow by her side laughed. A dwarf. "She's got fire, at least," he said. "Don't worry, girl, we won't hurt the mule. Just hand over your valuables and be on your merry way."

"You are more than welcome to them," Briar said, gathering her courage. "They are for you."

The dwarf blinked. So did the rest of the band.

"Wish all our marks were this obliging," said the dwarf.

"I have more, if you'll listen to my proposal."

The dwarf looked up at the man who still held the knife to her throat. He nodded, pulling the blade back. Briar got to her feet. "My name is Briar-Rose. I'm the princess of Verona."

The weather-beaten man raised an eyebrow. "That's a foolish thing to tell us."

"Is it? I imagine my parents would pay very handsomely for my safe return."

"I'm listening."

"I'm under a curse," she said. "You might have heard about it. It was very public."

"We've heard rumours."

"Well, I should very much like *not* to allow the curse to come into fruition."

The leader scoffed. "Doesn't matter much to us, girlie."

"But does money?" She removed a small ruby from her pocket, and tossed it towards him. She had been careful to only bring a little, just enough to whet the appetite. "I want you to teach me how to fight."

The man laughed. "Our ways of fighting are not fit for a princess."

"Good! That's what I want. I doubt the evil fairy is going to challenge me to a duel."

The dwarf stroked his beard. "She's got a point there, boss."

"Please," said Briar. "It needn't be you, yourself. Any of your men could teach me. I'm a diligent pupil, and can pay in gold."

The leader rubbed the ruby between his fingers. "I think, little Briar," he said, "that I might be warming up to you…"

The bandits took her back to their den, a series of damp and earthy caves besides a lake. The caves may not have been ideal, but the location was beautiful. Briar had never seen such an expanse of water before. The glimmer of sunlight along the surface was mesmerising.

"Even gold doesn't glitter like that," she breathed.

The slim one with the long dark hair laughed. "I am Lorenzo, Princess." He gave a sweeping bow. He was very graceful, and despite the calluses on his hands, his fingers still possessed an elegance that didn't fit with the rest of the mucky crew.

"You… you weren't always a bandit, were you?"

He shook his head.

"You were a noble?"

"One of the lesser families," he said. "I was at your christening. My parents were thrilled for the invite, but then your parents invited everyone."

"*Almost* everyone," Briar corrected. She looked at him. He could barely have been more than a boy, then. "Why... how came you here?"

"I had a disagreement with my family," he said. "So I found myself a new one."

They were a strange looking family, but Briar thought it would be rude to point that out.

"Let me take the donkey!" said the little boy. "We have a brush somewhere, and some apples–"

"Don't waste apples on the donkey, Ezio," the leader snapped.

Ezio pouted. "It's not wasting..."

The older man sighed. "Lorenzo, make sure he doesn't use all our supplies."

"Roger, boss."

The dwarf helped Briar down from her mount, with some difficulty due to his stature. "I'm Rogan," he declared. "Don't let the boss be too hard on you."

Hard, Briar thought, *is probably what I need.*

People were always too easy on princesses. Only Margaret had ever really pushed her, and she'd learnt more as a result.

She looked up at his leathery face. "What's your name... boss?"

"Anton," he said shortly. "The boy is Ezio. Rogan and Lorenzo have already introduced themselves. That just leaves Benedict." He hollered into the back of the cave. "Benedict! Company!"

A scrawny, light-haired man emerged from the gloom. He was as white as a ghost, his footsteps just as insubstantial. He had the pale, pinched look of a man who spent a lot of time indoors.

He tilted his head at the new arrival, but the surprise barely registered. "Who is this?"

"A young princess who wants us to teach her how to fight."

"Naturally." He gave her a curt nod. "A pleasure, Princess."

"Give her something to eat," barked Anton, "and then take her back for the day. We don't want the kingdom in uproar if she's discovered missing."

Benedict nodded. "As you wish. Come this way, Princess."

"You should know," Briar started, "there are knights in the forest looking for you."

Rogan snorted. "Looking, but not finding."

"We are leaves in the wind," said Lorenzo, pirouetting on the spot. "Catch us if you can."

After a very light luncheon, Benedict escorted her back to the castle, complimenting her on her disguise.

"A maid helped me," she admitted. "I didn't think of it myself."

"So you have learned something." He gave her the slightest of bows in the stable where she deposited the donkey, and was gone before she could turn around.

She went back through the servants' entrance, finding the maid to help her redress.

"I covered for you," said the maid.

"I clearly owe you more than a fencing lesson."

"Perhaps you can teach me what the bandits teach you?"

Briar smiled. "I'm sorry," she said, "but I don't know your name."

"It's Talia," the girl replied.

"It's pretty."

Talia shrugged. "It's a very common name in these parts."

6
Ogres AND Allies

T he darkness was unfathomable. The air pulsed with it. Leo held out his hands and found his arms robed in shadow, thick tendrils coursing round his fingers like smoke. How was it he could see himself, and nothing around him?

There was something else in the darkness. Whispers. They gushed past him like vicious ghosts.

"Not quite like his brothers, is he?"

"Foolish. Stupid."

"Not strong enough. Not smart enough."

"Such a disappointment."

The darkness morphed into the giant spider, which rose to greet him with its pincers snapping before dissolving into a thousand, million tiny monsters, which scuttled about him, splitting into the blackness. He could feel them crawling all around him–

A roar, a howl, a scream. Flashes of fang, of fur, of bloody flesh. White bones strung in a web, his sword beside them.

Death. Failure.

Then a voice, cutting through the dark, calling his name, as soft and lilting as the wind. The darkness parted, and he found himself in a courtyard thick with ivy. A beautiful woman stood at the centre. She had thick, chestnut hair, a silvery glow to her pale, milky skin, and blue eyes almost a shade of violet.

"Are you going to set me free?" she asked.

Leo's knees went weak, and he felt he would do anything – anything – she asked of him.

She smiled, and was immediately swallowed up by the darkness. Leo tried to cry out, but the heaviness of the shadows crushed against his chest.

He woke struggling to breathe.

Talia stood over him. "Are you all right?"

He choked on the air, spluttering, managing a weak nod.

"Are you sure?" she pressed. "You were thrashing a great deal."

"Just a nightmare."

"What about?"

"Spiders," he said, half-truthfully.

Talia bit her lip, and pressed him no more. "Breakfast is ready," she told him. "Come. I've–"

"Already eaten, yes, I know." He wondered if she had a thing about eating in front of people, or if someone had tried to poison her in the past and she didn't trust others to prepare meals for her anymore. Maybe she just didn't like waiting for him to get up. She'd been alone for a long time. Perhaps meals were no longer social occasions, in her mind. Besides, they spent enough time together during the day.

They resumed their journey after Leo had eaten, making the most of the cool morning. Despite the ache across his back and his burning muscles, Leo felt lighter today. It helped that Talia was keeping pace with him, not barrelling on ahead as if his company were scalding her.

They swapped ballads and folktales. Leo amused her with stories from his youth, of the scrapes he and his brothers had gotten into over the years, like the time they were chased by a badger.

"A badger?" Talia's nose crinkled.

"Yes, do you not have those here?"

"Yes, but I've never been chased by anything as benign as a *badger*."

Leo scowled, but he barely meant it. "I assure you, that badger was not benign. It was a demon in furry form."

Talia laughed. "Your country," she said, "what other than badgers dwells in its forests? I've not heard you mention any magical beings."

Leo shrugged. "We don't get many. The assumption is that they were all drawn here, but that wouldn't account for the lack of other magical beings. Good ones."

"You don't have any fairies in your court?"

"Gods no. Some people are starting to doubt they ever existed in the first place, although Wil was convinced our old tutor, Madame Syra, was one. But mostly I think that's because she always knew when he was lying and wouldn't let him get away with stuff."

"Strange," Talia said wistfully.

"The rumour is that the Queen of the Fairies is limiting their contact with us mere mortals," Leo continued. "Ever since…"

"Since one of them cursed a kingdom?"

He nodded. "It's not just that. Or, perhaps I should say, it wasn't just that one. Far too many have been… taking liberties. Or so I hear. Which isn't much."

"Hard for me to imagine, a land with so little magic."

It was hard for him to imagine her in one. "Were you born in the forest?"

Talia raised an eyebrow. "Yes, Leopold. I popped out of the ground here. I am not human at all, but secretly a very good-looking troll…"

Leo snorted. "A *very* good-looking one…"

Talia blinked at him, giving him a few moments to realise what he'd just said.

"I mean, er, you know, because trolls are supposed to be *really* ugly. Not that I'd ever–"

"You can stop talking now," she said, biting back a laugh.

"Happily."

For a while, they walked on in silence, Leo glad that the exercise hid his flaming cheeks. He had no idea why he had said that, or even if he really meant it. Talia was hardly beautiful, but she certainly wasn't unpleasant to look at. Not, of course, that any of that mattered.

It didn't matter because she – along with everyone else – was worth more than their outward appearance.

It didn't matter because even if he *did* find her attractive, she was unlikely to reciprocate any desire, and, if their quest was successful, he'd end it engaged to another woman.

There was no point in dwelling on any thoughts that lead to anything happening between them.

As the day wore on, they came across a pool shaped in a perfect circle, a deep, unnatural hole in the earth. Talia avoided it entirely, although Leo felt a strange tug towards it.

She held up an arm. "Don't."

"What is it?"

"The Pool of Desire. It has claimed countless lives."

"By showing you your desire?"

"By ensnaring you with it." She pointed to a nearby mound of earth, to the flash of yellowish white protruding through the muck. It took Leo a moment to realise what it was. Bones.

"You become so enamoured with the vision that you starve to death, or fall in and drown.

Leo was not ashamed to admit, that heavy as the price was, he understood the appeal. To see your utmost desire, not just hold it in some foggy misshapen thought, but to experience it before you...

"You're looking way too tempted. You heard the part about starvation and drowning, right?"

"What would you see? If you looked in?"

"A very personal question. What would *you* see?"

"That's easy. My triumphant return to Germaine. Wil and Ingrid's wedding. The princess and I falling in love with one another. Her laughing at my jokes."

She smiled. "Simple desires."

"From what the stories tell us, love is rarely simple."

"Is that what the stories tell us?" She raised an eyebrow. "I always thought they made light of love. Made it seem like a thing as common as leaves in a forest."

"A wonderful sort of common," he said. "But I don't mean the type of stories found in ballads and poetry. I mean the real stories. The ones buried in tales of epic ballads, or spoken by old women at the hearth."

"You sound like a secret romantic."

He shrugged. "Perhaps I am. Or a hopeful one."

She shook her head, but her smile lingered. "Come along, prince, before you fall prey to your desires."

"A wise course of action," he said, tugging his gaze away from the pool.

"I would see my family," Talia said, when the glade had faded behind them. "I would see them happy, too."

"Nothing for yourself?"

"I did not say that."

He wondered what she truly desired, deep down, and if any of them had a hope of ever coming true.

They stopped to make camp a few hours later. Talia instructed him to make up a fire while she went to fish.

"But... you don't have any tackle."

"I have my ways."

A short while later, just as the fire was starting, he heard a song drifting from the direction of the stream, a warm, light-hearted tune reminiscent of summer rainstorms. He abandoned the fire and made his way towards it.

Talia stood on the edge of the bank, twirling in the shafts of evening sunlight, her voice bending like the river itself. He had not seen her look like this, had thought her expressions limited to raised eyebrows, stony stares and wry smiles. Here she was a picture of serenity, a creature of the forest, so at peace with the world around her that for a moment, he forgot there was any darkness in the world at all.

As she sang, fish leapt out of the water and onto the ground beside her.

"How are you doing that?" he asked.

Talia stopped, without a murmur of embarrassment. "I'm not," she said. She turned back to the river and uttered a few clear notes. Three heads rose to the surface, composed entirely of water.

"River nymphs?" he guessed.

She nodded. "They'll happily offer you fish in return for a song."

"May I try?"

"By all means."

He sang an old tune that he'd known since childhood. A small fish, decidedly smaller than the ones Talia had received, flopped onto the bank. One of the nymphs giggled.

Talia laughed too. He crouched down on his knees, scooped up some water, and flung it in her direction. She gasped.

"I'm so sorry," he said quickly, "did that violate your no touching rule?"

Talia whistled three sharp notes, and the nymphs hurled a small wave at him.

He stood dripping on the bank. "I'm going to have to get naked again now, you do realise?"

The three nymphs giggled. Talia smiled wryly. "Oh no, what a terrible shame."

He plucked the fish from the bank. "I'll get these on the fire first."

That evening was the lightest he'd spent since leaving Germaine, the lightest he'd spent in a long time. He couldn't think of many evenings he'd spent staying up late, staring at the stars and not wanting to sleep because he was enjoying another's company so much. It reminded him of a night long ago when he was just a boy, and he and his brothers had dragged a bunch of pillows out onto Wilheim's balcony to sleep beneath the open skies. Jakob had fallen asleep naming the constellations, and was dozing open-mouthed on Leo's shoulder. Wilheim was telling some old story about heroic deeds and brave feats; the only kind of story he knew.

"You must miss them," said Talia, as he recounted the memory.

"It's only been a few days."

"Sometimes it's worse then," Talia sighed. "It's more raw. You haven't yet realised you can go on without them."

He shrugged. "You've been keeping me too busy to miss anyone."

"Even now, when you have nothing else to do?"

"Even now."

A soft silence spread between them.

"The nymphs liked you," she said eventually.

"I am a handsome and charming prince. Despite my singing abilities, there is little about me not to like."

"There's your humour."

"That is one of my finer traits and you know it."

Talia grinned across at him. "Nymphs are surprisingly good judges of character, you know. They won't aid anyone with a dark heart."

"Well, they soaked me, so I'm not *quite* sure I charmed them as much as you believed."

"They were teasing you."

"As were you."

Talia turned away from him. "You are quite deliciously teasable."

He frowned. "Did you just call me delicious?"

"Goodnight, Leo."

"Yes," he said, "quite."

The following morning they resumed their journey deeper into the woods. Things brightened around midday when the trees gave way to a more mountainous region.

Talia started to sing a jaunty tune, spurring him on as they climbed uphill. He stopped at the top to catch his breath, resting besides a boulder. "How can you sing so well marching uphill?" he panted.

"I have been doing this a lot longer than you."

"Still, I–"

"Stop talking."

"But–"

Talia held up her hand. "Stop." Her face was grave.

Leo felt something shift behind him, a dark, cold shadow rising from the earth. He turned. The boulder was gone. In its place was an immense, stony creature, like rock made flesh. It had huge limbs and a tiny head, dwarfed by massive tusks protruding from its thick, grey lips. Leo was no expert on magical creatures, but from Jakob's notes he knew this was a perfect representation of an ogre.

"Run," hissed Talia.

Leo bolted from his spot, but another boulder rose up in front of him. He let out a shriek and jumped back, colliding with another. Cold, leathery skin smacked against him.

"Leo!" Talia darted around them, trying to draw their attention. Clubs and fists swung through the air. Leo could barely dodge them. The air was thick with punches. Green, blue, brown, all the colours of the forest were reduced to mere snatches. The grey of the ogres' gigantic forms dominated every flash of vision.

"Talia!"

He swung his sword wildly, trying to reach her.

"Run!"

"Not without–"

Something heavy collided with the side of his head, sucking sound from his skull. Something hot and liquid dribbled into his ear. For a moment, he was certain he was fine, that nothing was wrong, despite the white and terrified face of Talia in front of him. She was screaming, but her voice was silent.

I'm fine, he tried to say. *Don't be scared, I'm fine, it's all right...*

But then his legs turned to putty, and the floor raced up to greet him.

"You don't have to do this," Wilheim said, the night before he set off for the forest.

"I know," Leo replied, swallowing the tremor in his voice. "But I think... I think I want to."

"You want to, or you feel obliged to?"

"Does it matter?"

Wilheim looked at him, a long and palpable ache in his eyes. "Yes," he said. "A great deal."

"You won't talk me out of it."

"All right," Wilheim said sternly, "but I should like to know your reasons."

Leo sighed. "You love Ingrid. You want to marry her. I don't love anyone–"

"You can't do this for me–"

"Maybe I'm doing it for her," Leo snapped, but then softened. "She's a lot prettier than you are, after all."

His brother laughed.

"I... I understand that you want to protect me. I'm your little brother after all. But this is something I can do for you that you can't do for me. And it's not *entirely* selfless. I don't want to see you or her mope around for the rest of your lives."

"I'm fairly sure that reasoning still comes under the blanket of 'selfless', Leo."

"Well, maybe I *want* the glory of rescuing a princess."

Wilheim raised an eyebrow.

"Fine. Maybe I don't. But... I am *bored,* Wil. I'm bored of..." *Of being considered mediocre next to you and Jakob. I'm tired of not knowing my strengths. Of not knowing myself.* "Of lying around this castle, never earning my keep." He finished. "An adventure is absolutely required. Then I can laze about for the rest of my days, boring people with my stories whenever they think I've done nothing to deserve my good fortune."

"It's all right to be scared, Leo."

"You wouldn't be."

"Are you serious? The thought of going into those dark woods where few ever return from? Leaving behind you and our parents and... Ingrid?" Her name escaped his lips like the echo of a wish. "Thank you," he said.

Jakob appeared at his elbow. He was fifteen, but he looked a lot younger, especially next to the muscled and foreboding form of their elder brother. He was slighter and lighter than either of them, with huge green eyes, almost bug-like. He looked like a soft breeze could have blown him away. There was never a question of him going.

"Ogres aren't very smart," he said, pushing his glasses up his nose. "Don't insult centaurs. Plug up your ears if there are sirens nearby. Use candle wax or tree sap or mud. Don't make any wishes on anything. Keep an eye out for snakes."

"My, Jakob, anything else?"

"Yes." He withdrew a folded scroll from the inside of his jacket. "I've compiled a list in order of danger..."

It was several feet long.

Ingrid parted from the company of women she'd been conversing with, and put an arm around the young boy's shoulders. She was of average height, with watery hair and kind eyes, if sometimes a little stern. She was the court historian, and had been Leo's tutor for a while, although Wilheim had been too old by the time she arrived at the castle. Leo had liked her long before Wil had noticed her, although never in the same way. She was one of the few women who didn't fawn over any of them. She was practical and no-nonsense and treated everyone equally regardless of station. Leo knew she would make a fine queen, although being of lower station an official declaration had not been made.

But if Leo married well... no one would mention it. He hoped.

He really, really wanted Ingrid in the family. His country would be better for it, his brother would be happier for it. And Ingrid *wanted* him. Leo wouldn't exactly call himself a romantic, but it was sweet when two people matched like that. There was not a great deal of it at court. He would be a terrible brother – a terrible person – if he didn't do everything he could to enable their union.

"He's spent a long time compiling that," said Ingrid proudly. "So you'd do well to read it."

Leo stared at the enormous list, and began to wonder if

perhaps Jakob wouldn't have been a bad choice after all.

"Thank you, Jakob. I'll read it carefully."

A feast was being held to bid him farewell on his travels, but Leo hadn't the stomach for it. With the exception of some of the knights and courtiers, everyone skirted around him as if he was very ill and didn't know it yet. It was like attending his own funeral.

He went to bed early, penned a letter to his family, and read Jakob's list.

He did not sleep well, waking in the early hours of the morning, and decided to leave before any forced fanfare could be arranged to see him off. He woke the knights and helped saddle the horses himself while they were getting ready.

"Leaving without saying goodbye?"

Leo buckled. Ingrid was standing in the stable doorway, dishevelled, still in her nightclothes, with nothing but a shawl to guard her from the morning chill.

"W-what are you doing here?" he stuttered.

She raised a single incredulous eyebrow. "Jakob isn't the only smart one in the family."

Despite the occasion, Leo found himself warmed by her words. Ingrid *was* one of the family, and he was glad she saw herself that way. "But... why have you come?"

"I'm trying to work out who I love more, you or your brother. I'm struggling a great deal. I may love him to his bones, but you wind me up less."

"Ingrid..."

"Don't worry, I won't cry. I'm tougher than that."

The lump in Leo's throat tightened. "I... I'm going to come back, Ingrid. And when I do, you're going to marry Wil, and have lots of incredibly smart, brutally strong children, who are going to be the joy of your life and the bane of his."

"What if they're all beastly?"

"Then, as their uncle, I shall have strong words with them. But they won't be. They'll have you for a mother."

He tightened the straps on the stirrups, and tugged his mount from the stall. Ingrid's hand flew up and brushed against his arm, as if any stronger a movement would have rendered her incapable of letting go.

"Leo?"

"Yes?"

"The princess better deserve you."

He felt her gaze on him as the party descended, felt it long after she faded from view. He was a tangled nest of festering fears and hopes; he hoped he deserved *her*, that she wouldn't be disappointed to wake up to *him*... that he made it far enough for disappointment to even be an option.

Fear was much easier than hope.

Consciousness, or some remnant of it, slowly crawled back inside his skull. His left eye – the one closest to the wound – was proving difficult to open. His head was pounding, and he felt like he wanted to be sick. One half of his head felt numb and distant, plugged up with foam.

Blearily, he cast his distorted gaze over his surroundings. He was inside a cave, wrists and ankles bound, his weapons lying out of reach. His captors, the three ogres, were outside, heating a large cauldron. His stomach churned. He knew exactly why it was so large, what it was supposed to fit. The floor of the cave was littered with bones, including a few human skulls.

Talia.

He wriggled in his bonds, searching the rest of the cave. She was nowhere to be found. Had she managed to escape, or...

Or had the ogres already eaten her?

No, he thought. That wasn't possible. None of these bones were fresh, and the cauldron didn't smell like anything was cooking, yet. She wasn't here. They hadn't got her.

Relief sloshed against him, but it was short-lived. Had she abandoned him, then? He could hardly blame her. She was far from helpless, but taking on three huge ogres by herself was no simple feat. It would be the smart, logical thing to leave him to his fate.

He hoped it wasn't a choice she'd made easily, though. That she'd felt a little conflicted, at least.

No, if he was going to escape, he was going to have to get himself out.

He shuffled forward on his knees, slow as a snail. His vision was still drifting. He felt like his brain had turned to syrup. He stopped halfway towards his weapons, unable to move any further and fighting the urge to be sick. He'd hoped to cut his bonds on his hunting knife and slip away while they were distracted, but he wasn't sure he had the strength to stand.

I am NOT going to be eaten by ogres, he told himself, pulling himself back on his knees. He tried to remember anything from Jakob's notes, but all he recalled was his comment about them not being smart... and their penchant for human flesh, which, oddly enough, was not a detail easily forgotten.

"Food," a voice boomed. "Food is moving."

A huge fist grabbed Leo by the legs and dragged him out of the cave. He let out a muffled cry, lost as the ogre yanked him up. "Pot ready?" the ogre asked the other two.

They made a few grunts, a few gestures Leo couldn't make out while his vision was still so hazy. It sharpened back into focus when it fell on the form of a slight, muddy girl, crouched on a ledge a few feet away.

Talia.

The pot rose towards him.

"Salt!" Leo shouted. It was the first thing that came to mind.

The ogres stopped. "Salt?"

"Have you salted the water?" Leo blurted. "You really should flavour the water first."

"Got no salt."

"I have," he said swiftly. "In my pack, over there. There's a little pouch of salt and herbs. Right at the bottom. I promise you, I'll taste much better salted. It would be a shame not to make the most of me."

The ogre looked at his fellows, who nodded in agreement. Leo was dropped to the floor. The ogre stomped back to the cave and snatched up Leo's pack, rattling it. He tore it up with clumsy fingers and dumped the contents on the ground.

Leo glanced back at Talia. Whatever she was planning, he hoped it was soon.

A monstrous howl sounded in the distance, followed by an enormous, guttural roar. The ogres stopped, their tiny ears pricking. There was a sudden rush, like the wail of wind, and into the clearing poured a dozen fearful apparitions, shapeless ghosts, blurs of angry colour.

One of them pounded into Leo's shoulder, but he felt nothing. It was an illusion, nothing more.

The ogres didn't seem to understand that. There was a mad stampede. The cauldron knocked to the ground, the contents spilling. Scalding water jumped against Leo's leg, but his scream was lost to the wind. It was like being caught in a typhoon. If he couldn't get out of the way, the ogres would squash him–

There was a sharp crack, and a small, green-haired girl appeared at his feet, flashing a knife. She sliced through the ropes in seconds and pulled him to his feet, with surprising strength for her tiny stature.

Another person materialised by his side, a taller, older woman, with gold, eagle-eyes. She reminded him of a governess.

"Who–" he started.

"Hold onto me, boy."

There was another crack, and the world vanished, like it was being sucked down a drain. It was a sheer and awful relief when it jolted back into focus beside a lake, and Leo's body finally gave up trying to fight the nausea. He turned away from his rescuers just in time to retch upon the bank.

The smaller fairy patted his back gingerly, while the older one righted him and placed a warm, glowing hand to the side of his head. It felt fuzzy, which was only slightly better than numb. At least the sight in his left eye was returning.

"Talia," he said, when his stomach returned to normal, "she was–"

"She'll be here, have no fear," said the little one.

"Where... where are we?"

"Not far away," said the stately one, her gaze still fixed on Leo's wound. "Transportation magic is not easy, and you were not in the best condition to be travelling via it."

"You think?" he said. "Who are you?"

The green one smiled. "I'm Ophelia. This is Margaret."

He looked at the two of them. They were both dressed in floating gowns, softer and simpler in style than anything in Germaine, and although they both looked mostly human, their eyes were far too bright, and the green hair on Ophelia was most unnatural. She was half his height, but she wasn't a child, and what he'd first took to be a cape on her back trembled and glittered. Not a cape. Wings.

"You're... you're fairies?" he muttered.

"Well, technically we're *Fey*. I'm mostly pixie with a bit of nymph thrown in..." said Ophelia. "And Margaret is a siren... *not* the type that live in water. Very different. But sure, fairies is close enough!"

There was a flash of light, and another being appeared in front of him. A tall, willowy woman, with white-gold hair and a cunning smile. "Did you *see* the looks on their faces?" she cackled. "I was all over that clearing. In every bush and every crevice, I flamed amazement!"

"*That's* a full fairy, in case you were wondering," said the little one.

Margaret sighed. "It was a bit ostentatious, Ariel."

"It was *perfection!*" she giggled. She dropped down to her knees in front of Leo. "Why, hello!"

"Umm, hello. Thank you for the, er, assistance."

"Oh, he's awfully sweet."

"Ariel!" said Margaret.

"Brown hair and green eyes. One of my favourite combinations. If only he wasn't destined for another–"

"'Destined' isn't quite right," said Margaret. "But leave the poor boy be, Ariel. He's been through enough."

Leo turned to Ariel. "Talia," he said. "Was she–"

"I'm here," said Talia, appearing almost as suddenly as the fairies. Her eyes didn't meet his. She looked at the others first. "The ogres have been successfully driven off. We should be reasonably safe here."

"Of *course* they've been driven off," Ariel pouted. "Did you not *see*–"

"We saw," said the other three, groaning in synchronicity.

"You really should be preserving your magic, dear," said Margaret. "It's wasteful. We shan't have nearly enough to help out if–"

Ariel snorted. "You're no fun."

"I'm pragmatic."

"My point still stands."

Talia's gaze finally drifted back to Leo. It warmed him far more than Margaret's magic touch.

"Is he... is he all right?" she asked. There was a tremble in her voice Leo wasn't familiar with.

The stately fairy tutted. "With a bit of fairy magic and some rest, he'll be right as rain. You're lucky you found us, girl. Head wounds can be nasty."

"But he'll be all right?"

"Yes, dear, he'll be fine."

Talia knelt down by Leo's side, closer than she'd ever been before. He flashed her a faint smile. It really was good to see her again.

"For a moment," he said, "I thought you might have abandoned me."

"No such luck," Talia replied. "I must be going soft." She raised a hand as if to stroke his hair, but thought the better of it. "I'm glad you're all right," she said.

Part 2

Night

By Nature's law, what may be, may be now;
There's no prerogative in human hours:
In human hearts what bolder thought can rise,
Than man's presumption on tomorrow's dawn?
Where is tomorrow? In another world.
For numbers this is certain; the reverse
Is sure to none; and yet on this perhaps,
This peradventure, infamous for lies,
As on a rock of adamant we build

--Edward Young--

7

Sirens and Secrets

The fairies spent a few hours with the two of them, doctoring Leo's wounds, force-feeding him like a trio of overbearing wetnurses, and transporting them to a nearby cave along with Leo's rescued belongings.

"Are you benign forest dwellers?" he asked.

Margaret scoffed as if she had never been more insulted in her life. "*We* are members of the fairy court!" she said. "We are here to oversee the end of the curse. Hopefully. Talia was very fortunate to find us."

"I wasn't sure forest nymphs would have been quite enough..." Talia added weakly.

Leo snorted, imagining scantily-dressed women darting through the clearing, offering the ogres garlands of roses. It probably would not have had the same effect.

Margaret stared into his eyes. "You seem to be feeling better. We should probably depart, ladies."

"Wait," said Leo. "I don't mean to sound impolite, but... were you there when the curse began? I know it was a long time ago–"

"We were," said Margaret.

"What happened with the wicked fairy? Rumour says she's in the castle too."

"She is," said Ophelia, barely suppressing a shiver.

"But... how? Why is she trapped there too?"

Four pairs of eyes darted around the cave, none of them meeting his.

"Oh, sure, don't share the secrets with the person who's come to break the curse, that makes perfect sense."

Margaret sighed. "You'll learn soon enough. It is not our story to–"

"The princess refused to go down without a fight," said Ariel. "And that's all I will say."

It was the first time he'd ever met anyone who knew the princess, who knew more than rumour and myth. "What... what's she like?" he asked. "Briar. What kind of person is she?"

"The sort that doesn't go down without a fight," Ariel repeated. "Didn't you listen?"

"But is she... nice? Does she like horses? Is she funny? Did she suggest this whole marriage bargain, or did someone else? What–"

Thunder clapped in the distance. All three of the fairies prickled, standing to attention like dogs on the hunt.

"Excellent questions," said Margaret, looking out at the sky, "but we must away to the castle."

"I don't suppose you could transport us all the way there?"

Margaret shook her head. "Transporting humans is difficult, as you found earlier. Short distances are manageable. A mile would probably melt your mind."

Leo gulped. "I do prefer my mind unmelted..."

"I hope we see you at the end, young Leo." Her smile was both warm and grim.

"Bye!" trilled Ophelia.

Ariel waved. "Take care, handsome."

They vanished once more, and he was alone with Talia. He sighed, slumping back against his pack. "Is there something going on at the castle I don't know about?"

Talia went quiet. "The fairy," she said, "Thirteen. The time of her awakening is at hand. Her powers are growing. The good fairies are trying to keep her at bay."

"But what can she do, if she's trapped?"

Talia's face was grim. "You would be surprised." She came

to sit beside him.

"I was worried the ogres had eaten you," he told her. "Then I realised you're far too clever to be eaten."

Talia laughed. "You were pretty clever yourself, trying to delay them by getting them to season the pot. I might have laughed if I hadn't been so terrified."

"You... you were scared?"

"The thought of watching you boil to death lacks any appeal it might once have had..." Talia looked down. "I'm growing rather fond of you, you see."

Leo smiled. "It's mutual, if it helps."

Talia did not respond.

He stared back into the cave. It had been used before as some kind of home or den. There were crates behind them, a couple of barrels. Someone had even drawn on the walls... little stick figures, one of a girl with a long braid.

"Is that... is that you?" he frowned.

She nodded.

"Did you draw that?"

"No. I was never an artist. My... my friend drew it."

"Your friend?"

"Honestly? He was more like a brother." She sighed, and he sensed it would not be wise to push her further. Whatever had happened to him could not have been happy. He saw the figure next to hers. A small one. He couldn't have been old.

"Tell me more about *your* brothers," she said.

Leo was only too happy to oblige. "Jakob is about a thousand times smarter than anyone you'll ever meet," he said, unable to hide the swell of pride in his voice. "And I have no doubt that whatever he ends up doing with his life, he'll be a huge asset to his country. Wil is... not that smart. Luckily Ingrid – his would-be fiancée – really is. Putting aside his occasionally terrible advice, he has a big heart. He's fiercely brave and loyal and will no doubt make an excellent king..." A sudden thought struck him, rendering him speechless.

"Leo?"

"Sorry, it just... it just hit me. If... if I rescue the princess... they'll make *me* king one day, won't they? Admittedly, not the ruling monarch, but, but still... I've not been trained for that."

"You'll have years to prepare," she said. "I hope. The king is not old."

"I don't want to let anyone down."

She smiled at him. "You'll be fine, Leo."

"You don't know that!"

"You managed to keep your cool today when ogres were about to eat you. That bodes well for life at court."

She spoke about it like she knew something of it, but that couldn't be right. He shook it away.

"You should rest," she said. "I'll go see if we can stock up on food."

Despite whatever fairy magic Margaret had used on his head, she had advised the two of them to rest for at least two days before picking up the journey again. Leo was secretly glad of it. The pounding had been replaced by a dull ache, but he still felt unsteady on his feet, his eyesight not as sharp as it was, and the urge to be sick hadn't completely vanished. He didn't want to think about the state he'd be in if it wasn't for Margaret's magic. Wilheim suffered a head wound during a training accident once and was laid up for weeks. He'd sounded like a mad person for the first few days. Talia clearly knew a little something of this; she kept engaging him in conversation, as though testing his sanity.

"What's your name?"

"Leopold. You know this."

"Place of birth?"

"Blenheim Castle, Germaine."

"Your parents' names–"

"Talia, I'm not losing my mind. Stop asking pointless questions."

She sighed. "If you could be anything, what would you be?"

Leo stared at her.

"What? It's not a pointless question."

Leo pondered it. No one had ever asked him that before. What was the point? He was a prince. Most paths were closed to him forever.

"I have absolutely no idea," he said, after some reflection.

"What do you enjoy?" she asked.

"Riding," he said. "Reading on occasion. Singing, albeit not as well as you. Dancing... but with the right people. I know you might not believe me, but when I'm not knee-deep in mud and sleeping on rock, I actually rather enjoy nature, too."

Talia laughed.

"Nothing I can imagine making a profession of, alas. What about you? If you weren't a guide, what would you be?"

"A wandering minstrel," she proclaimed, gazing wistfully out of the cave to the lake below. He could see that, actually. A happier, freer version of Talia, roaming about the world, singing stories of brave damsels, fantastic creatures, heroic deeds. The path should not have been closed to her, but there was something in her voice that suggested she was as wedded to these woods as he was to his kingdom.

Perhaps it was her aversion to people, but he doubted it. There was something else.

They passed a pleasant enough evening, playing word games, swapping more folk tales. He and Talia tried to find a ballad they both knew to sing together. It wasn't easy. Talia's tended to be very old, or variants of the ones he knew. They ended up mashing a few of them together to create something both hilarious and awful.

He couldn't remember the end of the day, but he knew he dozed off listening to the sound of her voice.

Sleep came easily, but the dreams were anything but. Thick, cloying visions, nightmares pasted to the back of his eyelids. He half woke several times, unable to call out, before being dragged back down into the painful dark.

It was a relief to wake.

Talia was off somewhere, which he was glad of. He was covered in sweat and didn't want to think about what he looked like. He stumbled down to the lake, stripped off his clothes entirely, and waded in to waist height, dousing his body in the cool, refreshing waters. He shivered; it was too cold, really. Perhaps this wasn't the best idea.

He looked up. Talia was on the bank, staring at him like he'd grown a second head.

"What?" he asked. "Is it the bare chest? Are you suddenly noticing how toned and attractive I am?"

Leo expected a laugh, but Talia's face didn't waver. "No," she said. "I noticed that when we first met…"

"What?"

"What?"

Leo blushed furiously, but no such spot of pink prickled Talia's cheeks. She did, however, look away. "You don't look well," she said.

"I got hit by an ogre yesterday!"

"I meant…" she gestured to her own face and body.

Leo glanced down, and realised his arms and torso were covered with bruises and scratches from his run-in with the ogres and his fall into the rapids.

"The reeds there,"—she pointed to the bank—"their roots are good for pain relief. That's what I came to tell you. You should chew them into a paste. There's bandages back at the cave if you need them. That's all."

"Thank you," he said.

"I'm off to hunt."

Leo didn't spend too long in the lake, the chill quickly creeping into his bones. Talia must have set up a fire before she left, because there was one blazing outside the cave when he returned. He sat down beside it to dry off, pulling his shirt back on. There was little to do without her around, so he investigated the supplies at the back of the caves. Some very old rum, dried spices, blankets, cooking equipment, basic living supplies. Someone had spent a lot of time here, once.

There was an ancient map rolled into one of the crates, that showed what the forest must have been like before the curse. Someone had added layers of notes over it, citing points where various creatures were likely to dwell. Was this Talia's hand?

Leo studied it for some time, having little else to do. There was a road once that led straight to the kingdom, but it was swallowed up by the forest years ago. Several new routes had been charted to avoid new obstacles; burst lakes, landslides, rock falls... he could see why the map had been abandoned. There was so little of the forest that was left behind.

He heard a voice rising from the lake. Talia?

No, not her. This voice was sharper, colder. Still hauntingly beautiful, although devoid of any kind of warmth.

The voice in the back of his head that should have warned him about investigating the source of the sound, vanished as the tune increased in volume. He had to seek its owner. He had to see her.

Someone was bathing in the lake. A thin, graceful woman, with silvery skin and long damp hair. She smiled at Leo, still singing, and his legs went weak. He bent beside the water.

She swam closer, and his body trembled with each stroke she made. He wanted to call out, to beg her to come closer, faster, but his voice had deserted him. The weakness in his limbs grew, the heaviness absolute. He wanted to sink in the water with her, to be one with that beautiful song.

Her arms rose up to pull him in.

"Leo! Leo, no!"

Under the water, her sisters swam beside him, just as beautiful, just as lovely. The song went on, and on. His chest tightened, but it didn't seem to matter. They smiled at him, their gazes radiant and wonderful.

The song grew darker.

Somewhere, far away, a voice was calling to him. Over and over, they rushed his name. Such a racket, compared to this beautiful melody. He wished they'd stop. Who was this 'Leo', anyway?

He felt nothing when the smiles widened to reveal sets of razor-sharp teeth. He was fearless as their fingers sharpened into talons and fastened around his clothes. There was nothing to fear, not even as they dragged him deeper into the murk.

Something cut through their song. Another voice. Just as beautiful, but painful and desperate. Impossible to ignore.

Leo took a sharp breath, choking on water, and struggled upwards.

What was he doing?

All at once, the faces turned monstrous, devoid of any beauty, any humanity. His scream was lost to the roar of water. He lunged away from them, breaking the surface with huge, gulping breaths.

"Leo!" Talia broke her song to scream his name, but he could barely cry out to her before being dragged under again. Down, down into the dark.

He dug his fingers into the silty bottom, and his hands drove into something. A skull. A very human skull. He swallowed a gasp, conserving the little oxygen stored inside his lungs, and plunged his hands deeper into the murk in search of something else. His fingers fastened around something cold and metallic. He knew the feeling.

A sword.

The blade was too rusted to slice, but he stabbed at his attackers, catching one in the shoulder, the other in the arm. He kept thrusting until the water was bloody and they released their hold on him, deciding he wasn't worth the effort.

He didn't watch them go. He climbed to the surface, dragging himself out on the bank, coughing and spluttering.

Talia stood a few feet away, immobilised, white-faced, stricken. "I... I thought you were dead," she said numbly.

Leo vomited up lake water. "No such luck," he said.

Talia didn't laugh. She turned her back, her shoulders shuddering, and fled behind a tree.

"Talia?"

"I thought you were dead," she repeated, out of sight. "I've... I've watched too many people die. Far, far too many."

He stumbled upwards, making his way towards the sound of her voice. "It's all right, I'm fine–"

"Today, yes! Yesterday, yes! But what about tomorrow? The day after? Nothing's all right, don't you see? I've lost so many people. Not one more. Not one more!"

She darted away from him, deeper into the woods.

"So, what's the plan? You're giving up? Going to abandon me here? Because I'm a lot more likely to die without your help."

"I'm a terrible guide," Talia shuddered. "I should have checked the lake before I left you. They don't usually come this far south–"

"You are *not* a terrible guide," he insisted. "I'm the fool who came in here by myself. Strength in numbers, right?"

Talia sniffed. "Right."

He held out his hand towards her. "Come back to the cave. I need to dry off... again."

"Are... are you going to get naked again? Because maybe I should wait."

He laughed. "Just... close your eyes, if it bothers you."

"I make no such promises."

They walked back to the camp together, where a handful of berries, nuts and mushrooms had been abandoned beside the fire. Talia turned her back to give him some privacy while he changed out of his sodden clothes.

"Do you think they'll come back?" he asked, as he draped a blanket around himself.

"I don't think so. The lakes here are all connected; there's plenty of other places for them to go. I don't think they'll be interested in you since you managed to repel them." She paused. "How *did* you manage to repel them?"

Leo felt hot around the neck, and was glad she couldn't see his face. "I heard you singing."

"I'm surprised that worked, if I'm honest. Siren voices are supposed to be impossible to resist."

"Yours is prettier," he said.

Talia turned. "What?"

"What?"

They both laughed.

"You'll forgive my clumsy attempts at compliments," he said. "I scored shockingly low in the 'charming prince' part of my education..."

"I don't believe that for one moment," said Talia wryly. She went quiet for a moment. "Leo, this whole… self-deprecating sense of humour you have, is it…"

"Yes?"

"Is it just that? Just for humour? Or are you secretly afraid you aren't good enough?"

Leo paused. "A bit of both, if I'm honest. I… I enjoy making people laugh, and I know I'm not… I know I'm not *terrible,* but yes, sometimes I worry I'm not good enough."

"For what?"

"Everything. I worry I'm not a good enough prince, that I don't use my power or privilege wisely… and that I'll never learn how. I worry I'm not strong or smart enough to survive this place, and that I doomed an entire kingdom to save a handful of lives. I worry that… that even if I *am* good enough to survive all this, that I won't be able to wake the princess because I'm not worthy, or… or that…"

"What?"

"That I will wake her, and she won't like me. Or we won't like each other."

Talia turned away from him.

"Silly, right?"

"Yes," she said. "But not for the reason you think." She went quiet. "You shouldn't question your worth, Leo. You are worth so much more than you give yourself credit for."

Leo stood stunned. "That… that was… was that respect?"

"Grudging. Grudging respect!"

"You *like* me!"

"You *know* I like you. But I could revoke my opinion. Quite easily."

Leo grinned. "It's all right," he said, "I think I might like you, too."

"You *think* you might?"

"I need a few more compliments, just to be sure."

"You shall not get them."

It was only later, as he was trying to sleep, that he realised something strange.

"Talia… how did *you* resist the siren's call?"

Talia paused. "Their voices don't work on women."

Leo could not remember hearing any such thing before, and he ached to check Jakob's notes, but sleep tugged at his eyelids, and by morning he'd forgotten.

While Leo might have been glad for the respite, Talia was not so at ease. She clearly wasn't used to sitting still. She paced about the cave constantly, unable to stay immobile for long. It was like she could feel the walls scraping against her skin.

"You can go for a walk, you know," he said. "I won't wander off. It's all right if you need to be by yourself."

"You won't almost get eaten by ogres? Or drowned by sirens? Or–"

"I won't even leave the cave, if it pleases you."

Talia twitched. "I won't be gone long."

Leo nodded. He hoped she might eat something if she went out. She'd barely touched her breakfast and she hadn't eaten much the day before. He hoped she wasn't trying to conserve their supplies and really was just grazing as she scavenged, like she said she was.

He re-read Jakob's notes religiously, hoping they were accurate, and quizzed Talia about them when she returned. She seemed impressed, and her mere flash of a smile turned his insides to jelly.

Night came. Another evening of falling asleep, listening to her voice as she told a tale of sunken ships and lonely sailors. It was as soft and soothing as a lullaby.

His dreams were not. He dreamt he was in the Castle of Thorns, only it was *his* parents sitting in the sleeping throne room, his brothers at their feet. Only they weren't sleeping, they were dead. The entire court turned to dust before his eyes, before he could so much as reach out a hand to touch them.

He was alone. He had failed.

The beautiful woman with the chestnut hair and the violet eyes appeared before him.

"You failed, Leo," she said. "You were born to fail."

He woke shaking.

It was still night. The cave was swimming with blackness. Not a hint of dawn slithered in through the mouth, although just enough moonlight illuminated the place to ascertain he was alone. He craned his neck. Talia was down by the bank.

Certain sleep would evade him, he crawled onto his feet and slid down to join her.

"Bad dreams?" she asked.

He nodded. "You?"

"Something like that."

He followed her gaze out onto the lake. The surface was as perfect and unbroken as a mirror. Fireflies skipped along it, and the shimmering moonlight made the whole glade glisten with impossible light.

"I had no idea the darkness contained so many colours," he breathed.

"Sometimes I feel I could stare at sights like this forever."

"What changes?"

She shrugged. "I already feel like I have been staring at them forever." She stretched out, and lay back against the bank. "I... I don't like being alone," she admitted. "I know that might seem strange but... don't ask me why I have to be. It's just the way it is."

"But, if there's something I could do–"

She shook her head. "Eye on the prize, Leopold."

"I do wish people would stop calling her that."

"What?"

"The princess. Everyone keeps referring to her as some kind of reward. People can't be rewards, rewards are things. She's a living breathing person who might be just as annoyed about this arrangement as I am."

Talia blinked. "I meant prize as in goal, as in the quest, but all right."

He watched her gazing at the sky, a thousand million stars dancing in her eyes, her skin lit by moonlight.

"You're beautiful," he breathed.

Talia sat upright. She gave him a cursory once-over. "Have you been poisoned? Did you hit your head again?"

Leo's cheeks started to burn. Had he really just said that? "I... er... I am *so sorry*. I have no idea why I said that–"

Talia was still checking for injuries.

"I'm fine, Talia!"

"You are," she said, half-laughing. "But I'm not. I'm not pretty, Leo. I'm not bothered that I'm not, either. Beauty is overrated and makes people act like idiots."

Leo, glad to have something to talk about other than the embarrassing compliment he'd just spluttered, readily agreed.

"Have... have people ever been silly around you, because you're so classically handsome?" Talia asked.

Leo blushed again, but for an entirely different reason. He didn't mind Talia thinking he was attractive. He actually rather liked it.

He nodded. "For the most part, of course, it might have been more the fact that I was a prince that had women act... strangely around me." He chewed his lip.

"What... what did they do?"

"Oh, it was mostly harmless," he said. "Not leaving me alone at parties. Following me about the grounds. Occasionally being a bit... um... grabby... if ever they found themselves alone with me."

Talia balled her fingers into fists. He carried on.

"My first kiss was with a woman I barely knew. Some rich courtier, older than me. She had too much wine and grabbed me in the gardens. She seemed amused that I was so flustered. I don't think... I don't think she knew what she had done. She laughed and went back to the party. I didn't. I cried. Wilheim found me not long afterwards, and I told him everything. He... he didn't get it. He didn't mind himself. He said maybe I should just try and enjoy it. That I should be grateful for the attention. I don't think... he didn't mean to be so dismissive, but... I thought maybe he was right, for a while. That I was being foolish. Maybe I *should* have been grateful–"

"No, you shouldn't," said Talia shortly. "What changed your mind?"

"Ingrid," he said. "She received attention too, and once... someone went too far. She slapped him in the face, publicly shamed him, and he has since been exiled from court. Wilheim never once told her she should have been grateful for the attention, a fact she spat at him herself when I told her about my experiences. He was very sorry after that."

Talia's face was rigid. "I... I'm sorry. That that happened to you."

Leo shrugged. "I suppose it's just another cost of privilege."

"No one should ever make you feel uncomfortable like that," she said. Her hands were digging into her thighs, and he remembered her rule about touching, and then felt even worse for bringing up this tale, when he suspected she had experienced something far worse.

"Talia–" he said, readying an apology.

"I... I want to tell you something," she said. "Yet I am afraid of your judgement."

"Please tell me. I can hardly think what you can tell me that I would judge you for."

Talia sighed. "A... a while back, I was guiding a group of men through the forests. A few days into the journey, they set up camp, and started laughing about what they'd do if they reached the castle. One of them... one of them suggested not kissing the princess immediately. Said... said they might have... have a bit of fun... before waking her up. What was the harm, right? She'd never know..."

Leo felt physically sick. He swallowed.

"Almost worse than that was the fact that most of them *laughed.* Not one spoke out. Not one voiced disapproval. They just laughed with him."

"What... what did you do?"

"I left without a word," she said. "I don't know what happened to them. If they gave up and turned back, if they died... I've never tried to find out." She looked up at him. "Do you think me a murderer?"

"No," he said. "I think I would have done the exact same thing." He paused for a moment. "Do... do *you* think you're a murderer?"

She shook her head. "No," she said. "I think they got what they deserved, but for some strange reason... I care what you think."

"Were you testing me?"

"Perhaps," she said. "Maybe I just wanted to tell someone."

"You... you've never told anyone?"

"There has never been anyone worth telling."

No wonder she lived alone, he thought. If you'd interacted with people like that, how easy would it be to imagine similar monsters lurked under the face of everyone you met?

"Let's go back to the cave," she said.

"I'm still not tired."

"Nor am I, but sleep is a necessity." She got up and moved towards the still-glowing embers of the fire at the mouth of the cave. She lay down beside it, and Leo next to her, as close as he dared. She did not tell him to move further away.

"You told me about your first kiss," Talia whispered in the dark. "Were there other, better ones?"

Leo smiled. *"Much* better ones."

"What happened?"

"Well, I'd place my lips against theirs, and–"

"That is not what I mean, and you know it."

He sighed. "I didn't want to lead anyone on, and I never found myself matching with any of them. Not all were after my title, but I don't think they were really interested in *me,* if that makes sense?"

"It does," she said quietly. "After all, I can hardly blame them for losing interest once they got to know you..."

"Oh, very funny," he said, wishing he was allowed to dig her in the ribs. "You can stop pretending you don't like me, now."

"But I *like* pretending I don't like you."

"Why?"

Talia went silent.

"Has... there ever been anyone like that for you?" he asked instead.

"A few," she said. "It never worked out, for one reason or another. No match, like you said. Although..."

"Yes?"

"Before you, there was a man I guided through the forests. Edelvard. I... I liked him. A great deal. It wasn't love, not quite, but... I imagined it could grow to something, if... if we'd had more time."

"What happened to him?"

"He died," she said. "All the monsters here and he was crushed by debris during a storm while we tried to seek shelter. We weren't far from the castle. Close. So close. And... and he didn't die quickly. I had to watch. I stayed with him until he wasn't him anymore."

Leo's throat was tight.

"Have you ever watched someone die?"

"No."

"I've watched four that I really, truly cared for. Dozens of others. Each time, it's like they take a bit of your soul with them to wherever you go next. You don't quite fit into the shape you were before. They've snipped off a bit of you won't ever get back."

Her eyes lined with tears, but they did not fall. No wonder she pretended not to like him, or anyone. No wonder she preferred to be alone, solitary but unhurt. Leo wanted so badly to take her in his arms, to let her strengthen or shatter there, whatever she preferred, but he remembered her rule. It beat against the walls of the cave, like the thump of a heart. He was not allowed to touch her. He must not.

"Talia–"

"You don't need to say anything. I just... I wanted to tell you."

"I don't want to say anything," he said. "I want to hold you."

Talia turned toward him, her eyes like silver spoons, wide and shining.

"I want you to hold me," she said. "But..."

"It's all right," he whispered. He placed his hand beside hers. Not touching, not quite. "You don't need to explain."

It was only after, lying awake at night, that he wondered if the reason she was so frightened of something happening to him was because he reminded her of this other fellow. How much had she liked him?

He rolled over, trying to convince himself it was foolish to be jealous of a dead man.

Foolish to want Talia to like him in that way at all.
Foolish to like her back.
Foolish, foolish, foolish…

8
Poisons and Daggers

Every week after meeting the bandits for the first time, come rain or shine, Briar would slip away from the castle, into the forests, and go to the bandits' caves to train.

Anton was hard on her. She could tell almost instantly that he didn't expect her to last long, that he thought if he pushed her enough, she'd give up and go.

Briar did not. Every time he ran her ragged, every time she went home with her fingers bruised and blistered, every time he pushed her to the point where she was so exhausted she could barely sit up in her saddle, her resolve only strengthened.

"He sounds like a monster," said Talia, wrapping her hands in gauze. "Tell me more."

"I think he's just a man," Briar explained. "Neither good nor bad but somewhere in between."

Talia shook her head. "He shouldn't run you so hard. What will your parents say about your hands?"

"I'll just tell them I've been training. These are not the first injuries they've seen me with."

Talia sighed, with the breath of a woman far beyond her years, a kind of aged governess. "You are a lot of trouble, for a princess."

"I disagree. I think more princesses should be trouble." She grinned. "Would you like another lesson?"

"But your hands–"

"Need toughening up. Come on, grab the swords."

On her first training session with Anton, he gave her a huge broadsword and told her to hold it over her head for as long as she could. She'd only wielded rapiers before. Strong as she was, the sword was stronger. A handful of seconds was all she could manage.

He sighed, and sent her to chop wood with Rogan. She almost broke the handle in her fury.

"Are you angry at Anton?" asked the dwarf, swinging his axe beside her.

She split a log in two. "I am mad at myself."

"You can't be brilliant overnight."

"I know that. And I'm mad at myself for being mad at myself, too."

Rogan snorted. "That sounds exhausting."

"You should take up meditation," said Benedict. "That many emotions will drive a person insane. Hone your mind before your body."

Briar looked at him sharply. "I want both," she said, "and I already know how to meditate."

"Then both you shall have. Come with me, child. Your hands are in a terrible state."

Benedict guided her towards one of the caves beside the lake. It was stacked with baskets of herbs, vials of liquid, jars of dead creatures and other accoutrements. He sat her down on an upturned crate, smeared a colourless paste over her fingers, and bandaged them carefully.

"You're a healer?" she asked.

"An apothecary," he corrected. "I make poisons as well."

"How came you to be here, among these folk?"

"I liked deciding who I poisoned."

Talia stared up at him, trying to decide if he was serious or not. There was a playful smile in his cheeks, but his eyes were grave.

"You were an assassin?"

He nodded. "Part of a fine guild. Unfortunately, I developed something of a moral compass when my employer asked me to brew up something for his pregnant mistress, against her will. I helped her escape him instead, and here I am."

"Have you... have you killed anyone since?"

He shook his head. "We avoid killing. Wounding, weakening, some light maiming... that's all fair game."

"No one has ever taught me those before."

Benedict laughed. "Unsurprising! You're royalty. I think the idea is you'll always be able to pay someone to do it for you."

"I think, if you want someone dead, you should do it yourself," said Briar. "So you understand the weight of what you ask."

Benedict raised an eyebrow. "A wise thought, for one so young."

"I read it in a book."

"But you agree with it?"

She nodded.

"And you still want to be queen?"

Briar thought for a moment. No one had ever asked her, in thirteen years, what she actually *wanted* to be. She was the sole heir. She had no choice. And yet–

"Yes," she said, "I think I do."

"Why is that?"

"So I can find ways of resolving issues *without* killing people. So I can lead my country to peace and prosperity. So I can make things better for as many as possible, in the time that I have."

"I see. And... the evil fairy?"

"Oh, I'm killing her," she said. "I'm not *completely* idealistic."

Benedict laughed. "Would you like to learn about poisons?"

Briar's eyes gleamed. She felt hungry with desire. "I want to learn about *everything*."

By the fourth time she visited the bandits, Briar could hold the sword over her head for a full sixty seconds. It was difficult to tell whether or not Anton was impressed by this. The only time he elicited any emotion was when she placed payment in front of him. The rest of the time his face was fixed in its leathery scowl.

"You can try swinging it now," he instructed.

Briar took a huge swing at his head. He dodged it easily and smacked the blade out of her hand with the flat of his own.

"Did you honestly think that would work?"

"No. I wasn't *actually* trying to decapitate you."

"Don't swing a blade unless you're prepared to do some damage."

Briar tried to go for a punch instead. He caught her fist and flipped her over his shoulder. "What did you intend to do, if I caught you?" he asked.

Briar picked herself up. "I don't know. I didn't think that far ahead."

Anton took a swing at her. She darted out of the way, but he stuck out his leg and she toppled over. "Always think ahead," he said. "Ask yourself constantly; what is my opponent's next move likely to be? Will they duck, swerve, counter? Which direction will they go in?"

"What if you're wrong?"

He slid a knife out of his sleeve. "Then you have a back-up plan."

She ate lunch with the rest of the bandits. Anton was nowhere to be seen.

"Does he ever smile?" she asked them. "Does he ever say

anything nice to anyone?"

"No," said Rogan, Lorenzo and Benedict all at once.

"He's nice to me," said Ezio. "He took me in."

"You're too young to remember that, Ez," said Benedict.

He nodded, as if this merely proved his point. "I remember you coming, and you coming, and you coming. But Anton has always been here. He says the forest would have eaten me up if he hadn't found me."

"I think you might need to readjust your definition of 'nice'," said Briar, ruffling his hair.

"Well, *you're* nice," he said, and bit the food straight from her fingers before scampering off, his golden eyes gleaming.

"Where did he come from?" she asked the others.

Lorenzo shrugged, stroking his dark ponytail. "No one knows," he explained. "We thought, at first, with those eyes, that he might be part fairy, but the benign spirits of the forest said otherwise. Most likely his family mistook him for a changeling and abandoned him to the woods."

"That's horrible!"

"Better he doesn't remember it," Lorenzo said coolly. "He has a family now that would never do such a thing."

Rogan poked at the remains of her rabbit stew. "Are you going to eat that, lass? You need to hurry up if you're to get back to the castle on time."

She sighed, not feeling like eating any more. "You finish it, Rogan. I'll make my own way back."

She clutched the sword by her side. There was nothing in the woods fiercer than she was. Nothing at all.

9
Nymphs and Nightmares

Talia was not happy to resume their journey the following morning, which surprised Leo. She had been itching to move the day before, but by dawn her reluctance was clear.

"You look awful," she said. "Are you sure you wouldn't benefit from another day's rest?"

He shook his head. Rest would not come easily, either way. "I didn't sleep well," he said.

"You never seem to sleep well."

"Soft prince, remember? Not used to the hard floors."

"Leo..."

"I'm *fine*. Let's just get moving."

They replenished their supplies from the stores at the back of the cave, and resumed their trek through the forest. Leo realised his bag had been repaired after the ogre tore into it. Had Talia done it? Or one of the fairies?

"It really is a shame they couldn't transport us all the way there..." he said as they walked.

They stopped for a moment and Talia scooted up a nearby tree to get a better idea of their heading.

"Shouldn't a forest guide know where we're going at all times?"

"Did you know every nook and cranny of your castle?"

"No..."

"Well, exactly. And the forests are considerably larger and liable to change."

"What, really?"

She leapt down again, landing soundlessly in front of him. "Major things tend to stay the same – mountain passes, lakes, the caves and buildings. But some of the trees can move, there are these thorns that block off sections of the land entirely... and even a skilled mountain troll or a strong water creature could alter certain aspects irreparably."

"You really are worth your weight in whatever I'm eventually paying you."

Talia laughed. "He says, after nearly dying several times."

"Nearly dying is not *actually* dying," he insisted. "But if we can stay on the side of *nearly,* that would be excellent."

"Understood. We're going the longer route."

For the next few days, they trekked through the forest. The terrain was difficult, but they rested often, and avoided trouble entirely. Talia told him stories of past exploits, of having defeated monsters here, avoided death there. She even told him a little of the others that had walked this path before him, of the family she'd once had.

It turned out that one reason Talia travelled so light was that she had hundreds of little caches dotted about the forest, some with emergency food rations, others with medical supplies or fairy charms to ward off certain types of evil. One had a vial of anti-venom.

"Hmm, we should probably take that. There's a basilisk running wild in these parts."

"Basilisk?" Leo tried to hide the tremor in his voice. "Don't those turn you to stone? Does the anti-venom work against that?"

Talia looked moderately impressed with his knowledge. "Alas, nothing can save you once the petrification is complete.

But it can still poison you. It, or its underlings. They tend to attract regular snakes."

Leo stared at her, and then packed the anti-venom without another word.

"Is there anything *nice* in these forests?"

"Other than my company?"

"Oh, very funny."

Talia flashed him a grin. "Yes," she said, "and if you pick up the pace, I can show you one before sunset."

Leo opened his mouth to ask what exactly this would be, but then shut it again; Talia would tell him when and if she wanted to.

Sometime later, he heard the sound of music drifting through the trees. A playful, jaunty tune, flutey, willowy, beautiful. Talia smiled back at his surprise and crept slowly towards it, gesturing for him to follow.

The glade ahead was aglow with light, warm and soft and fiery, as if the sunset had been splashed around the space like paint on a canvas. Around a campfire danced dozens of slight, tiny, mostly naked women, clad only in what the forest could provide. Several short men with goat legs piped their music, to which the women moved and twirled in their wild, untameable dance. It was all at once perfection and utter discord, endless and ephemeral, flawless and free.

They circled around the glade like ribbons of sunlight bending in the breeze, or drifting blades of grass, untethered and wondrous. They looked like they could have taken flight at any moment. Were they creatures of earth, or air, or even water? Their bodies bent like part of a current.

They were splendid and magnificent, human yet completely unearthly. Although they were short in stature, they came in every size and colour, round as peaches, thin as reeds, pale as shafts of moonbeams and as warm and earthy as the forest.

Unable to tear his gaze away, he could only incline his head towards Talia, who stood almost shoulder-to-shoulder with him. "Nymphs?"

"Yes."

"They're beautiful," he breathed.

She smirked. "What? Like I am?"

"I could learn to dislike you."

"Please don't," she said. "I rather like you liking me."

A hotness rose under Leo's collar. "Dance with me," he asked.

Talia bristled. "I–"

"We wouldn't have to touch. They aren't. Please?"

Talia opened her mouth, but shut it again within a fraction of a second. She bobbed her head. "All right."

They slid into the glade together, and were welcomed with a chorus of smiles and laughs. A garland of flowers was placed upon Leo's head, and one nymph offered him a large bloom to drink from.

"Should I?" he asked Talia.

She threw back her head. "You might as well. Not too much, though!"

The liquid tasted like honey and sunfire, hot and refreshing all at once. It was hard to resist, and it made the colours around him brighten like lightning. A haze covered everything, making it even more beautiful, even more perfect.

The music sang itself to life, and Leo began to move, Talia beside him. They kept perfect pace with the nymphs, turning in the circle, backwards and forwards, out and in. The colours intensified as the sun set, and he found himself dancing still, even as the moon rose high above and bathed the dancers in silvery light.

He was plied with more sweet nectar, stuffed with fruits and berries, and danced with until his feet should have burned. He was never far from Talia's side, even with the haze of other faces and bodies surrounding him. Hers stood out as brightly as the moon in the sky, her eyes alight with energy, her smile burning, turning his insides to pure molten lava.

When the dancing finally stopped, and she stilled in front of him, he knew if she hadn't forbidden it, he would have kissed her and let the world explode into spark and flame.

When he woke the following morning, the glade was still and quiet. The nymphs and the satyrs had vanished, leaving nothing behind but the embers of their fire. The forest was green and still again.

Talia's head rested beside his on a log. He could not remember the rest of the evening, couldn't remember falling asleep so close to her that they were almost entwined. He had never seen her asleep before. Mud patches aside, she looked incredibly peaceful.

Her eyes flickered open.

"Good morning," said Leo. "I was beginning to think you never slept."

"I was not sleeping. I was just... resting."

"Sleep is a necessity, Talia. Not a weakness."

She sighed, and shifted up. "You look brighter this morning."

"I *feel* brighter." Dreams, if he'd had any, had been simple, shapeless things. He wondered if the nectar had anything to do with that. It was the first restful sleep he'd had since he left Germaine.

"Come on," said Talia. "Eat something. We need to resume our travels. There's a storm coming, according to the nymphs, and we'll need to seek shelter before it hits."

"Thank you," he said.

"For what?"

"For taking me to see the nymphs last night. I doubt it was on our way."

Talia shrugged. "It wasn't much of a detour."

"I needed it. To see something good. So thank you."

Talia looked down, and he fancied a ghost of a blush flashed across her cheeks. "You're welcome."

They set off again shortly afterwards.

Something good, he had said. 'Good' did not contain what that night had been. Parts of it were covered in a mist-like haze, but other slivers of it felt like a brand against his heart, such as Talia's rapturous smile. He could imagine himself as an old man, holding that memory close to him still, gazing at it like one might the portrait of a dead spouse. He wondered if he would ever stop thinking about what it would have been like to kiss her.

"You're quiet this morning," said Talia.

"Too much nectar last night."

"It isn't like wine, you know. You can't use that excuse."

"Does the forest have other wonders like that?"

"Some."

The sky started to darken, the clouds converging overhead.

"We haven't long until the storm hits," she said. "Let's not waste time."

They reached a mountainous region of the woodlands just before midday, and took shelter in the caves there, Talia giving it a check for any creatures first. It was a small, low cave, sheltered from the wind but affording barely enough room for two. There was some dried wood at the back which Leo used to start a fire. It grew cold quickly.

The rains came before the fire could work itself into a flame, the struggling embers hissing and spitting as the droplets bounced into it. The mountain transformed into a riverbed, the skies heavy, the rock slick and silvery with water.

"You know, I usually quite enjoy the rain," said Leo, hugging his arms. His skin prickled. The coldness in the air was intense. "Being inside and watching the raindrops fall against the window pane... one of life's simple pleasures."

One side of Talia's face shone with watery light. "And now?"

"It's awfully cold," he said. "But... the company is all right, I suppose."

Talia smiled, and sang a song of storm clouds as the thunder rolled overhead. A tiredness tugged at Leo's eyelids. It was too soon for sleep.

"You can rest, if you wish," said Talia. "You had little last night."

"Neither did you."

"I don't need much sleep."

He snorted. "Not much sleep, not much food, not much anything." He yawned. "Sometimes, Talia, I wonder if you're even human."

The rain had gone by the time he woke, replaced by a thick, palpable fog, that pulsed around the entrance to the cave.

"Talia?" he bolted up.

She was nowhere to be seen. The rock seemed to ring with her absence. He called again, out into the fog.

A voice called back.

"*Leo...*"

Soft, chilling, and as unavoidable as the sirens. He fancied for a moment that it was Talia's voice, and was moving before he could think.

"Talia?" He skidded across the rocks, through the murky fog, his hands searching. "Where are you?"

"*Leo...*"

"I'm coming!"

The fog cleared, just a fraction, and he saw the same woman as before, with the dark brown hair and violet eyes, only she didn't seem as beautiful as she once did.

"Hello, young prince."

"Who– who are you?"

"Your prize, of course."

"You're... you're the princess?"

"Would you like me to be?" she smiled. "I can be anything you want. I can *give* you anything you want. You don't *really* want the princess, do you? You want freedom. Peace."

Talia.

"Just turn back, Leo. Let the time run out. Make a wish on your way out. I will grant it, without repercussions. You have my word."

"You... you're the fairy."

Her smile widened. "Surprise!"

"You're supposed to be asleep."

"Aren't we all?" She stared at him. "Well? Will you do as I ask? Will you let me go free?"

Leo thought about it for a second. He could wish for his country's protection, for its everlasting peace and prosperity. Perhaps he could wish to save the lives of everyone trapped within the walls of Verona. This was surely a better guarantee than moving forwards, with only a faint hope of success, and yet–

"No," he said.

"Whyever not?"

"I... I have to try."

"I could cast a spell over your kingdom. I could make them believe you'd defeated me. You could go home with glory–"

"But I wouldn't. *I* would know. I would know and I have to *try.* I have to try and stop you."

The fairy scowled, and then rolled her eyes. "You are *so* like her. Foolish prince. Foolish *princess.* You will both fail. You already *have.*"

"What–"

The smog grew thicker and thicker, and the fairy fell back into it. Something else rose from behind her, dark and huge. A scaled column towered over him.

A monstrous snake lunged forwards.

Leo snapped awake, choking. He was still in the cave. The rains had parted, the fire was going. He was not alone.

"Talia–"

"It's all right–"

"I think the evil fairy visited me in my dreams."

Talia froze. "Right."

"You... you don't sound too surprised."

"No. I knew you were having nightmares, I didn't think... I hoped..."

"Has this happened before?"

She nodded. "A few of them."

"Why didn't you say anything?"

"Your dreams are your own," she said. "I didn't want to pry if you didn't want to talk, and... I didn't want to be right. I didn't want to scare you."

"What... what happened to the others that had nightmares?"

"Some turned back. *Most* always turned back. Only Edelvard... he kept going. They got worse as we got closer. I think... I think that's why she sends the dreams. To confuse and exhaust and disorientate. I sometimes wonder if he was too slow because of them. If... if he'd be alive if he'd been allowed to rest."

Leo swallowed. "But... but she can't hurt me? In the dreams?"

Talia shook her head. "No. You're safe from that."

Leo breathed deeply. He looked outside the cave. It was hard to tell what time it was. The rains had gone, but fog had barred the sky. Not a sliver of sun was to be seen.

"Should we try to cover more ground?" he asked.

Talia shook her head. "This is but a lull in the storm, and the ground is too slippery and wet to traverse safely. We'd get nowhere before nightfall. It is best to stay here, for now."

Leo fiddled with the hem of his tunic. Nightfall meant sleep, meant more of *her,* and whatever else she conjured for him. "Do you ever have nightmares?"

She was quiet for a moment. "All the time. Sometimes they're so bad I'm afraid to sleep."

"How do you convince yourself to?"

"By reminding myself I'd go insane if I didn't."

"So... you give yourself a stern talking-to?"

"Yes."

Leo chuckled. "That sounds like something you'd do." He sighed. "Not sure that'll work with me."

"I could try."

"Please don't try to shout me into sleep. I'm scared enough of you as it is."

Talia bristled. "You're scared of me?"

"You're very intimidating. You have a kind of 'I could kill you in your sleep' intensity about your stare."

Talia looked down. "That's not why I stare."

"Is it because I'm incredibly handsome?"

Talia glared at him.

"Ah, yes, there it is again."

"I... I'm just trying to figure you out. Work out what sort of person you are. I've never had... none of the others were so noble in their intentions. I half think you must be some kind of trick."

"How could *I* be a trick?"

"Well, exactly. I've come to the conclusion that you must be honest after all."

"But why would you think I was the trick? Why would I want to trick you?"

"I don't know. I think maybe I've been in the forest too long. I don't trust that there's kindness any more. I think every good thing is an illusion sent to torment me."

"Talia," he said softly, "do you trust me?"

"Yes," she returned. "I think I do." A ghost of a smile twitched in the corner of her lips. "And do you trust that I'm not about to murder you in your sleep?"

Leo laughed. "Yes, I do. Whether or not you'll murder me while I'm awake, however..."

Talia chuckled. "I'd let you arm yourself first. Give you a fair shot."

"I think I could take you."

Quick as a flash, Talia leapt across, her dagger glinting in the fire light. He jolted backwards out of the cave as the blade stopped a few inches before his throat. He breathed heavily. The blade wasn't all that was close. Talia's face was next to his, her grey eyes blazing with colour, her skin dangerously close to brushing his.

"Are you sure about that?" She smiled.

"I... I wasn't ready..."

He reached for his sword, jerking it free of its sheath and slashing at her, but she leapt easily away from him. No matter how carefully he thrust, she twisted out of the way. It was like aiming for a feather, drifting in the wind. Not even the wetness on the ground deterred her.

"You're fast," he said.

"You're strong," she returned. She took two swift swipes towards him. He dodged both, stumbling back, his feet catching a loose log. He tumbled backwards. "I'm smarter."

The tip of his blade rested in the remains of the fire. "Are you sure about that?"

He flipped the tip, aiming to set a few sparks flying, just enough to distract her, but he misjudged the angle and sent the embers jumping towards her face.

He braced himself for the scream–

It didn't come. Just a strangled gasp. Talia leapt backwards. He shot up. "I'm sorry, I didn't mean to–"

"It's fine."

"Let me see–"

"No." She took another step away from him. "You can't... no touching, remember?"

"Right." He stopped short. He'd forgotten... or maybe, maybe he'd hoped that the playfight meant that some touching, at least, was allowed. She didn't sound angry though, more sad. Like... like she regretted the rule. Maybe that was progress.

"I'm sorry."

"Don't be," she said. "I'm fine. No harm done."

"I was sure–"

"Luckily your aim is as bad as your form."

"I wasn't... I wasn't aiming for you–"

"I know." She smiled. "I'm just teasing. Feeling more tired yet?"

"No, not remotely." He glanced back at the fireside. "If it's all the same to you... would you mind if we sat down and talked some more, at least for a little while?"

She bobbed her head. "I will concede defeat in the talking department. You are a much better conversationalist than I am. We shall play at your game for a while."

"Not everything is a competition, you know."

Talia shrugged. "Life's more fun if you pretend it's a game."

"More fun?" Leo frowned.

"Bearable," she corrected. "And with that happy thought, I hope you have a charming one."

"How about an honest one?"

"Hmm?"

"I shall exchange you a thought or a fact of mine for one of yours."

"Now that *is* a game," she said slyly. "And I accept."

"Very well," he said. "I am convinced that horses are the finest of creatures, I frequently wonder what it would be like not to be a prince, and I am terrified of something happening to my older brother, but for all the wrong reasons."

Talia frowned. "What are the–"

"That's three," Leo counted. "Your turn."

Talia's lips thinned. "I find kittens to be the sweetest creatures in existence, I used to dream about flying, and sometimes... sometimes I think I made a mistake... becoming a guide."

"Why would you–"

"Tell me about your brother, first."

Leo sighed. "Don't confuse my meaning; I love my brother. It would be easy to dislike someone who is *so much better* than you at pretty much everything, but I don't. He's never boastful and honestly, him being such a great leader means there's less pressure on me to do anything, but–"

"If something happened to him, all that would fall to you." Talia nodded, as if she completely understood. "And you're worried you would fall short in that case."

Leo bowed his head. "I can't help but feel that whatever the future has in store for me, I won't be well prepared enough. That I'm going to fail at some task I'm not even sure of. Does... does that make any kind of sense to you?"

Talia was quiet for a moment. "It makes perfect sense. You've no idea..." Her voice faded. "I don't like being a guide. The woods hold little joy for me anymore, and... and I'm lonely. But I've forgotten how to be anything else, and sometimes..."

"Yes?"

"Sometimes I feel lost. And trapped. Like I would do

anything to be free." A chill emanated from her. "Even something evil."

"Should I go back to sleeping with one eye open?"

Talia laughed. "You are safe from me, have no fear."

"In all seriousness though," he continued. "If... if you don't want to be a guide any more, don't be. After this is over, be whatever you want. I'll help you, whatever you need–"

"You're kind," she said with a smile, "and I thank you for it, but like I said, I am not sure of what else I can be."

The Best Birthday

"I swear, sometimes you're not even human!" Ezio proclaimed, watching Briar dispatch the small mountain troll Anton and Rogan had caught for her to practise on. She executed it as easily as the last seven they'd found for her. She was getting increasingly used to stabbing things.

Briar grinned. "You only say that to excuse yourself from practising."

"No, I don't!" He scowled, his golden eyes flaming with indignation.

She smiled at him instead. "Read to me."

Ezio sighed, and turned to the passage before him. They'd struck a bargain almost three years ago; he would teach her how to trap if she would teach him how to read. She'd mastered trapping a long time ago, but she was glad he'd wanted to continue with his lessons. Helping him access words was far more rewarding than learning herself.

"*Many long, long years later, once again a prince came to the country. He heard an old man telling about the thorn hedge. It was said that–*"

Anton appeared in the clearing, flanked by Rogan and Lorenzo, who glanced at her kill approvingly. "Finished already?" the grizzled leader asked.

"I think I need something more challenging than a

mountain troll."

A rare smile twitched in the corner of his leathery cheeks. "We'll see about getting you a giant spider next time. Maybe an ogre."

Lorenzo rolled his eyes. "Those are not easy to come by."

"We'll find her something. That's what she's paying us for. She needs little in the way of tuition anymore."

It was as close as she got to a compliment from him.

"I'm going to wash off before my lesson with Benedict," she said. "Can you boys handle the clean-up?"

"Again, it is what you pay us for."

Briar dusted herself off and went to splash herself with lakewater before heading to Benedict's cave. He had a series of potions laid out for her to distinguish from smell and sight alone. She managed to identify nine out of ten, and grumbled to herself.

"I need to be better."

"Nine out of ten is a worthy score," he said. "But, as it happens, the tenth is impossible to distinguish from its cousin by sight or smell. How could you work it out?"

"Taste?" she asked. "A droplet; no more."

He nodded, bringing out another vial. "Try this one with it. Can you work out the difference?"

Briar followed his instructions, spitting out each sample on the ground outside the cave. Her mother would be disgusted.

"The first one's sweeter," she said. "Which makes it... celamin? The hallucinogenic?"

"Excellent."

She smiled, and helped him put away the equipment. She knew that she would be missed if she didn't head back soon, but she was not keen to depart.

"I can't come next week," she told him.

Benedict nodded. "It's your birthday, isn't it? Lorenzo's been whining about his missing invitation for weeks."

"My sixteenth," she said. "The last one, until..."

"The last one." He bowed his head. "Would it help if I reminded you that you still had a year?"

"No," she said. "A year doesn't seem so long, anymore."

"A sure sign you're growing up."

"I don't feel like I'm growing up," said Briar. "I feel like I'm getting smaller and weaker. That shouldn't make sense. I *know* I'm getting stronger. But it just feels like… like it's not enough."

Benedict squeezed her shoulder. "There are precious few who can ever understand precisely how you feel," he whispered, "but there are many who will listen whenever you wish to talk."

"I'm not sure all this training will matter," she said. "I doubt Thirteen will try to slip poison into my food. She'll probably be prepared for a physical attack. She is older and more powerful than I will ever be. I can't shake the feeling that I'm going to fail, no matter what I do."

"Will you give up?"

"Of course not."

"Why not?"

"Because this is all I can do," she said. "Teach me something else."

The ball to celebrate her sixteenth birthday was a lavish affair. No expense had been spared. The throne room was drenched in candlelight, bedecked with banners and streamers. A glorious feast was prepared, stuffed birds, roasted pigs, honeyed wine, sweet treats. The finest musicians were arranged, and every noble in the kingdom and its surrounding allied lands was invited.

It was every bit as awful as she'd anticipated.

Briar understood why her parents celebrated her birthday with such aplomb. It was the same reason they allowed her less-than-princessly pursuits and yet never, ever spoke about them. Her parents didn't like to talk about upsetting things. They liked to paste over them with pretty nonsense. 'Nothing's amiss here, everything's fine!' might well have been the royal motto.

The only thing different about this birthday ball, as

opposed to any others she remembered, was the sheer number of young men that kept talking to her. Not just dancing, but *talking.* Edging into conversations at every opportunity. Prattling at her for hours on end. Smiling at her from afar. She barely got a second to herself.

Many she'd met before, but some were complete strangers. She began to suspect her parents might have extended the guest list further than she first thought.

Eventually, it was all too much. She excused herself from a dance with a particularly rambunctious young lord and marched to her mother's elbow.

"Mother," she said, taking care to keep her voice low, "a word."

Queen Eleanora was chatting away with the Duchess of Pigna, and barely seemed to hear her at first. "Oh, darling, can't it wait?"

"No," Briar insisted, "it cannot."

Her mother looked at her, nodded at the duchess, and swept her away to one of the balconies. "What is it, dearest?"

"Did you invite all these young men here tonight to court me?"

The queen paused. "Yes."

"Mother! Without consulting me?"

"I was afraid you'd say no."

"Of *course* I would have!"

"Darling, think logically about this. If only true love's kiss will break the spell, it makes sense to... widen the pool, as it were."

"This is giving up."

"You have your back-up plans," said the queen, bristling, "and I have mine."

"This won't work."

"Why not?"

"Because I'm never going to fall in love with any of them! Or at least, not like this. I'm not going to fall in love with someone at a ball. I need to get to know them slowly, to understand the person they really are. Plus, Mother, most princes are terribly dull and spoilt and arrogant and in love with the sound of their own voices. I want someone kind, brave, intelligent, witty, thoughtful–"

Her mother laughed. It was half teasing, half sad. "Oh, darling. You ask for too much. You'll never see all of that within a few moments of meeting them."

"I don't want to have to accept less than what I desire. The right person will be worth waiting for."

Her mother sighed. "But we don't have all that long, dearest."

The tears that had been threatening to fall all day, suppressed with the false joy, gathered behind her eyes. But she did not let them fall.

"I'm going for a walk," she snapped. "Please tell my guests I have retired."

"Briar–"

"It's my *birthday*, Mother! Don't ruin it any more than you already have."

She turned before she could see the hurt in her mother's face, gathering up her skirts and fleeing down the steps towards the stables, where she asked a groom to ready her horse immediately. No one dared defy her, not even as she flew off into the night, unescorted, the powder blue gown trailing out behind her.

She would have galloped all the way to the bandits' hideout if her horse could have managed it, but she arrived in such a state she looked as if she had anyway.

All five of them were seated around a campfire, even Ezio, despite his tender years. Lorenzo was playing a flute. He stopped immediately when Briar burst into the glade.

"What's going on, lass?" said Rogan, racing forward to settle the horse. "Is the castle under attack?"

No, just me. Just my life, my choices, my future, my dreams.

She felt foolish now, childish. How silly she was to run away, to make such a fuss. But still the unfairness, the frustration, the impossibility of it all struggled to the surface, and the words gushed out of her like air from the lungs of the drowning.

"I don't want to get married to someone I don't love and I'm not even sure I want to fall in love, but I'm afraid I don't have a choice, but also that I won't be able to and I don't understand what I'm scared of all of the time and I know I'm supposed to be patient but I've been trying really hard for a very long time and I'm not sure I have the strength to keep going. I'm running out of time and I don't want to fall under a curse but I don't have a choice." She stopped to take a deep, shuddering breath. "I don't have a choice," she whimpered. "And today's my birthday. I just hoped... I hoped I could forget today. Just for a moment, a little while, I wanted to forget." She wiped her nose and eyes with the back of her sleeve. "I'm being foolish, aren't I? A stupid, spoiled princess."

The bandits stared at her solidly for several minutes, then Lorenzo got up and offered her a handkerchief. Benedict marched back into the den and came out with a lute, which he started to play. Rogan fetched his pipes while Ezio took the horse to be watered and Anton cleared the logs away.

"What... what are you all doing?" Briar asked.

"It's your birthday," said Anton gruffly. "We're having a party."

Lorenzo appeared with a tray of tankards. "I put a bit of the nymph nectar in it," he winked. "Sip slowly."

Briar seized the tankard and gulped down a few mouthfuls of the sweet, foamy liquid. Lorenzo shook his head. "I really hope you don't regret that."

Briar didn't. Though parts of the night faded to mist, others were preserved with crystal sharpness, like dancing with each of her friends, or Rogan showing everyone a fire-breathing trick. She tried a pipe for the first time. Lorenzo and Benedict sang a stirring ballad. Anton even smiled, though his tough face almost broke with the effort.

Somehow, it became the perfect night.

Ezio curled up in her arms at the end of it, as they watched a silent lake shimmer with starlight.

"I like your dress, Briar. It's very pretty."

"Thank you, sweetheart."

"If you don't want to marry someone you don't know, I'll marry you when I grow up!"

She stroked his hair. "That's very kind of you."

"I'd offer, if you wanted to shock your parents by marrying a disgraced nobleman," said Lorenzo. "But it would be a sham. You really are not my type."

"Too young?"

"Too female."

Briar had suspected this for years, and laughed.

Rogan and Benedict expressed similar sentiments. Anton did not.

"We should get you home," he said. "We don't want them to send out a search party. If they haven't already."

"Take this with you," said Benedict. "A sleep potion. One night of pleasant dreams."

She sighed. Time to leave fairyland behind.

11
The Marshes

Somehow, Leo got through the rest of the evening, talking with Talia until the day folded into night, and sleep became irrepressible.

The nightmares came again, worse than before. Pits of spiders and snakes, his brothers screaming, trails of blood he could not follow.

He screamed himself awake several times, but Talia was there.

"I didn't mean to wake you."

"You didn't."

She talked with him again until he drifted off, no matter how many times it took.

He was exhausted by morning. He felt hollow and slightly sick. Even the breakfast Talia prepared was a chore to swallow. She, of course, looked as fresh and raring to go as ever. He began to wonder if his comment about her not being entirely human was accurate. She *looked* human enough, but then so did most fairies and spirits. Was that the reason she couldn't leave this space, the reason she rarely needed sleep or sustenance?

He hoped it wasn't the reason, and he was afraid to ask.

"Don't try to tell me to rest," he begged.

"I wasn't going to," said Talia, avoiding his gaze. "I just…"

"What?"

"I wish there was something I could do."

Leo's insides twisted. He had the fleeting urge, foolish and childish, to ask her to hold him. He knew how weak and pathetic that made him sound, like a boy with skinned knees seeking comfort in the arms of his mother.

His mother.

She and the castle, and any remnant of childhood, felt a long time ago now. It had been two weeks at most since he'd bid her farewell, yet the feeling of her arms had faded entirely. Other things had dribbled away, too. The scent of hay in the stables, the bookish smell of Jakob's room, the clanging of steel in the armoury where he'd spar with Wilheim. Memories so misted they might as well be someone else's.

But if he could just hold another person, just for a moment, he'd be anchored once more. Just a touch, just a second–

But he couldn't ask this of her. Partly for her judgement, and partly for her rule. He didn't know which was more prominent.

"It's all right," he said, shrugging it off. "We can't be too far away now, can we?"

Talia did not meet his gaze. "No. Not too far."

They set off at a slow pace, Leo still waking up, his feet tripping over themselves. Neither of them spoke much, although Talia opened her mouth several times as if she were going to, but had second thoughts. He wasn't in the mood to chip away at her armour, so he stayed mute. She could talk to him when she wanted. It wasn't up to him.

After a few hours, they came across some hoof prints in the mud.

"Wild horses?" he queried.

"Centaurs, I think. Heavier than horses." She looked pensive.

"What is it?"

"They were running from something."

Fear crackled inside him. "Can you be sure? They weren't just… galloping for the fun of it?"

"Centaurs rarely do anything for the fun of it," she said. She stared in the direction the trail began.

"Let me guess, that's the quickest way to the castle?"

She pointed to a nearby tree with an arrow. "Yup."

"Terrific." He paused. "You look more worried than usual. Why?"

"The centaurs don't run from anything. Things run from *them*. If they decided to flee…"

Leo gulped.

Talia paced about the glade, her features twisted in thought, her fingers moving through the air as if she were tracing an invisible map.

"Right," she said eventually. "Three options. We blindly continue on this route and hope for the best. Second, we backtrack and go another way. Will add at least two days to the journey, maybe more. Third, we risk going through the Fear Marshes. It's quicker but… well. It's called the Fear Marshes."

"Marshes that… conjure up your worst fears?"

She nodded.

He sighed, and flung up his arms. "Well, I've already had spiders!"

"So… Fear Marshes?"

"Fear Marshes."

"You are a brave man."

"I'm a tired, impatient one."

Talia reached out a hand towards his cheek, but dropped it away. "I'm sorry," she said.

"Don't be," he said, trying to ignore how desperately he craved that touch, craved more of her than that. "It's not your fault this is happening."

Talia turned away.

A few hours later, the mist began to thicken again into that deep, tangible quality. The kind of fog that permeated the deepest crevices of your bones.

"Strange," said Talia. "The fog shouldn't be this close…"

Leo gripped the hilt of his sword, for what good it would do. These manifestations, whatever they would be, could not be cut away. He was starting to think he would have preferred the spiders.

She whirled round. "Stay here for a moment," she said. "I'm

going to scout ahead. Do *not* move from this spot, no matter what you hear. Understood?"

"Why would–"

"Rule number one!"

He swallowed his question, and nodded grimly. He watched her fade into the fog with a wretched, twisted feeling. Something tugged within him, like a hand on one of his ribs. *Don't let her go. Follow her.*

But the old man's voice rose inside his head. *"Listen* to her."

She was gone a long while. The silence intensified with the thickness of the fog. Each tiny sound seemed voluminous. The plop of a frog in the marshes, the rustle of a creature in the undergrowth... it might as well have been a stampede. He would almost have welcomed the disruption to this endless white nothing.

Eventually, a grey shadow formed in the distance. Leo inched towards it, before realising the figure was too small and wide to be Talia. A bent, wrinkled old woman emerged, breathless and gasping.

"Help me, help me!" she shrieked.

He remembered Talia's warning, but the old woman's cries were hard to ignore.

"Who... who are you?" he asked. She looked human enough, dressed in rags and caked in mud. A forest-dweller, or a human-looking spirit?

"There's something... there's someone..." the old woman spluttered. "There's isn't much time–"

"What do you mean?"

"You have to help!"

A scream split through the air.

Talia.

"She fell in," said the old woman. "I tried to pull her out, but I wasn't strong enough!"

The scream ripped through him again.

"Talia!" he screamed back.

Everything inside him wanted to bolt into the fog. Only a tiny part of him, the part that remembered his promise to stay, held him back. This was a trick. An illusion of the marshes.

"Leo!"

But what if it wasn't an illusion? What if it was real? What if Talia *died* because he didn't go? Was he willing to take that chance?

No, he realised. He wasn't. He was never, ever risking her life for anything.

He ran into the fog.

Talia's screams reverberated around the walls of what appeared to be a small valley, sounding both far away and incredibly close. He could see nothing, just patches of wetness, reeds, snatches of path, and... and milky bodies, floating under the surface. Bones of other, unfortunate explorers.

He should not have come.

Something, someone, gurgled and choked nearby. He saw a shape on a patch of dry land ahead of him, an armoured man with dark hair, impaled by a huge spike.

The form called out to him.

Wilheim.

A trick. An illusion. Not real, not real.

"I'm sorry, Leo," said the shadowy form. "I came to help you."

"You... you're not real."

"What... what are you talking about?"

"You're not real!" Leo insisted, not daring to move any closer. "You're a vision of the marshes–"

"Leo, look around you," the illusion cried. "I didn't come alone."

Leo looked down, and realised the bodies were those of the knights he'd dismissed.

No.

Not real, not real...

Wilheim's illusion held out his hand. "Please, little brother. Take the sword..."

The sword of the crown prince.

"I... I can't."

"It's up to you now."

His fear twisted into grief. *Not real, not real, but...* but it felt real. It *looked* real. That was Wilheim's face, Wilheim's tears.

Wilheim who never cried–

"Take care of them," he said.

His eyes sank shut.

"No!"

Leo bolted forward, but something snatched the body into the water before he could reach it. Someone sighed behind him.

"Such a shame," said his father's voice. "He was always my favourite son."

"I *know* that's not true," Leo returned.

"But what you know, and what you feel, are two different things," Talia spoke now, rising from the fog beside him. He reached out to grab her, but she dissolved into mist. Her voice continued to haunt him. "I'm not real, Leo, you do know, don't you? I'm just a fantasy you've conjured up. A dream. You're all alone here, all alone…"

You have always been alone.

"That's… that's not true," he insisted. "You're wrong!"

"Am I? Think about it, foolish boy. When have you ever seen me eat? When have you ever *touched* me? Have you ever even seen me touch anything else?"

Leo thought desperately, trying to find some loophole in this logic. She must have done. He would have noticed if she'd never…

Yet, even when they'd fought, he'd never felt the swish of her blade. Her body emitted no warmth, no matter how close she got.

"No," he said. "No!"

A dark, thunderous cackle. "You were born to fail, little boy. Why even try?"

Leo breathed, filtering through his whirring thoughts. "Because that is one thing I'm really, *really* good at."

A giant spider rose out of the marsh. A green, distorted, slimy version, slick with weeds. Leo raised his sword to slice through it. He preferred this to taunts of Talia.

The fog seemed to understand this. Voices rose up instead, faces of people he knew. Relations, friends, courtiers, teachers, past lovers, servants.

"Not the smartest, not the strongest…"

"Little more than a pretty face…"

"Awkward…"

"Cowardly…"

"Impossible to teach."

"Out of touch. Looks down on us. Just as well he'll never be king."

"I prefer his brother."

"I think everyone does!"

"I only like him because I'm lonely…"

Talia. No. She wasn't a fantasy. If she was, he would have conjured up a kinder one. One whose feelings he never doubted.

She was real, and she was somewhere, and he was going to find her.

He closed his eyes, blocking out the face. He could still hear their vicious taunts, but he wasn't going to listen. He remembered Talia's voice, cutting through the siren's song… and he started to sing.

Something, anything, a nursery rhyme. A childhood ditty. A ballad of heroic deeds. Any verse to block out the noise.

I see nothing, I hear nothing, I fear nothing.

"No," said a rasping voice, rising over the sound of his own. Someone stamped their foot in front of him. "This will not do. No!"

Leo opened his eyes. The old woman stood in front of him, her face distorted and grizzly and barely human, her bony limbs protruding from her shoulders at sharp, unnatural angles. She swiped at him, raking her nails down the flesh of his arm. Leo drew his sword and plunged it under her ribcage.

Thick, hot blood oozed onto his hands as he jerked the weapon free and she slumped to the ground. A few minutes of guttural choking later, she was dead.

The mists vanished.

Talia stood at the end of the valley. Her scowl darkened as she marched towards him. "You came in."

"I heard you screaming!"

Talia seemed a little taken aback by this. "You heard… me?"

"Yes."

"What was I doing?"

"After the screaming? Being rather mean."

"Your fear is me being mean to you?"

"Amongst... amongst other things."

"Other things?"

"It's complicated. But actually, you being there made me realise it was just that, an illusion. So–"

"How?"

"How what?"

"How did me being there help you realise it was an illusion?"

"It's... complicated."

She threw up her hands. "Fine," she said. "Have your secrets."

He gestured to the body sinking in the marsh. "Please tell me I didn't kill an old lady."

"A borda," she said. "A fear witch. And well done."

"You could sound a *little* more impressed...."

"You could have *died!*"

"I know," he said with a sigh. "But I thought you were going to. I... I couldn't risk it. I'm not *particularly* sorry about that."

Talia looked down at her feet. "We've been through this before," she said, her voice feather-light. "Don't risk yourself for me. You're more important."

Leo shook his head. "Leaving aside the fact that the chances of me making it safely to the castle without you are slim to say the least, I don't feel more important than you. And I don't say that to be self-deprecating. I say that because you're more important to *me,* and rules aside I just don't see myself being able to stand idly by while I think you're in danger. I... I care about you a great deal. Too much, probably." He stopped. "So... so there."

Talia still didn't meet his gaze.

Look at me, he begged. *Say something. Say you feel the same, or say that you feel nothing. Crush me so that I can forget you.*

At the same time, a deep, desperate thought squirmed in the back of his mind. *I will never forget you. Not in a hundred years. Not in a thousand. You are etched into me. If all we have in our long lives is a few weeks in a forest... it'll be these days I return to in my dreams.*

"I... I have something to tell you," said Talia.

Leo's heart smashed against his ribcage, but a sound cut through her words. A horse whinnying, followed by a strangled cry, loud and wretched. Human.

"What–"

"Come on," she said.

They sprinted out of the valley. The cries grew louder as they tore through the undergrowth. A bolt shot through the trees.

"Hold!" said Talia. "We come in peace!"

A figure appeared, sporting a crossbow. A man's face, olive-skinned and human apart from the slightly flatter nose and the pointed, fur-topped ears. His bare, scarred torso ended with a dark horse's body. A centaur.

"Talia." He sniffed.

"Oakfoot."

"You're friends?" asked Leo.

"Allies is a better term," Talia explained. "Is someone hurt?"

He nodded. "Acre. There's nothing you can do."

Something grave flickered in the corner of Talia's face. She knew him. "May we see?"

Oakfoot tensed, as if he didn't want his friend's final moments sullied by their presence, but he moved aside and let them pass. Two more centaurs were in the clearing, one crouched on her forelegs, tending to another sprawled out on the ground. Acre. He was panting hard, his eyes closed, beads of sweat running down his forehead. A blackish wound pulsed on his hind. Talia crouched beside it.

"A snakebite?" she deduced.

The other two centaurs nodded gravely.

"One of the basilisk's brood," said Oakfoot. "We were separated from the others."

"How long ago?"

"An hour," said the other one. "Even if we could find the herbs, we'd never brew anything in time."

Talia's eyes slid to Leo's pack. He shucked it off without a second's thought.

"Will this work?" he said, fishing out the vial.

The centaurs' eyes gleamed. "Is that–"

Talia nodded.

Oakfoot reached out to grab it, but held back. "Your price?"

"The same as always. A favour."

"We accept," said Oakfoot, without hesitation. He snatched it from Leo's palm and tossed it to the other centaur, who quickly applied a few droplets to the wound. It smoked around the blackened veins. Acre groaned.

"Hush now, young buck. You're going to be fine," said the female. She pressed the rest of the vial to his parched lips. "You need to drink."

Acre did.

"You have our gratitude, Talia-of-the-Woods," said Oakfoot. "I hope you don't ask too much in return."

"I'll let you pick the favour," she said.

He snorted. "Generous. I might just give you an apple and be done with it."

"I could go for an apple," said Leo.

Talia glared at him.

"What? I'm hungry."

The female centaur laughed. "What say we make camp together? There's plenty of daylight left but you're wounded too. Acre cannot go anywhere. Shall we combine our forces?"

"Will this be the favour?" asked Talia.

"More a mutually beneficial arrangement."

Talia glanced back at Leo's arm. "All right," she said. "I'll scout the area. Make sure it's safe."

"I'll gather firewood," said Oakfoot. "You, human, watch Swifthoof whilst she doctors Acre. Then you."

"Umm, yes, sir."

He snorted. "Sir, eh? Don't think I've been called that before. Where did you find him, Talia-of-the-Woods?"

"Leave him alone. He's polite."

"You always prefer the polite ones."

"*Everyone* prefers polite ones..."

They carried on bickering until they'd disappeared into the trees. Leo turned to Swifthoof. "You've known Talia long?"

"What feels like forever. It has been a long time since we saw her, though." Her calloused hands passed over Acre's wound. She started to clean it, now that it was certain he would live.

"Where... where does she go, when she's not guiding people?" he said. "Does she have a home here?"

"She did, once," said Swifthoof. "But it has not been home since her family died."

He was reminded of how little he knew of her. It seemed strange, to know so much and so little of a soul, to feel them so much a part of you and yet baffled by the shapelessness of what they'd bared. And he wanted to know *everything*.

"You have come to break the curse?" Swifthoof asked.

Leo nodded.

"You have done well, so far."

"What do you mean?"

Something flickered in her eyes. "Not many make it this far," she said, after a pause. "Many give up, or perish. You've just passed the Fear Marshes. Impressive."

He wasn't sure that was it, but it seemed rude to push. "I've been lucky. And I listen to Talia. Mostly."

She smiled. "Usually a recipe for a longer life. Not always."

She finished doctoring Acre and came over to inspect Leo's wounds. She had almost finished by the time Talia returned. Her face broke into a smile when she locked eyes with Leo, and his heart trembled inside him.

"Safe?" he asked.

She shrugged. "Safe enough," she said, and came to sit beside him.

He flexed his bandaged arm. "How is it that whenever we run into danger, I barely escape with my life while you escape scratch-free?"

Talia's eyes darted away from his, just for a second, as if she were ashamed of her indestructibility. "Well, I *am* much faster..."

Leo chuckled. "So fast I swear sometimes it's like you can

teleport."

"Wouldn't that be something?" She glanced at his wound. "I'm sorry," she said. "Does it hurt?"

"A bit," he lied. He wasn't often injured, wasn't used to pain. People always went easy on a prince, and although there had been a few scrapes over the years, he'd never been injured this many times in succession, and had access to a small army of healers. Wilheim, he was sure, would be better at dealing with this than him.

"I wish I could help," said Talia softly.

He smiled at her. "You *are* helping."

Talia frowned. "How?"

By being here.

"Er, by, well, not yelling at me for a change."

"I yelled earlier."

"True," he said, wishing more than ever he could reach out and take her hand, "but not now."

Acre regained consciousness a few hours later, much to the relief of his friends. He could not put any weight on his injured limb, but he was able to sit up and managed to eat a few mouthfuls of something Swifthoof had prepared.

Leo was surprised. One of his brother's friends had been bitten on a hunting expedition. He'd been delirious for days and laid up for weeks.

"Centaurs are much stronger than humans," Talia explained. "Natural resilience for such things."

"How else do you think we survive in these woods?" Oakfoot asked.

"Sheer dumb luck?" said Talia.

He snorted.

It was actually quite pleasant to spend the evening amongst company. As the night grew darker, Oakfoot brought out a set of pipes. He wasn't as skilled as the satyrs from a few nights ago, but it was a sweet, summery tune. Talia and

Swifthoof sang to it. It was just as easy to get lost in Talia's eyes as it was her voice, whenever she sang. The whole of her seemed to light up and pour out of those stormy eyes, like fire and ice. He'd never met anyone with that look about them before. He doubted he ever would.

"You smile a lot, human," said Swifthoof, as Talia sang another ballad by herself. "Although perhaps it is *what* you are smiling at that I should comment on."

Leo blushed.

"It would not hurt to tell her, I think."

"Wouldn't it?"

The centaurs fell asleep first, but Leo was wide awake. He could tell Talia was too. No sleeping person was that still. Too still.

"Talia," he started.

She turned her face towards him, her eyes large and luminous. "Yes?"

Are you human? Are you a ghost? Are you real?

"Nothing," he said. "Let's get some rest."

He didn't want to know. He didn't want his fears confirmed. If she was a dream, he wanted to keep dreaming her.

Just a little longer.

The Cursed Dagger

One year. She had one year left. Twelve months, fifty-two weeks, three-hundred-and-sixty-four days to come up with another back-up plan, one that didn't hinge on her magically falling in love with one of her mother's chosen suitors, or hoping the fairy gave her a chance to defend herself.

She turned to the library. There was not a great selection on fairy curses, and much of what she did find was poorly-researched hearsay little better than children's stories. Briar blasted through most of it in a month. She wrote to other libraries in neighbouring towns and kingdoms, but anything they sent forward was just as vague and disappointing.

Briar was glad of the distraction at first; it gave her a way to avoid her mother and an excuse to avoid looking into suitors. But her excuse was quickly waning. She was running out of material, and out of options. Desperate, she penned a letter to the one person who might still have some ideas for her.

"Is there anything I can do to help?" Talia asked one night, having found her slumped over her desk yet again.

Briar rubbed her bleary eyes, and held up the smudged letter. "Could you see this sent out in the morning's post?"

Talia frowned. "Who's it for?"

"My old tutor, Margaret. It's a plea for any texts she has on curse breaking."

"Wouldn't she already have read everything?"

"She might have missed something."

Talia sighed. "You'll stop at nothing, will you?"

"It's one of my finer qualities."

The maid took the letter from the princess' fingers, shaking her head in defeat.

Two weeks later, a trunk arrived at the castle with the following letter:

Dear Briar-Rose,

I assure you that I have gone through every available resource on curse-breaking and have found nothing that will aid you. However, as I know you are unlikely to believe me, I have included every text that we could spare in the hopes that you will see that I am, as always, correct. If nothing else, it will give you something to do for a while.

Take care and try not to do anything foolish,

Lady Margaret, Royal Governess

Talia unpacked the tomes stacked within the trunk, and lay them out on the floor of the room so that all the titles were visible. There were around thirty huge volumes, some handwritten in minute, almost indecipherable scrawl.

"This is going to take us a while," said Talia.

Briar agreed, half-wondering if Margaret had included enough just to keep her occupied until her time ran out.

Talia picked up the first one. "Oh well. No time like the present."

It took them weeks to work through what Margaret had sent. Briar grew so tired of reading the same information over and over that she seemed to learn *less* with every word she glanced over. She could feel her mind dribbling away each night she stayed up late, her eyes bleary with exhaustion, still frantically searching for some new, unknown piece of knowledge. But nothing new appeared within the pages, just stories of curses broken by time, by loopholes in the wording, and, of course, by true love's kiss.

On the day of her seventeenth birthday, the princess will prick her finger on a spinning wheel, and fall down dead.

Her father had taken care to remove spinning wheels from the castle, because if she could not prick her finger on that, she could not fall victim to the curse. The same applied to the date; if she could avoid it, the curse would never come to pass.

There was also the counter curse.

Little princess, you shall not die as the curse commands, but fall into a sleep like death, to be awakened by the kiss of one with a noble heart. In this slumber you shall remain for one hundred years, and awake as if no time has passed at all.

If she could not be awakened within that time frame, she would perish entirely. Thirteen's magic had been too much to grant more than an extended timeframe.

Maybe Margaret was right. Maybe there was nothing she could do.

"Have you *thought* about maybe trying out your mother's suitor idea?" asked Talia, lying on the bed flicking through one of the dustier books. "Some of the options were quite attractive."

Briar pressed her head against the desk. "Some of the options were quite insufferable."

"Lots of people are insufferable at first glance," said Talia. "Maybe even you."

Briar lifted the pillow off the back of her chair and threw it at her friend.

There was a knock at the door, and Talia scrambled upright as Queen Eleanora slipped inside.

"Your Majesty–"

"It's all right, Talia. As you were."

Talia looked about her, as if hoping to right the dent on the bedcovers with her gaze alone.

"May I have a moment to speak with my daughter?"

Talia said nothing, bobbing her head and hurrying from the room with the book still in her grasp.

Eleanora sat down on the bed.

"I'm sorry," she said, "about the suitors. I shouldn't have invited them without talking to you first... I was just desperate to do something, anything. I... I'm not like you. I'm not strong enough to wield a blade and I don't know what good that would be. I'm only good at parties and people... which means I should have been smart enough to know that you wouldn't want that. That's what *I* would have wanted. I'm sorry."

Swallowing, Briar got up from the desk and came to sit beside her mother. Without saying anything, she lay her head in her lap. Eleanora brushed back her hair.

"I'm sorry too," said Briar softly. "For storming off. Not for anything else. I just... it feels like giving up. Surrendering myself to fate."

"I understand that now," the queen continued. She took a deep breath. "Your father wants to issue a proclamation before your next birthday, promising your hand to anyone who can free you. To... incentivise them into the journey. The forest may well grow quite wild with no one to patrol them. I've asked him not to do it yet, but..."

"We're running out of options, aren't we?" Briar buried herself further in her mother's lap. "It's too soon," she murmured. "It's too soon and too late and I don't know what to do!"

"I know," said her mother, her voice trembling. "I know exactly how you feel."

Briar took a deep, shuddering breath. "Maybe you better line up those suitors after all," she said. "What harm can it do?"

It did no harm. It also did no good. There was nothing objectively wrong with any of the young men her mother picked out. There was also nothing special about them. They could hold a polite conversation. Several shared similar interests. Most did not approve of the fact she could beat them in a duel, and none of them could match wits with her. It was like teaching someone to play chess when she wanted a partner.

And none of them could make her laugh.

"Tell me, Talia, am I asking too much?" she asked one night, as they lay together on her bed, poring over the most informative volumes yet again.

"Yes," said Talia, "but also no."

"What do you mean?"

"Your expectations are high, but they should be. You shouldn't have to settle for anyone that makes you feel less than extraordinary. *They* shouldn't settle for less either. They may not be your match, but they might be someone's. And if the fairies are correct, and only true love's kiss will break the spell, *of course* your expectations need to be high. Have any of these men seemed truly noble to you?"

Briar shook her head. "Noble in body, maybe in mind... certainly not in heart." She sighed. "What does a 'noble heart' even look like?"

"It doesn't look like anything. It's something that you feel. And I believe that one day you will. You'll find it, and it will be everything you've hoped for and more."

Briar laughed. "I wish I had your optimism."

"Well, you're about to have some more." She handed over the book she was reading, pointing to the illustration of an intricate dagger. "It's called the Curse-Sharer," she said. "It's an ancient Fey blade. If someone under a curse stabs another with it, they share in whatever curse they are under. So if you stabbed the fairy–"

"She'd also share in my hundred-year sleep," Briar nodded. "She wouldn't have a chance to stop any would-be rescuers or attack the kingdom while it slept..."

"And you'd get to stab her," said Talia. "That part sounds

fun."

"Sometimes I worry about your humour."

"You should. It's just like yours."

Briar snorted. "I thought about it myself, when I first read about it. But the dagger has been lost for decades."

"Have you asked that bandit leader of yours? I hear he's quite the treasure-hunter."

"Anton?" she shrugged. "I suppose it never hurts to ask."

She went back to the woods the following day to do just that. It had been some time since her last visit; she had been too busy with research and entertaining suitors. Anton was out hunting when she arrived, and Lorenzo demanded a blow-by-blow account of every young man to which he added a running commentary.

"Oh no, you can't *possibly* marry a Da Lini, Briar dearest, have you seen the state of their estate?", "No, the Van Housans are terrible employers, I forbid it.", "The Menanis? They're tolerable, I suppose. Terrible dressers.".

Finally, Anton returned. Briar handed him the book. "I know it's unlikely, but do you know anything about this?"

Anton stared at the image, carefully. "Hey, Lorenzo, does this look familiar to you?"

Lorenzo snatched the book from Anton's grasp. "That's one of my father's daggers."

Briar's heart leapt. "You're sure?"

"That or a very convincing copy. But believe me, I know it. He dragged me into his private collection enough times."

"Would he sell it? I'm sure I can–"

Anton shook his head. "Your trinkets might fetch a fine price for me, but men like Lorenzo's father do not part easily with objects they prize."

"If I went to my parents–"

"This object… it doesn't allow you to avoid the curse. It allows you to punish the one responsible. You think your parents would be willing to let you risk yourself further?"

Briar looked down at the floor. Maybe. But not certainly. And they would never allow her to wield the dagger herself. And it *had* to be her. She had to be the one to fight for herself.

"I didn't think so."

"We could steal it," Lorenzo said.

Anton shot him a fierce look.

"Not for free!" he added hastily. "But honestly, I would *love* to take something of his. Again."

"I don't suppose you could just ask nicely?"

"My father hasn't done a nice thing for anyone and disowned me over personal preferences. The language I would use to describe him isn't suitable for my mouth to utter, let alone a princess to hear. One does not ask an ass nicely. You simply step away from it and hope it doesn't sh–"

"I'm all up for a quest," said Rogan, swinging his axe onto his shoulder. "Benedict?"

"Will I have to poison anyone?"

Lorenzo clapped his hands together. "Oh please!"

"We'll need everyone," said Anton, stroking his chin. "Even you, Ez."

Ezio leapt into the air triumphantly.

"I want to come too," Briar announced.

Anton sighed. "It's a two week trip. What will you tell your parents?"

Briar's mind whirred through over half a dozen excuses. She'd need a good one to visit another kingdom, and she'd never be able to go alone. If she secured a direct invitation from Lorenzo's father, she'd be chief suspect, and if she stayed elsewhere, she'd be closely guarded. There was a way, there was always a way–

Anton placed a hand on her shoulder. "Sometimes," he said, his voice unusually soft, "the best course of action is to rely on other people. You don't have to do everything yourself, you know."

Briar swallowed, because true as his words were she didn't feel them. She *wanted* to do everything herself. She didn't want to have to rely on anyone to fix this mess for her.

"All right," she said. "How much will this cost me?"

Anton's eyes glinted. "You'll still be paying us when you're queen."

Lorenzo whispered "knighthood" behind his back.

Briar was a nervous wreck the entire time the bandits were gone. She had little to distract herself with and nothing held her focus for long. She wrote a letter to Margaret, telling her what was going on, half-hoping she'd be able to offer assistance and desperately hoping she wouldn't disapprove.

Every other day she rode into the forest. The date of their expected return had not yet passed, but the woods were the only time she ever felt a fragment of peace. That and she occasionally came across a troll she could dispatch. She wondered what it said about her that killing things made her calmer. What sort of person did that make her?

She imagined the Thirteenth Fairy's unknown face every time she did so.

I cannot kill you, so I will kill these other dark things.

The day they were supposed to return came and went. There was no news, not that they could really afford to send it. She kept her ears pricked for anything from that part of the country, half-interrogating any suitors that might have passed that way. If Lorenzo's father had caught them, surely he'd be boasting?

Or maybe, if the captured party contained his disgraced son... he wouldn't want to.

Who could she write to that might know more?

She was halfway to madness when a report reached her that a noble had been robbed in the woods.

They were home.

She saddled her horse with barely more than a rushed word to Talia to cover for her, and galloped off. She arrived just after nightfall.

Ezio was the first to hear her. He ran out of the cave and she half-fell off her steed, stumbling to meet him. She pulled him into her arms and rained a shower of kisses on his face. Rogan and Benedict were next out, followed by a dishevelled-looking Lorenzo. Her heart stopped when Anton did not join them.

"Anton," she started, "is he–"

"Asking for further compensation? Yes," said a familiar gravelly tone. He hobbled into the dim light, his thigh strapped in a bandage. "Your little dagger was not easy to get hold of, Princess."

Briar's heart soared. "You got it?"

He nodded, and drew it from his belt. "Took a short detour to have its authenticity tested. It checks out. The Curse-Sharer is yours."

"Thank you," said Briar, disentangling herself from Ezio's arms and going to each of the others to thank them properly. "Thank you, thank you, thank you."

Anton waved her away. "I'll take coins instead of kisses."

Briar grinned and planted a loud kiss on his cheek, before drawing a coin and flicking it into his nose. "You can have both!"

She turned her attention to the rest of the party. "You're all unhurt?"

"A few cuts and scrapes," said Rogan. "Nothing serious."

"I tore my second-best shirt," sighed Lorenzo. "A travesty."

"Why do you even care? No one can see you in them, lad."

"I can see myself! They make me feel nice. Briar, help me out here."

"I shall buy you a new shirt. The finest money can buy."

"See?" He threw an arm around her shoulders. "Briar understands."

She clung onto him tightly. "I missed you," she said. "All of you."

"We missed you too, lass." Rogan grinned. "Now, shall we open that cask of ale?"

It was late by the time Briar finally returned to her chamber and placed the dagger all her hopes were pinned on inside her bedside cabinet. She unbuckled her sword and slid onto her bed, lying still for a few moments, wondering if she had the strength to undress.

A voice rose from the darkness. "Why on earth would anyone have their bedroom in the *tallest tower?*" it said. "Is it supposed to be safer up here, or something? Do you have any idea how many stairs I would have to climb if I couldn't teleport?"

Briar leapt upright and scuttled to the other side of the room, unsheathing her sword. Standing on her balcony, illuminated in the faint light, were two fairies; a tall, willowy blonde one, and a little green impish creature.

"Put down the sword, Princess," said the tall one, "we've come to help."

Briar kept her grip firmly on the hilt.

"Who are you?"

"My name is Ariel, Princess. We've met before. I was at your christening."

"You're not... you're not *her*, are you?"

"Ha! No. I am pleasantly benign. I gave you your wit."

Her grip loosened, but only slightly. "My best trait."

"You're welcome."

"I was at your christening too," said the little green-haired one. "I gave you song."

"Well, I thank you both, but... what are you doing *here*? Now?"

"I have a gift for you," said Ariel. "More a loan, actually. The fairy queen would like it back eventually." She clicked her fingers, and a box materialised in Briar's hands. Inside was a small but intricate golden pendant. "Margaret wasn't sure whether or not to give it to you."

Briar frowned. Margaret had always seemed like a great supporter. "Why not?"

Ariel's bright face dimmed. Even her golden wings seemed more subdued. "If you use this, there will be consequences. I cannot tell you what, precisely. You could be opening yourself up to a great deal of heartbreak, but… it might be your best last resort. A way to control your destiny even if the worst should happen."

A way to control things. To have some say in who came to rescue her? To stand a chance of rescuing herself? For a moment, Briar felt a sliver of what her mother must have felt all those years ago at the well. The feeling of being willing to do anything.

"I'm listening," she said.

Ariel smiled. "Tell me, have you ever heard of astral projection?"

13
Den of Thieves

T he nightmares came again, darker and more twisted than ever. Leo drifted in and out of sleep all night, trying not to yell, not wanting to disturb Acre or any of the others. He gave up at one point, heading out of the glade in search of water. His throat was parched.

He dropped to his knees in front of a stream, guzzling greedily.

A face appeared in the water. Talia.

"They're getting worse, aren't they?" she said, dropping down beside him. She looked pale and ill herself. "The closer we get."

Leo nodded.

"I wouldn't think any less of you, if you wanted to turn back."

He snorted. "I'd think less of myself." He glanced at her. "Are you so eager to see the back of me?"

"I am eager not to watch you suffer."

At that, Leo managed a smile. "You can be nice, at times."

"When it comes to you, I find I can't help myself."

Leo tried to ignore how her words warmed his insides, spreading outwards to every inch of him.

"I didn't like that, at first," she said.

"Didn't like what?"

"Liking you. It's distracting. After... after so many losses, I just… I stopped trying to see the people I guarded as human, because it hurt so much when they failed. I didn't want to care about you, even though…"

"Even though what?"

Talia swallowed, her jaw tight.

She couldn't say it. He understood why. Because it didn't matter if she *did* like him. It didn't matter if he liked her. There couldn't be a future for them, just a painful separation.

Although, did they have to say goodbye? There was nothing to stop them remaining friends, especially as he was likely to have to remain in Verona for a time, and the woods were the only home she knew. He wasn't to be a prisoner there. He could come out here as often as he wished.

"Talia–"

But could he? Would that not hurt more, in the long run? Was that fair to her, or himself, to only have a fraction of what he really wanted? And what of the princess? It would certainly not be fair to her, even if nothing ever happened between him and Talia…

It wouldn't be fair, because he'd always, always be wanting it to.

She blinked at him. "Yes? What is it?"

"What… whatever happens, if we make it to the keep or I succumb to madness–"

"Don't say that!"

"It was worth it," he said. "I'm glad we met."

Talia was reticent for a moment. "I'm glad we met, too." There was a sadness to her words, like she was holding something back. He wondered if she was thinking of the others, of ones she lost. Was she glad she met them, or had loss ultimately eclipsed fondness?

He sighed and fell back against the bank. "I don't want to fall asleep."

"I know," said Talia faintly, "but sleep you must. If… if it helps, I am right here. I'll wake you if they get too much."

"How will you know?"

She smiled. "I'm a light sleeper."

"I wouldn't want you to–"

"Don't finish that sentence," she said. "I am here, I am going nowhere, and I will help you. Close your eyes."

"But–"

"Rule number one, Leopold."

He sighed, closing his eyes, certain it would not help. But when she started to sing, it did.

The centaurs packed up and left shortly after dawn, with only a brief farewell. Leo joked and asked for a lift. Swifthoof and Acre gasped. Oakfoot looked ready to murder him.

"Offer you a lift? Do we look like mules to you, boy?"

"I, er–" Leo floundered, remembering something in Jakob's notes about not insulting centaurs. "I never meant to–"

"Relax, little princeling. I shall not murder you. But seriously, never compare a centaur to a horse again. The next time will be your last."

They parted ways not long after.

"How's your arm?" Talia asked, as he slid on his pack.

"Better, thank you. Did it look deep enough to scar?"

"I doubt it."

"Drat. I'd love to have at least one to show Wilheim. He's got dozens."

"Each with a heroic story attached to it?"

"Well, there's one from when he fell through a privy... but he doesn't like to talk about that."

"So you bring it up at every available opportunity?"

"You *do* know what it's like to have a brother!"

Talia's gaze dropped to the floor.

"What was he like?" Leo asked. "Your brother?"

"He wasn't really–"

"I know," said Leo, keeping his voice soft, "except he was, wasn't he?"

Talia smiled, still not meeting his eyes. She stroked the end of her braid. "Yes. He was."

"Younger than you?"

"Yes. By about seven years. He was... a wild thing. But so caring. To a fault, almost."

"How did he die?"

"He didn't," she said. "He left."

"Why didn't you go with him?"

He expected her to say she couldn't, to hint once more at whatever bound her to the forest, but she didn't.

"Because he needed to get away from me," she said, her glazed eyes dark.

Leo suppressed a shiver. "You're not secretly a werewolf, are you? You don't turn into a monster or something during the full moon?"

Talia snorted. "Don't be ridiculous."

"So, why would he need to–"

"We should get moving," she said. "We lost too much time yesterday."

"But–"

"Rule number two, Leo."

He gritted his teeth, swallowing his suspicions, and followed her out of the glade.

"She doesn't love you, you know," said the fairy softly. "Oh, it's nothing personal. She just doesn't care about anyone anymore. She can't. You're just a means to an end for her."

"You're wrong."

"Am I, though? You already know she's lying to you. How much do you really know about her, little prince? Can you really trust her?"

"I... I trust that she cares for me."

The fairy sighed. "I broke her. It took a while, but I did it. I will break you, too. I will break your bones, I will break your *mind*. Nothing left of you will crawl out of this place."

Leo's insides chilled, but his resolve tightened. "Bring it," he said. "Do your worst."

"Oh," said the fairy, "I intend to."

Blackness engulfed him. He was launched backwards, falling through the air, grasping at nothing. He couldn't stop. He couldn't scream. He tried to kick himself awake, felt seconds from it, only to be pulled back into the slippery dark. It was inescapable, endless, unyielding. He was going to fall forever. Fear pulsed through him. He struggled through the nothingness, fighting for a conscious thought. Every now and then he caught a sliver of it, when he thought he was awake again, but he could not move. His voice was gone and his limbs were paralysed. He slid back into the blackness.

It was all part of her torture, to make the fall worse, to remind him what gravity felt like only to crush him further when it began again.

He was unravelling. Names slipped away from him. Faces, memories... blurred and gone. Every good thing was erased, leaving only a faint fragment of an idea, just enough to know what had been lost. He remembered the feeling of company only so that its absence could crush him.

There was a name, a name on the tip of his tongue, but he couldn't remember it. Everything was shapeless and gone.

He woke gasping, as if crawling out of a shipwreck. He was starved for air, choking on the dream.

"Talia!" His hand stumbled for her, but grasped only air. He was still dreaming, or not awake enough. For a moment, he was sure–

"I'm here," she said, her voice as light as he dreamed her touch was. She hovered by his side, and it took all of his restraint not to reach out and grab her, to cling to her like she was an island in a storm. "It's all right," she continued. "You're here now. You're safe."

"I thought... I was... she was..."

"She cannot harm you anymore."

But he knew that wasn't true. Maybe she couldn't reach out and harm him physically, but she was there every time he closed his eyes, her image pasted to his lids. Inescapable. She would be back again tonight.

"How many more days, until we can reach the castle?"

Talia swallowed nervously. "Six days, at a push," she said.

Six more nights of this, each one crawling him closer to insanity. The thought alone sickened him. He was afraid of vomiting in front of her.

Talia stood uselessly beside him, her face deathly white. "Tell me what to do," she said. It was the first time he had ever heard her sound uncertain. Talia *always* knew what to do.

But what he wanted violated her rules, and he would not violate her, not even for this.

"Talk to me," he begged, praying his voice was steadier than he was. "Tell me a story, something good, tell me about yourself, just... speak. Banish the silence."

Talia's mouth floundered while she searched for the words, and for a moment, he was sure she was rooting for an excuse, but what came from her lips was far from it.

She began to sing.

A soft, gentle tune, a lullaby as light as air, but her voice was strong enough to cut through the sharp, slithering darkness. He felt like he could lean upon that voice as surely as one could a rock. She kept going, singing line after line, with such power he was surprised the glade didn't fill with starlight.

Finally, her voice faded away.

"I've run out of verses," she said. "But I can find another."

"That was beautiful."

"Thank you. My mother used to sing it to me."

It was the first time she'd ever mentioned her parents. "Tell me about her."

"She was... well-meaning," Talia said, smiling. "Kind almost to a fault. Everyone seemed to adore her, though. Especially my father. He was the stricter of the two, but I still got away with a lot. Mother was obsessed with my romantic entanglements, flinging me at suitors as soon as I came of age..."

This story didn't seem to fit what he already knew about her, that she had been a guide for years. How long ago had she 'come of age'? It was sixteen in Verona, same as Germaine. He supposed she could be older than she looked, but it also didn't fit that she'd had suitors, which was more a term nobility would use. He'd push the inconsistencies, but he didn't want this side of her to vanish, and besides, the honesty was pouring out of her.

"Did you like any of them?"

"Who?"

"The suitors."

Talia smiled. "No. They weren't all awful, but... most of them were dull. Or awkward. And not in the sweet way that you sometimes are."

"What?"

"What?"

"Did you just say I was–"

"No." But she was grinning when she looked at him. "Did your parents ever try to inflict you on anyone?"

"Don't you mean did they ever try to inflict anyone on me?"

"No."

They grinned at each other.

"There were some suggestions, over the years," he said. "But we've been at peace for decades. Our alliances hold strong. There was never a need, and so never a push."

"Did you like any of the suggestions?"

He shrugged. "I didn't know any of them. I didn't..." He looked across at her, stifling a sigh. "I didn't match with them. Even the ones that were charming and lovely. I didn't feel we were a fit. And none of them made me laugh like..." He reigned back his words just in time. "I hope the princess has a sense of humour like yours."

Talia blinked. "I'm sorry?"

"The princess. I hope she makes me laugh. I think... I think that's the best in a person, don't you? I obviously have every intention of returning the favour."

"Laughter," Talia continued incredulously, "that's what you want? You want her to make you *laugh*?"

I want her to be like you, thought Leo, glad he caught the words before they spilled out of him. *No, no, that will do no good. Don't fall for her. That way lies nothing but heartbreak.* "Well, obviously it would also be wonderful if she's much, much nicer than you. You can be mean."

Talia hung her head. "I wasn't always."

He felt bad for trying to make a joke of it. "You have many other admirable qualities," he said, doubting she would want him to list them. "I can't think of any right now, but–"

Talia laughed, at the same time the fire crackled. It was no good to deny it. It didn't matter how funny or pleasant the princess was. It was *Talia's* laugh he craved, her company. The days were marching on far too quickly now, and he wanted to grab them and stretch them out into a hundred. He wanted more time with her.

At the same time, he wanted to run away. This was the scariest thing the forest had thrown at him, and it would only get worse, the deeper they went. Talia and he would have to part ways eventually. His chest tightened at the thought. When they went their separate ways, something inside of him would snap, and nothing in the world would plug the gap she left there.

Stupid. Foolish. A schoolboy's crush, the product of spending too much time together in a dangerous situation. It was nothing, nothing–

But then Talia smiled at him, and he wondered if she felt at all the same, and which answer would hurt less.

He didn't go back to sleep. He couldn't. They started again at first light, Leo unable to eat and begging her to push him as hard as possible.

"Leo–"

"I mean it," he said. "Push me. I'm stronger than I was."

"I know you're strong," she said. "But–"

"Could you, just for once, please listen to me?"

Talia swallowed. "All right."

He followed her into the growing darkness. The trees wound closer together, tight as vines. All remnants of a path vanished. It took hours to cover minimal ground, the undergrowth snaking around his ankles.

Then they arrived at a thick wall of spiny brambles, almost impassable.

"Are we... are we here?" he asked.

Talia shook her head. "Huge patches of it spring up from this point forward," she said. "That's why it takes so long to reach the centre."

"No way round?"

"No way round."

He drew his sword. "Onwards, then."

He hacked away at the thorns. It was like cutting through stone. Ineffective, back-breaking, endless. Each strike seemed to push him further back. His lungs felt like iron. His palms blistered. The hilt stung his raw skin.

"Leo–"

He carried on cutting. He didn't want to stop. He didn't want to stop and think about the pain, or think about her, or have a moment to acknowledge how exhausted he was, how sick he felt, how his muscles burned and his joints felt like jelly. He had to keep going. Another swing, another half-step closer.

Endless. Endless thorns.

And it was dark, so dark.

And he was tired, so tired.

"Leo!"

He sank to his knees, placed his head in his hands, and sobbed.

"I can't," he said. "I'm sorry."

Talia stood in front of him. He stared at her mud-caked boots, and realised she was trembling too.

"Don't you *dare* apologise to me!" she hissed. "Not for this, do you understand? And if I ever hear you say you can't do something again, Leopold, I will kill you myself!"

She sat down beside him in the tiny space he'd cut away.

"Catch your breath," she said. "Rest. Eat. We're going another way–"

"No detours," he begged. "Please."

"This one will be worth it. I promise. You'll get at least one good night's sleep."

One good night's sleep sounded worth anything. At that moment, he'd have sold his soul for real, true rest. A quiet, still blackness was everything he desired.

"Bind your hands," she instructed. "We've still a little more to cut through."

Before nightfall, they arrived at a thicket beside a lake. Several wooden structures were perched in the treetops and wrapped around the bases of the trees. Some were connected by shredded ropes; the remnants of what once must have been bridges. Ivy and moss clung to every surface.

"What is this place?" Leo asked.

Talia was silent. "Home," she said eventually. "Or it was, a long time ago."

They descended into one of the structures at the foot of an enormous oak. Underneath the swathes of ivy, he could make out a sink, a cauldron, pots and bowls. This had been a kitchen, once upon a time.

"Down," Talia pointed.

There was a sloping hole in the ground, leading to a lower floor, a dark and earthy chamber lit by crystals. A hundred jars and vials of potions and herbs lined the walls. Talia swept towards them, surveying every faded label.

"That one," she said, pointing to a small vial of colourless liquid. "A potion for a dreamless sleep."

"How many are there?"

"Five," she counted.

Leo wasn't sure if he wanted to sob with relief or shiver with fear. Five was not quite enough to get him to the castle. But five days of relief... After a break, he could handle another night or two. If only he could sleep for a bit...

"I... I can't brew anymore," Talia said. "Most of the herbs were destroyed, a long time ago. If I could, I would."

"You brewed these?"

"Some of them."

A whisper of natural light stirred at the end of the chamber. He craned his neck. The lake. It wasn't a chamber at all, but the back of a cave. He could see something dancing on the surface of the water.

"What are–"

The shapes vanished.

"Illusions," Talia said. "Perfectly benign. Memories you can summon with a thought."

Leo crept closer. A vision rose from the depths. His parents, his brothers, smiling and laughing.

"Your family?" Talia guessed.

He nodded. "Mother, Father, Wilheim, Jakob."

"They look... happy."

"They were. They are." He paused. "We were." He looked back towards the abandoned structure of Talia's former home. "You aren't happy to be here."

Talia cast her eyes downwards. "Home isn't home without a family."

"I'm... I'm so sorry, Talia. I know I said that before, but I really, *really* feel it now. Whatever happened to them... whatever happened to *you*... I wish it hadn't. I wish there was something I could do–"

"I'll go and find us something for dinner," she said. "Stay here. You should be safe. I won't be long."

"Talia–"

She did not reply, vanishing back into the woods. It would have been easy to stay beside the lake, to summon sweet, beautiful visions, but he was more interested in the truths packed into the walls of this forgotten place.

He stumbled back up to the ground level. A ladder had been cut into the trunk of the tree, still usable despite the years. He pulled himself up to the next floor. It was a weapons' room, full of rusted blades, discarded bows, none of them usable. How long ago had this place been deserted?

There were two bridges leading out to other trees, other structures, but both had rotted away with age. He continued upwards, arriving in a bedroom. He could make out five or six bunks under the foliage. The ceiling of this room was painted. Most of it had chipped away or faded over the years, but a handful of images still survived. A whisper of a dragon, half of a lagoon, an eagle. Each brushstroke spoke of a passion, of a love that outlived the hand that crafted them. Someone had been happy here. *Talia* had.

On the trunk of the tree, someone had carved six names. *Lorenzo, Anton, Benedict, Rogan, Ezio.* The sixth had come away, through nature or a hand, it was hard to see.

With one final look at the paintings, he went back down to the kitchen and started to clear through the debris, hacking away the ivy, sweeping out the swathes of leaves. It was as good a task as any to occupy himself with.

After an hour or so, he heard a wittering, whispery kind of chatter from outside. He leaned his head over the windowsill, and saw a campfire going. Three tiny brown-skinned creatures in red caps were stoking it, chattering to themselves.

He went outside.

"Hello–" he started.

The creatures stopped their task immediately and darted behind a fallen log.

"It's all right, I won't hurt you."

Talia appeared beside him. "They don't like being watched."

Leo jumped. "Where did you come from?"

"The forest. I've been hunting."

She gestured to a nearby bird.

"You…" He shook his head. "Never mind. What are they?"

"Brownies. Wild ones. They're helpful spirits, aid with domestic tasks, etcetera, but they don't like being watched. I suppose…" Her eyes glanced towards the den. "We should go inside."

Leo nodded, leading the way.

"You cleaned up," said Talia upon entry.

Leo scratched the back of his neck. "I just felt… I wanted to do something."

"Thank you."

Talia looked around at the ruined pots, the salvaged crockery and mouldy furnishings. Her eyes misted.

"Talia?"

"Yes?"

"You don't have to tell me, and I won't pry, but… if you wanted to tell me what happened here, I would listen."

Talia swallowed. "Follow me," was all she said.

14
The Spindle

The day before her seventeenth birthday dawned with no aplomb, no grandeur. It was just another day.

Just another day. Not the last, not the last.

She woke painfully early and went to the armoury to train. Her mother was up early too, and kept drifting in to ask about last-minute party decisions.

"Shall we have the blue banners, or the pink ones?"

"Are you quite sure you want *lemon* sponge?"

"Have you had breakfast?"

Seeking an escape, Briar saddled her horse and rode wild through the woods. The weather was grey with expectation, the morning dew clinging to the leaves like pearls, a light fog swallowing up every lake and clearing.

She arrived breathless at the bandits' den, where Anton silently put her to work. None of the bandits could engage her in conversation, though Ezio read to her for a while. Benedict gave her a potion to help her sleep, and Lorenzo gifted her with a fine embroidered handkerchief.

She was muddy and exhausted by the time she returned home, although once she'd bathed and swallowed a supper, energy was returning. She did not want to sleep. Benedict's potion glinted at her bedside, but she could not bring herself to take it. The very thought of sleep was a taunt.

She tossed and turned for hours, too hot, too cold, too exhausted, too awake, until finally a dribble of sleep occupied her body. It wasn't enough, and she woke several times.

The third time, her mother was next to her. She panicked at first, thinking the wicked fairy had materialised beside her, before she recognised the soft features of her mother's face.

"Mother, are you... watching me sleep?"

Eleanora nodded, stroking her nose. "It's a thing mothers do."

"To their babies, maybe..."

"You will always be my baby." She paused. "You'll understand one day."

Briar stiffened, not sure that she ever would.

"You know..." her mother continued, "the few nights between your birth and your christening, I barely slept at all. I was so afraid you'd vanish in the night. I couldn't take my eyes off you. In a way, the curse was almost a blessing. I knew I would have you for seventeen years. But now that those years are up..."

"Mother..."

"It was my fault. It's all my fault. If I'd just asked what she wanted from the start–"

"Casting blame accomplishes nothing," said Briar swiftly. "And I don't regret your bargain. Not at all."

"You... you don't?"

"If she'd asked you upfront for your first child, would you have said yes?"

"I... no. No, probably not."

"Then if you'd refused her, I wouldn't be here. And I really, really like being here. Almost all of the time."

Her mother smiled wearily. "You never wished we would have let her take you?"

Briar raised an eyebrow. "Exciting as a life of magic and adventure would be... she sounds rather mean. Not ideal mother material." She launched herself forward and into her mother's arms. *Let me be a child again, just for a moment. Just for a little while longer.* "You're ideal mother material," she whispered. "Most of the time. Thank you for wishing me into existence."

Eleanora let out a sigh. "Thank you for being everything that I wished for." She paused. "Most of the time. And... and some things I didn't wish for, too."

Briar laughed, and buried herself further into her mother's arms.

There was a quiet, almost imperceptible knock at the door. Briar whispered a response, and her father appeared in the crack.

"I thought I heard voices," he said. "Is there room for one more?"

Briar smiled, and shifted aside to make room for him. She had not shared a bed with both of her parents since she was a tiny child, and even then, it had been infrequent. She knew she was lucky to have many memories of it happening at all, that most royals were far too busy for their children.

Briar had rarely felt that. Even when her parents were occupied, she had understood why, and she had always felt that had she needed them more than their kingdom, they would have made time for her.

Like they had now.

I'm lucky, really, she forced a cheerful thought. *I'm not cursed, I'm blessed. Blessed, blessed...*

"Anyone fancy a picnic in Germaine tomorrow?" said her father.

"Very funny," returned her mother. "Germaine is several days away, and you know how much work I've put into this party–"

There had been talk, of course, of disappearing. Of dressing up another girl in her attire. They had put these plans aside, deciding that the fairy would not be fooled, that the location would not matter. Far better stay on their own lands, in their own castle, with their trusted servants and secret passages. Her father seemed unusually confident. Her mother was trying to pretend it was an ordinary day.

Briar felt neither. Her confidence was squashed, her training eclipsed by the overwhelming fear of Thirteen's magic. She was only a child. She could not stand up to her.

And yet she had to, because the alternative was giving in to fear completely, surrendering herself entirely to the might of another. And if there was one thing Briar was absolutely certain of, it was that she would not go quietly, she would not give in, and she would go down fighting.

She only wished she didn't have quite so far to fall.

The guests were arriving. The feast was being laid out. The castle was ablaze with music and the tantalising aromas of sizzling meat and baking pies drifted up from the kitchens.

Briar felt sick to her stomach, as if each waft of flavour was there to remind her that she would taste none of it that evening, and every note taunted her with the promise of any dancing being wrenched from her forever. She thumbed the fairy pendant thumping against her chest, wishing it was a ward to banish dark thoughts, rather than a failsafe she hoped she'd never have to use, and slid the dagger up her sleeve like Anton had taught her.

There was a knock on the door. Talia.

"You have the most adorable little suitor paying you a visit," she said. "Shall I let him in?"

Before she could usher a reply, Ezio had broken past Talia and rushed at Briar's middle.

"Ezio!" she cried, clutching him to her. "What are you doing here?"

"It's your birthday!" he declared. "I brought you a gift!" He drew back, and in his hands was a bouquet of wildflowers. Briar inhaled their sweet, earthy scent, all at once transported back to the quiet tranquillity of the forests.

"They're beautiful," she breathed. "Thank you."

"They aren't as pretty as you. I searched for a really long time to find the prettiest I could, though."

"They're perfect," she said, ruffling his hair. "As are you. But you can't stick around tonight, all right? I need you safe in the forest."

"Something bad is going to happen tonight, isn't it? The others were saying–"

"Don't you worry about that. You know how tough I am."

He pouted. "I'm tough too! Let me stay here. I can protect you."

"Which is why I need you away from here," she insisted. "You're part of my back-up plan."

He folded his arms, but relented when she gave him a kiss, and told him how important he was to her. He allowed himself to be steered away by Talia, who returned after escorting him safely off the premises.

Briar turned towards the mirror. She did not feel much like herself, though she'd picked out the sweeping midnight gown. It was simple and elegant, less girlish than a lot of her others, but the crown set aside for her seemed all wrong. She clutched Ezio's bouquet.

"Could you put flowers in my hair instead, do you think?"

Talia nodded. "Flowers on a princess instead of pearls or jewels? Your mother will have fit."

"That's if she even sees me."

Talia closed a hand over Briar's tightly-coiled fists. "It will be all right, Your Highness, it will. It may be hard for a while... but it will be fine. I promise you."

"Oh, Talia. You are so much better than I deserve."

The maid grinned at her as she unravelled the flowers and set to work arranging the buds in her hair. "I wouldn't say that."

Talia chatted about nothing in particular as she readied Briar for the festivities, teasing her over prospective suitors and whether or not she ought to let that little Ezio boy be one of them, when there was a quiet knock on the door. She went to answer, leaving Briar to her own devices.

Despite the flowers, the girl in the mirror still felt like a stranger. Even her room didn't feel like her own. In fact, what was that dark thing in the corner–

She froze. There was a spindle by the wall.

"I hope you don't mind, but I brought my own."

Briar wheeled round. Lying on her bed was a beautiful

woman with dark chestnut hair, violet eyes, and a red mouth fixed in a sneer. She had never seen her before, yet knew at once who she was.

"It's you," she said. "The Thirteenth Fairy."

The sneer widened. "Is that what they're calling me? Ominous. I like it."

"I– guards!" Briar shouted, turning in the direction of the door. Only then did she notice how still Talia was, she and the guards frozen in position.

"What... what did you do to them?"

"Oh, they're not dead," said Thirteen, sitting up and dusting down her dress. "They're just under a spell. Like you will be, shortly."

She crossed the room, and for a moment, Briar was paralysed. Something dark and frosty seemed to emanate from this woman, cold and violent and uncontrollable. It grabbed hold of her years of training and throttled it.

The fairy held out a hand towards her trembling cheek. "Such a shame," she sighed. "You are so beautiful. You would have made an excellent child."

Briar remembered the dagger in her sleeve, but before she could use it, the fairy had stepped away. She would only have one shot, and if the fairy saw her coming...

"Touch the spindle," she said. "There's no need to prolong this."

Briar stared at the spindle, and then back at the fairy.

"Touch it!"

Something cold licked at the corners of her mind, but she pushed back, as she had done a thousand times before with Margaret. "No," she said. "I will not. You cannot make me."

The fairy's mouth flickered. She looked almost impressed.

"Maybe I can't," she said, "but I bet they can."

The guards marched into the room, pulling out their weapons. Briar disarmed the first one before he could reach her, using his blade to parry the second. She jabbed the first in the ribs, but he did not flinch. He did absolutely nothing, even when she crushed the hilt against the back of his skull in a movement Anton would have been proud of.

"No..." she breathed.

The fairy laughed. She clapped her hands together, and the guards lunged towards her. Briar leapt out of the way, rolling along the floor and springing towards the balcony. If she alerted anyone, Thirteen would just manipulate them too, but if she could escape–

"Stop!" Thirteen yelled.

Briar chanced a look back into her room. One of the guards had grabbed an immobile Talia and placed a knife to her throat. A rim of blood dotted her neck.

"No," Briar choked, "please... don't hurt her."

"You really are a fiery creature. To resist me, to fight them... yes, you are everything I could have wished for. But your mother was insistent. Foolish girl. I always get everything that I wish for in the end." She reached out and stroked a lock of Briar's gleaming hair. "Touch the spindle, there's a good girl. Your life for hers. Then I will vanish from this kingdom and never be seen again. You have my word."

Her life was a small exchange for peace, and perhaps a part of her wanted to accept... perhaps it would be an awful lot less trouble than what was coming next.

"All right," Briar said. "I'll do it."

Thirteen smiled, waving a hand. The guard dropped Talia to the floor. Briar ran towards her, but the fairy stood in her path.

"Our bargain first," she said.

"Will... will I have time to say goodbye?"

The fairy shrugged. "A few seconds, maybe, given how resistant you are."

It would have to be enough. She had run out of other options. She clutched the pendant, and then stumbled towards the spindle, tripping as she went. She let out a quiet sob. *Let her think that I am weak.*

She raised her finger to the point, and pressed the tip down.

An ice-like sensation spread through her limbs, squeezing the air from her lungs. She fought against the tightness in her chest. A few seconds. That was all she had.

"It's all right, Princess, it will be over soon," said Thirteen.

"I... I'm scared," she whispered.

The fairy's smile was oddly warm.

"Hold me," said Briar, and fell into her arms.

Her body was warm beneath her, her embrace soft. It stiffened when she slid the dagger from her sleeve and plunged it into her middle.

Thirteen stumbled back, her eyes wide as she grasped at the hilt.

"Do you know it?" Briar asked. "Do you recognise what it is?"

"You... how did you...?"

"It doesn't matter, does it?" she said. "Sleep with me, witch."

The fairy grasped the edge of the balcony.

"You think you've won, don't you? You think you can just sit back and wait until someone rescues you? No. No one's ever going to come for you."

She raised a hand towards the sky, and black lightning shot from her fingertips. The skies overhead groaned, darkening into a thick storm.

"I will send out a beacon. I will fill your forests with every dark creature. Nothing and no one will ever break through. You are even more doomed than you were before..." She grinned back at her. "Foolish girl. You have destroyed your own kingdom."

She toppled over the balcony. The last thing Briar heard was the sound of screaming as her body hit the ground below, before the heaviness overtook, and she slumped against the bed.

She woke in the corner of her room, but for a moment, she was sure she was still dreaming. She could feel nothing; not a whisper of breeze, not the floor beneath her, not even her own clothes.

And she was staring at herself on the bed.

She looked like a corpse. Someone had taken the effort to arrange her like she was sleeping, turning her slightly to the side, but the drape of her dress, the perfectly placed flowers, the stillness of her flesh reminded her of a painting. There was so little life in her.

The guards, propped up beside the door, were similarly still. Talia was curled on a nearby chaise, small and kitten-like. An endless, unyielding silence pulsated around the chamber.

She got up and drifted towards the balcony. There was no unsteadiness, although she couldn't feel her limbs. Two turtle doves were dozing outside, their heads tucked beneath their wings. The courtyard, usually bustling with life, was as still as the graveyard. The servants were sleeping on the lawns, the stable hands drooped over the slumbering horses. The only movement came from a nest of thorns beneath her, which throbbed with dark energy, creeping slowly across the stones.

Ariel appeared behind her. "I know it might not feel like it," she said, "but managing to stab her... getting her to share your curse... that in itself is a victory."

"You're right," she said, her own voice feeling hollow, "it doesn't feel like it."

She slid down to the throne room, and watched her parents slumped in their seats, their hands outstretched, almost touching. It was a strange, unnatural slumber, utterly still apart from the rising and falling of their chests. She reached out to touch them, but her fingers fell through their flesh. She was no more than mist. A ghost, an echo.

And so she would remain, until someone set her free.

She wanted to cry. There was an urge inside her, an itch she couldn't scratch, a deep, unfathomable emptiness. She couldn't reach it, couldn't even skim the surface. How bitter the taste of nothing was. How endless.

The fairies gathered around her, and the silence of the sleeping kingdom was complete.

"I didn't think it would be like this," she said. "I didn't know what feeling nothing would be like."

Margaret swallowed noisily. "It is not forever, dear child."

"You're already hundreds of years old!" she snapped. "I'm...

I *am* only a child! I may have to wait decades... or a century. That is forever when you're seventeen." She looked back at her parents. How long would it be until she was with them again? "Happy birthday, Briar," she whispered. The name felt wrong, as if she'd be torn from her former self the second she pricked her finger. How could she claim to be a princess when she'd failed her kingdom so spectacularly?

"It wasn't your fault," said Margaret. "You did everything you could."

"If that was true, this wouldn't have happened."

Palpable silence filled the room.

"Don't do it," said Ophelia. "Don't stay... like this. Just sleep. You've fought enough. Just leave it to fate. Wait for someone to rescue you–"

"I... I can't," said Briar. "I'm still their best chance of making it through the forest. Did you hear what she was going to do? She's sent out a beacon, filling the forest with monsters. If I do nothing, people will perish in the attempt–"

"There's always us, pet," said a gravelly voice. "We can guard them through."

Briar spun towards the door. The bandits stood there, all five of them, looking out of place in the gleaming halls.

"Briar!" Ezio broke his gaze away from the shining marble and bolted across the room towards her. She opened her arms to embrace him like she'd done a hundred other times, not thinking, not remembering... and he went straight through her, slamming onto the hard floor behind.

She couldn't even help him up.

Ezio sniffed, climbing to his feet, rubbing his nose on the back of his sleeve.

"I... I'm sorry, Ez," she said, sniffing too. Again, some strange instinct, a remnant from when she had feeling. She still appeared to breathe even though she had no lungs. Perhaps her body upstairs was reacting on her behalf. She was, after all, only the echo.

"The woods are crawling with monsters," said Benedict. "You wouldn't believe the journey we had."

"And so it begins," said Briar, looking down at her muddy

reflection. "You should leave the forest. Go somewhere else. Anywhere else. Before it gets worse–"

"Are you mad, girl?" Lorenzo laughed. "Leave you? Couldn't contemplate such a thing, could we, boys?"

Anton gave a shrug of indifference, but the rest of them were all in agreement.

"You'll need someone to defend the princes that turn up on your doorstep," said Rogan, shouldering his axe. "And someone to defend you from them."

"I daresay any hero who attempts to brave the forest will need defending from Briar's sharp tongue more than anything else. She wields it as well as any weapon."

"You– you don't have to–"

"'Course we don't have to," said Benedict. "We *want* to."

Briar smiled gratefully, and looked at Anton. "I still have some jewels I can give you, but they'll run out–"

"Keep your jewels," he said. "We'll charge the men for safe passage, and rob the unworthy."

"You always were an excellent man of business, Anton."

He snorted. "Come, Princess," he said. "Let's get away from here."

"I'm not a princess," she said. "Not any more. You can't call me that around anyone else. Not if I'm to get to know them first. To find out if they're as *noble* as they need to be."

"You might have trouble convincing them you're anything else, in that ensemble," said Lorenzo.

Ariel drifted over. "You're quite right," she said, and with a wave of her hand, Briar's dress dissolved into forest gear, her hands flecked with mud, and her shining dark-gold hair was stripped to a dull brown.

"Oh, Briar, you look *ghastly*," groaned Lorenzo. "I love it."

Briar touched the pendant against her chest. Even that had been transformed, into something resembling a walnut.

"A glamour," Ariel explained. "I'll attach another charm to your body in the tower, in case you ever wish to change it–"

"I won't," Briar insisted, looking at her reflection, "this form suits me perfectly." She turned towards the bandits. "You need to stop calling me Briar, too. My name is too well-known."

"All right," he said. "What did you have in mind?"

"Talia," she said. "Call me Talia."

15
The Graves in the Grove

Talia took him round the back of the den, past an overgrown herb garden that long burst its borders, to a small clearing overgrown with weeds. Two wooden crosses marked with the names 'Rogan' and 'Benedict' were still just about visible, and between them sat a skeleton, bereft of flesh, more moss than bone.

"Anton," said Talia, her voice no more than a whisper.

"Your family?"

She nodded.

"Why didn't you..." He glanced at the skeleton.

Talia looked down at her hands. "I couldn't."

He hung his head. Either she hadn't been strong enough, or she hadn't been able to find the strength of will to do it alone. How would he have found the strength, if it had been one of his family? No wonder she quit this place. It was no longer a place of joy, but a place of death.

"I think I saw a spade earlier," he said. "I could bury him... if you wanted me to?"

Talia's eyes shone. "You would do that?"

"Of course."

"I– I– Thank you." Her body twitched. "I... I'm not sure I can watch."

He shook his head. "You don't have to."

It took a lot longer than he anticipated to cut a hole deep enough for a grave, although the body itself, picked clean, took up so little room. Freeing it from the undergrowth took longer, as did prying the smaller bones from the earth.

Anton had been here a long, long time.

He tried not to think about that. He told himself that he was wrong, that no matter what this place looked like, it hadn't been abandoned for decades. Because Talia couldn't be much older than himself. It didn't make *sense.*

He looked at the graves, and imagined another amongst them. A fourth. A body never buried, lost in some other part of the forest. Was... was Talia really alive? Or was she a ghost, some kind of spirit chained to the forest? Was the reason he wasn't allowed to touch her because he couldn't?

No, no. That can't be.

The words of the fear-witch rang in his ears, but he pushed them back, digging his spade into the earth.

She was real. She had to be.

Why does it matter? said another voice. *You can't be with her either way. Does it matter if she died long ago?*

He tried to convince himself that his desires were selfless, that he just wanted her to be free and happy and not trapped like she'd indicated so many times before, but that was a lie.

He wanted her to be real because even if their futures were never meant to entwine, even the faint possibility of one together was better than the crushing nothingness of nothing at all.

He pulled the last of the hand bones free of the soil. Something glinted in the dirt, a sliver of red. He pried it free. A ruby. He bit it, just to make sure. Real, all right. What was a bandit doing with such a jewel? Why was it clutched in his palm as he died?

Leo had no need for such an object, and it had clearly meant something to this man. He tucked it into the ground with the bones, and started to pour on the soil.

The mound complete, he went back inside the den and found a piece of string, roping together two branches in the shape of a rudimentary cross. He marked it with the name Talia had given him and set it in the earth.

He was sweating profusely, his hands were raw and blistered, and he was covered in earth. He went to wash in the lake before returning to the campfire. The brownies had gone. Talia was sitting silently beside the fire, staring into the depths of the flames. A half-eaten plate was beside her, and a full one laid out for him, along with a bowl of steaming water.

"For your hands," she said. "There's an ointment in it; it should help."

He sat down beside her and tucked into the meal. He was ravenous. He could hear his mother tutting as he shovelled the meat into his mouth.

"Try to leave a morsel for the brownies," she said. "It's polite."

He nodded, muttering a thanks.

"Is he... is it done?" she asked. "Did you bury him?"

"Yes."

"Thank you. You can't know... thank you."

She got up from her spot, and whispered an intention of visiting the grave, and slid away into the shadow of the trees. He watched her go, waiting for a fragment of dust to kick up beneath her boots, watching for a shadow, some clue that she was real and here and present.

There was nothing.

The meal lost its flavour after that, and it was easy to leave more than a mouthful for the brownies.

Talia returned to the campfire a short while later, her face white and studded with tears. He wanted to drop a blanket around her shoulders, if he couldn't hold her, but he was too afraid of the blanket falling through her.

"What is it?" she asked. "You're staring at me."

"Maybe I just find you pleasant to look at."

She raised an eyebrow. "Leo..."

"I... I have a question," he said, "but I'm not sure I want the answer."

"Ask it. I may not answer."

"Fine," he said. "Are you real?"

Talia's mouth opened, but she did not respond. Her lips hung there. That alone should have been answer enough. Anyone else would have denied it, laughed, said, "What?" in disbelief.

No, no, no... say something. Say anything–

"I... I have something to tell you," she said.

"You don't have to..." Leo's voice trembled. He didn't want her response, didn't want the truth to rip away what remained, that precious fragment of hope.

"I want to," she said, "but I'm scared, too."

"Of... of what?"

"Of losing you."

Leo's throat tightened. *You won't lose me,* he thought desperately. *You can't. Nothing you say holds that kind of power. Don't say it, don't say it if it does...*

"Leo," she started, "I–"

Something rustled in the bushes. Talia's head snapped towards the sound, holding up her hand for quiet. It didn't sound large. A rodent? A bird? A brownie?

She bolted upright, peering into the darkness.

"Sword," she said. "Leo, your sword!"

Leo swung his sword from its sheath just as something long and thin came slithering out of the dark. A snake? It leapt from the ground, straight for his face. A swipe of his blade cut it clean in two–

Not a snake. A vine.

Three more shot through the trees. He slashed through one just as another wrapped around his ankle, yanking him to the ground. The sword flew out of reach. Talia screamed, but the vines made no move for her. She dived for his hand as he was dragged back into the undergrowth, her face swallowed up by darkness, her desperate cries vanquished by the racing of leaves, the snapping of branches.

Thorns snagged at his skin. Logs smacked into his body. He could have been dragged for miles or minutes, but eventually the vines slowed, snaking over his limbs.

The vines will strangle you to death.

His body was jerked upwards and slammed against a tree. The vines pulled him up to the bark, hugging him. He couldn't breathe.

A figure stepped out of the gloom.

It was barely dressed, roughly human in shape but neither male nor female, and with a face devoid of anything like humanity. Its skin was colourless, neither beautiful nor ugly, and its long, dark hair hung in a woven braid.

It raised a long claw and stroked it down his face.

"I should probably let the vines dispatch you," it said. "That's what *she* would want. But a head as pretty as yours... I'm sure it has wonderful, wonderful dreams..."

It opened its mouth wide. Smoke rose from its throat as it laughed, its black eyes gleaming.

The laugh stopped, turning to a gargle.

The point of a sword glinted through the creature's chest. It fell to the ground with a wet thud.

Talia stood behind it, her eyes flashing. She cut Leo free of the vines.

"Come on," she said, and they raced back towards the camp site.

Leo swayed before collapsing in a heap. Talia was beside him instantly, grabbing his face, checking for any injuries. "Are you all right?" she asked.

He nodded. "What was that–"

"It doesn't matter," she said. She examined a cut on his brow. "Are you sure you're all right?"

"Yes." He reached up and took her hand, tingling at the warmth of her fingers. "You're touching me."

Talia smiled. "I suppose I am."

"I was... I was beginning to think that you couldn't..."

"That I couldn't what?"

"Touch anything. I thought... I thought you might be a ghost or something."

Talia laughed. "A ghost? Really? What a silly thought!"

It *wasn't* a silly thought. There had been plenty of evidence to suggest that she wasn't fully... fully human. But this didn't seem to matter anymore. Why even ask why she hadn't wanted to touch him before now?

He clung to her hands. "You're real," he said.

"Of course I'm real." She stroked his cheek. "I'm real."

He seized her in his arms, grabbing her as fiercely as he dared. He breathed her in, earth and woodsmoke and fresh, clean air. His body pulsed into disorder. He was undone by her touch. He rushed her name like a river over a fall, and pressed his mouth to hers.

"You're wonderful," he whispered into her. "I think I'm falling in love with you."

Talia's smile lit up his insides. "Good," she said. "Because I think I'm falling for you, too."

They woke the next morning inside the den in a pool of light, entwined in each other's arms. It didn't look nearly so bleak as it had the day before. In fact, it looked almost habitable. There was no carpet of leaves, no swathes of ivy, no inches of mud.

Talia smiled radiantly, and went to start breakfast. They feasted on wild mushrooms and leftover bird with a handful of berries. He kissed the juice from her mouth.

"I was afraid I dreamed yesterday," he said.

She kissed him back. "I was afraid I'd dreamed you up entirely." She slid her hands around his neck. "You're perfect, Leo."

They kissed for what felt like hours, his body glowing with warmth. Somewhere, he knew, he was forgetting something. He couldn't think what.

They spent the morning clearing out the den. They swept and mopped and cleared and tidied. They turned it into a home. What else had they to do? They didn't need to be anywhere. There was nothing outside of the clearing, outside of the two of them.

The light brightened as the day wore on. The lake shimmered with it, like liquid gold.

"Shall we go swimming?" Talia suggested.

He did not need any convincing, not when she was racing ahead of him, pulling layers over her head, discarding her clothes as she ran.

She dived into the water. He was by her side in seconds, gathering her up again, giddy and laughing. The air itself was intoxicating, the water the perfect temperature.

She tasted of honey and sunshine. He feasted on her laughter.

"You're magnificent," he breathed. "I'll never want anyone but you."

"You'll never *have* anyone but me," she insisted. She clung to his lips. "I want nothing else in the world."

The feeling of forgetting something trickled up inside of him. A sadness, a longing, a guilty twinge. But what was he doing wrong? He was meant to be with Talia–

She kissed his brow. "Don't worry," she said. "Nothing bad can happen, as long as we're together…"

They spent the afternoon drying in the sun. It was perfect, wonderful laziness. He drew circles on her bare back while she ran her fingers through his hair. He wished the days could always be like this.

"They can be," she said, as if reading his mind. The next kiss was so deep he swore he could drown. "Every day with you is perfect."

This could not be true, but he let himself believe it.

Hours bled into days, warm and hazy and utterly wonderful, over almost as soon as they began. He spent every second of it with Talia, next to her side. They tidied the old herb garden and planted a new one. Roses began to bloom. The plants hummed with life.

Something was missing from the thicket behind the den.

"Talia," he said, "what happened to the graves?"

She tilted her head. "Graves? What graves?"

A shaft of memory ruptured the light. His hands twinged painfully. He had done something here, something that hurt, but he'd been happy to do it–

She rose to kiss his cheek, and the memory fluttered away.

He was being silly, of course. Graves in the wood. What a dark, nonsensical thought.

They cooked a rabbit stew for supper, flavoured with wild garlic. He couldn't remember where the rabbit had come from. One of the benign forest creatures must have brought it for them. It hardly mattered. It was delicious.

"We should leave some out for the–" The name fell from the tip of his tongue.

"The what?" asked Talia.

He shrugged. "Never mind. It doesn't matter."

He sank into soft, luscious sleep, Talia curled up in his arms. There were no dreams. No nightmares, either. But why would there be? As Talia had said, nothing bad would happen as long as they were together. What even was a nightmare, come to think of it?

"I miss rain," he said one day, as they picnicked by the lake.

That evening, a thunderstorm blew through the glade,

shaking the very bones of the den. He and Talia stayed locked up inside as the storm battered against the boards, kissing to the rhythm of the wind. They stretched out beside the fire as dark descended, drinking wine from the stores below.

Divine. He needed no heaven other than this.

He needed nothing other than this.

And yet...

"Talia?"

"Yes?"

"Have we... have we forgotten something?"

"What could we have forgotten?"

He looked around at the wooden walls, and for the first time, noticed how small everything was. The wood seemed to shrink, the noise from outside dimmed. There was a nothingness outside.

"There's nothing out there," he said.

She laughed. "Of course there isn't," she said. "There's nothing else in the world but us."

But that wasn't right, wasn't true. There was a world outside, and other people too, somewhere, far away. They had come from somewhere...

A coin of dread pinged at the back of his mind.

What were his parents' names?

Four dark shapes haunted him as he tried to sleep. Four shadowy figures, just out of reach.

Mother, father, brother, brother.

A fifth shape. His brother's fiancée. His former tutor. Why couldn't he remember her?

"Tell me about your family," he asked Talia.

"They're gone," was all she said.

"Where did they go?"

"It doesn't matter."

"Yes it does," he said. "It used to upset you."

She smoothed down his hair. "Let's not be cross."

Leo seized her hands. "Be mean to me."

"What?"

"Say something teasing."

She grinned. "I love your smile."

"No, not like that. Say something... insulting. Abrasive."

"Why would I do that?"

"You used to."

She slid her arms around his neck. "That was before I fell in love with you."

His stomach turned to hot, fiery putty at the mention of those words, but the coppery dread was still there. These pretty words were just a distraction.

"What are my brothers' names?" he asked.

Her arms dropped away from him. Her face fell. "Wilheim," she said. "And Jakob."

Wilheim. He came here for him, loved him enough to risk his life–

Against what? What was there to be frightened of?

A spider wrinkled in the corner of his mind. A flash of fang and water. An ogre's club.

Many things. There were many things to fear.

So why had he come?

He had come to face a curse, to fight something, to free someone...

A princess. *The* princess.

Not Talia.

He clutched her in his arms, feeling that at any moment she was going to be ripped away from him. Her body seemed cold, her hair held no scent.

No, no, she's here, we're here, this is real...

"Talia," he said, "why do you love me?"

She eased back, blinking at him. "Because you're wonderful," she said, "you're perfect."

"These aren't reasons to love someone."

She gripped the front of his tunic, trembling. Fear coursed through her eyes, a bitter reflection of his own. "I don't need a reason to love you," she said. "I just do."

The wind howled around him, hissing at the wood. Any

minute now, it would break apart.

"I'm sorry, Talia," he said. "But this is only a dream."

"It's not!" She punched against his chest. "It's real! *I'm* real!"

"Is this your dream, or mine, I wonder..." He stroked back a lock of her gleaming, golden hair. "I suppose it would have to be mine, wouldn't it?"

"No!" she hit him again. "No! *No!* Don't wake up! I won't be there when you do! You know what happens when we wake. You know we can't be together!"

The guarded keep. A sleeping kingdom. Hundreds of bodies turned to dust. Wilheim saying goodbye to Ingrid. His weeping mother.

For a moment, almost worth it.

Almost.

"Stay," Talia begged him. "Please, stay with me! You don't want her. You want me."

"Of course I want you. I will probably die wanting you. But this isn't real."

"It feels real..." She clutched his hand to her chest. "Doesn't it feel real?"

Yes. No. Even now, her heartbeat seemed more like a sound than a feeling, her warmth more like a memory of a touch.

Dream as it was, he hoped he remembered it.

He kissed her forehead. "You really were a beautiful dream."

Part 3

Dawn

Day's sweetest moments are at dawn
Refreshed by his long sleep, the Light
Kisses the languid lips of Night,
Ere she can rise and hasten on.
All glowing from his dreamless rest
He holds her closely to his breast,
Warm lip to lip and limb to limb,
Until she dies for love of him.

--Ella Wheeler Wilcox--

16
After the Curse

The first few months after the curse were the hardest. Talia sank into something of a darkness, watching as the forests she loved became thick with monsters. One night, ogres invaded the caves as the bandits slept and nearly made off with Ezio. She started keeping guard over them, after that, when all pleas to desert her had failed.

The nights of standing watch in the dark ate away at her like a sickness. She could not continue. Finally, Anton snapped.

"If you won't sleep, and we won't leave, what can you do to make things safer?"

Talia held up her hands. "*I* can't do anything, remember?"

"Fine. What would you do if you had a body?"

She thought for a moment. "Build a safer den. Maybe... maybe somewhere else. Easier to protect. Less deep inside the woods."

"Good plan. Ezio!" Anton whistled. "Go grab that paper I stole for you!"

"Aye-aye, captain!" He vanished, grinning, returning a few moments later with a thick roll of parchment and some drawing implements. He spread everything out on the ground.

"Plan out a better base," Anton instructed.

"What?"

"Tell Ezio what to draw. You still have a mind, girl. Use it."

She had nothing else to do, so she let Ezio become her

hands. Alone, she scouted for the perfect location; somewhere closer to the outskirts so that they could better escort any travellers, somewhere with caves for Benedict, trees for shelter, water for sustenance. Somewhere beautiful.

Her search took her all over the forest, to the mountainous regions she'd barely visited, past dangers and beauties uncovered and hidden. The perfect place revealed itself beside another lake, one of the natural wonders that existed within the darkness. A lake that could conjure memories. She'd heard tales of it before, but never found it.

She would lose many hours in its waters as the years rolled by.

She brought Ezio back to the site, and together they planned a better base, one in the trees to guard them from the monsters, one not dark and dismal. One that looked like a home. The bandits set to work building it, liberating materials from the castle to furnish it. Lorenzo made curtains and proper bedsheets for everyone. Benedict planted flowers rather than just herbs. As the years went by, they crawled up the wood, making the treehouse look like a fairy palace.

The bedroom had a beautiful view of the lake, and on a clear day, you could make out the castle.

It felt like home.

The project complete, Talia realised she could do more. She turned her attention to mastering teleportation, to winnowing through the forest to help them hunt or scavenge, or alert them of danger. She learnt to fade back into her body and reappear at will, first to the sound of her name or the ringing of bells, and then just whenever she wanted, when she could pull herself out of a dream.

The first heroes arrived. Talia was hopeful to begin with, then apprehensive. Some parties they guided with no hope of success, merely to keep the level of monsters down. The forest widened and grew as the years rolled by, getting darker and more dangerous. Thirteen's power hummed in the trees, the closer they got to the kingdom. Few ever made it to her thorns.

Talia grew restless and faded into sleep more often, appearing at the den every few weeks, then months. The bandits barely changed at all, acting like she'd just nipped out to the market. Only Ezio ever said anything, bemoaning how long she'd been gone, and he seemed to change by the month. He stuck ever closer to her whenever she came, and they stayed up late at night reading to one another, or making up stories as they patrolled the woods.

He grew older. He grew stronger. He grew taller and smarter and wittier.

"You don't need any help with reading anymore," Talia said to him one evening, as they lay together beside the fire, long after the others had gone to bed.

Ezio grinned. "I haven't for years, but I enjoy this too much to ask you to stop."

"You do not need a reason to spend time with me."

"Yes," he said faintly, "I do."

She looked across at him. "I'd pinch your cheeks, but no hands."

He scowled. "I am too old for you to pinch my cheeks."

"I will still pinch your cheeks even if you're an old man by the time I'm freed."

"It will not take that long, Talia," he said. "I swear it."

Talia had reached something like contentment when, almost ten years after the curse was cast, she and Rogan went off on a hunting trip.

Rogan was her favourite hunting partner. Ezio was too talkative and they never caught anything. Anton said nothing at all and it was a miserable experience. Lorenzo hated hunting (or any long expeditions; he always complained about how tired he was or how muddy he got) and while travelling with Benedict was always a learning experience, Rogan and she just had an easiness, a good rhythm. He knew when to talk and when to be silent, and nothing between them had ever been awkward.

He'd entertain her with old dwarven tales and ballads when they were waiting to pick up a trail, and teach her hunting methods known only to his people. He had never told her why he'd come to live in the forest alone. She suspected some criminal dealings and a story of banishment, but he seemed very content with his life here. He teased Lorenzo something rotten whenever he complained about the roughness of the woods.

Rogan finished a particularly entertaining tale about a rowdy dwarf with a no-nonsense wife and paused to let Talia snort with laughter. "I've heard that one before," she said. "Ezio said it was one of his favourites. It's much funnier when you tell it."

"You'll break the boy's heart if you tell him that."

Talia frowned. "I don't understand."

Rogan shook his head sadly. "You ought to say something to Ezio, girl. Let him know if you're not interested."

"I think you're mistaken. Ezio's like a brother to me."

"Aye, maybe, but you're not a sister to him."

Talia hoped he was mistaken, but had little time to dwell. Something rustled in the undergrowth. Rogan barrelled on ahead. She stayed where she was, listening. Her skills in that area were unparalleled. Benedict joked she could tell the type of bird from the rustle of its feathers.

"What's the hold up, lass?"

"Do you hear something?"

"No, and my ears are as sharp as my dagger. Come on."

Talia grumbled something about him getting on in years, and teleported to his side. He jumped.

"Do you *have* to do that?"

"It's efficient."

"It's disconcerting, is what it is!"

"I—"

He held up his hand for silence. Something was moving in the distance. A lone deer. Rare. Perfect. Rogan's eyes gleamed as he reached for his bow.

The bolt shot loose, spitting against a rock. He crashed to the floor, a scream still at his lips. A snake slithered off into the darkness. She caught a glimpse of its pattern as it vanished from view.

A quick glance at Rogan's face revealed he knew the type, too. Venomous. Deadly. If Rogan didn't receive an antidote soon—

"Rogan!" Her gaze flew about the thicket, as if desperately hoping the antidote would pop out of the ground.

Rogan groaned, rolling onto his front and unbuckling his belt to stem the flow of the venom.

"I'll go back to camp," she said. "I'll get Benedict. I... I won't be long."

She vanished without a second's pause, reappearing in Benedict's cave.

"Rogan's been bitten," she babbled. "One of the red-crowned ones. He needs antivenom. He's–"

"Slow down," said Benedict, holding out his hands, "where is he?"

Talia gave him Rogan's location. Benedict's face turned grey. In his head, he was doing the calculation she'd tried not to. The one she'd pushed away.

"I'll get the others," he said. "Go back to Rogan. We'll be there as soon as we can."

She faded back to the thicket. Rogan was propped up against a tree trunk, his face was covered with a sheen of sweat. "The others are coming," she told him. "Can you stand? We need to try and meet them halfway..."

Rogan nodded, pulling himself up, clutching onto a tree for support. He took a few shaky steps before collapsing on the ground.

"Rogan! *Rogan!* You have to crawl. Come on, you're a *dwarf!* You're tougher than this! You're the toughest person I know!"

"You're... tougher..."

She didn't feel tough. She felt weak and stupid and useless. The truth hit her like a bolt to the gut; Rogan was going to die, and there was nothing she could do but watch.

"Don't cry, lass," said Rogan.

"I can't."

"You certainly have the look of tears about you."

"That's because I... because I..."

"Because you love me."

Somehow, her throat was too tight to speak. She nodded instead.

"It's nice, to be loved," he said. "I didn't know much love...

before I came here, that's for sure. I don't... I don't regret it. You... you better remember that... tell... tell the others..."

But what he wanted to tell the others, Talia never found out. He slipped into unconsciousness shortly after. The forest was filled with the sound of his laboured breathing.

"I don't know if you can hear me," she said, her voice trembling, "but I am here."

She sang him an old dwarven tune, because she could not find any words of her own. She was still singing long after he took his last breath, barely breathing herself, her notes singing themselves. A part of whatever she was, a sliver of her soul, had drifted away with him.

She was still singing long after the others found them.

Lorenzo sank to his knees beside his friend. Benedict checked his heartbeat, just to be sure. Ezio put his arms around Lorenzo, holding back tears as he looked at Talia, as if to say he was holding her too.

Anton crouched down beside her, putting a hand over her ghostly one.

"Talia," he said. "Talia, you can stop now."

It took her a moment to realise what he was talking about. Her song trailed off. "There was nothing... there was nothing else I could do..."

"I know, pet. You did everything you could."

"If I'd had body–"

"You couldn't have dragged him back. You couldn't have run any faster than we did. There was nothing to be done, girl. But you ensured he did not die alone. That's not nothing."

"It... it feels that way..."

Her hands started to shake, turning misty. She wanted to fade, to go, to scream, to cry. She could only do two.

"Talia–" Ezio reached out towards her, but she was already gone.

It would be a long time until she sang again.

It was the first time she watched someone die.

It was far from the last.

17
Lair of the Basilisk

L eo crept back into consciousness. He was still tied to a tree, the vines thick around him. He felt light-headed, woozy, like he'd lost a lot of blood. He blinked rapidly, trying to wake.

The creature sat crouched beside a campfire, soaking up the flames, its lips drawing into a snarl when it saw he was awake.

"You broke free of my dream!" it hissed. "That rarely ever happens."

"It was too pleasant," Leo sighed. "And she isn't."

The creature frowned, waving its hand. The vines tightened. Leo began to regret his decision to leave the dream. At least it had been warm and comfortable. He hadn't thought about what awaited him outside of it. Had he broke free only to die now?

"I could give you another, less pleasant dream," it said, gliding towards him. "It's harder to break free from despair..."

Leo suppressed a shudder. "If it's all the same to you, I'd really rather you didn't." His head felt very light again. "What... what did you do to me?"

"I fed off your energy," it said. "Your delicious dream... You would have been dead in another day or two."

"Another day or two?" Leo frowned. "How... how long have I been here?" Fear spiked through him. "Talia! Where's Talia?"

He looked desperately around the glade, dreading seeing

her shackled to a tree, hoping to see her hiding somewhere, waiting to free him like before.

The creature frowned. "Who?"

"Talia! She was with me when you–"

It laughed at him. "You were alone when I snatched you, human."

"I… no. No, that's not true–"

"Yours was the only mind I sensed. Believe me, I'd love to have another, especially one as lovely as yours…"

"You're lying," he said. "This is another game to you–"

"Everything in life's a game," it said. "But I am telling you the truth."

He knew something was wrong, something was different about her. The dream had been his own delicious fantasy, a construct born of desire. If Talia truly wasn't real, if she was only the ghost of someone who died long ago… what was the point in fighting, especially as he was trapped to a tree, too weak to struggle, unable to move? Why not fall back into a dream? Never mind that he had a job to do. If escape was impossible, then giving in…

Talia would want him to fight. Talia would yell at him to. She was probably somewhere close by, or getting help… alive or not, she wouldn't have deserted him.

He started to sing one of her songs.

"What are you doing?" the thing said.

Buying time. Signalling her. Trying to cling to life. Take your pick.

The creature came towards him, unhinging its jaw. "A nightmare it is, then."

Something huge came barrelling into the clearing, a monstrous serpent, each bluish-black scale the size of a fist. There was a flash of fang, but Leo forced himself to close his eyes. He knew what it was; the basilisk.

The creature knew it too. It let out a howl and raced off into the forest. Leo shut his eyes tighter, as if this would shield him from detection. He heard the screams of the creature getting further away. The hissing, slithering sound followed. It brushed past him, emitting a thick, cold kind of warmth.

Sound died away entirely.

"Leo," said a voice.

He opened his eyes. Talia stood in front of him. She darted back the second his eyes fixed on her, as if the proximity burned her.

"You're awake," she said.

He nodded. "What... what was that *thing?*"

"A djinn," she said. "A dream-demon. It traps you in a dream and slowly feeds off your energy. It's a powerful creature. Not immune to a basilisk's gaze, though."

"You lured it here."

She nodded. "It took me a few days to track it down."

"A few... days?"

"I tried looking for the centaurs at first. Then the fairies. I couldn't find either. I..." Her voice seemed to vanish, her expression dark and glazed, devoid of any of the warmth he'd conjured in his dream.

"What is it?"

"I think you should leave the forest."

"Are you crazy?" Leo strained against his bonds. They were looser now, but he couldn't think why. A few tugs and he was free. He sank to the ground, strength leaving him. "We're so close–"

"Something is happening. She's growing stronger. I don't think it's just a case of getting to the castle, anymore. She's... she's..."

"What?"

"She's too much for you!" Talia screamed. "You'll never be strong enough to defeat her, so you might as well give up now!"

"You... you don't mean that. You *can't* mean that–"

"I do. I mean that." Her words clawed into him, tighter than any vines. "You're not strong enough. You're going to fail."

He waited for her to say something else, something to dull the force of her words. *Say you're afraid for me. Say you just don't want to watch.* "Talia–"

"I'm not taking you any further," she said. "It's pointless. I'll... I'll find someone to take you back, but I... I can't..."

She disappeared into the trees, and he staggered after her,

only to find himself completely alone. She'd folded once more into shadow. "Talia!" he cried.

There was no reply. That didn't stop him. He stumbled forwards, calling her name until his voice was hoarse. "I'm not going!" he yelled. "I'm not leaving you here. *Please,* Talia!"

Still no reply.

He found his way back to the den without too much difficulty, and managed to rustle up something to eat. One of the potions in the cave below was labelled a 'strength restorative'. He took it without much deliberation; he was weak from lack of food, his body numb from underuse. If he was going to go after her, he needed all the help he could get. He was willing to risk whatever side effects the potion offered.

Within a few minutes of drinking it, he felt better, but there was still a sickness inside him. *Talia, Talia, Talia.* She should be here.

Despite the harshness of her words, he dared to believe she'd vanished in a strange attempt to protect him. He didn't want to think where his mind might have gone if she'd been taken for several days by that *thing,* that djinn.

How many days had it been, exactly? How many days did they have left?

He was losing track of time.

He didn't dally too long. He repacked his equipment, strapped on his sword, and descended once more into the dark. He had no way of tracking her, but he looked for the oaks, the signs pointing him further in the direction of the kingdom. He couldn't be sure she was heading in the same direction, but somehow he felt certain that she was. Their goals had been aligned from the start. Was she planning on entering the castle herself?

A stark figure stood in the undergrowth. He recoiled; the djinn. Only it was stiff and immobile, and even more colourless than before. It had been turned to stone.

The vines must have set him free when the basilisk caught it. He clutched the hilt of his sword and ploughed through.

Braying sounded in the distance, and Leo hurried onward. The sound was cut horrifyingly short, like the snap of a branch. He crept forward. He could make out the faint outline of a centaur, still and stiff as a statue. The basilisk was nowhere to be seen. He kept his eyes down just in case, avoiding its gaze, looking up only briefly when he passed the centaur. It wasn't Oakfoot or Acre or Swifthoof, whatever good that did to anyone else. Someone would mourn him.

For a brief, fleeting second, he wondered if Talia was right. Maybe he should turn back. His own family would mourn him. If it truly was fruitless...

And maybe it was fruitless. Because how could he possibly wake the princess when he...

But if the fairy was stirring anyway, he needed to face her. For his kingdom, but also for himself. He couldn't bear the thought of seeing two people he loved unhappy. How could he possibly face his entire country?

He only knew how to move forwards.

A rocky region rose out of the trees. The ground slithered beneath him. Not basilisks. Ordinary snakes, although he was willing to bet some of them were venomous. He wasn't about to get out Jakob's list and check.

Each step he took was a careful one, his sword drawn just in case.

The rocks were half-hollowed out, like a piece of sea sponge. Great round holes spread from one wall to the next. The basilisk's lair.

The stone vibrated. It was close. He forced his eyes down, and pressed forward, praying it would avoid him.

It slithered ahead, taking minutes to pass by. It was longer than the tallest tower he'd ever seen.

Keep moving, keep moving, don't look up...

The hissing subsided. The vibrating shivered away. The air behind him seemed to thicken. Hairs prickled on the back of his neck.

He raised his sword. Glinting in the blade was a dark,

shadowy reflection.

Leo gulped, and dived into a nearby tunnel, skidding into a pile of snakeskin.

The basilisk rolled behind him, crashing into the rock. By sheer, dumb luck, this tunnel was too small for it. He slid forward in the dark, searching for a faint pinprick of light. He emerged on another pathway, but the rock still hummed with the force of the serpent. Inescapable.

Something dropped down in front of him.

"You really are persistent, aren't you?" Talia groaned.

A flicker of a smile escaped him. "It's one of my finer traits."

Talia shook her head. "I'm going to distract it. You stab it. Don't–"

"Look it in the eyes, yeah, I know."

She flashed him a grin, and vanished into one of the tunnels. Leo turned the corner and watched its tail disappear. Seconds later, Talia emerged from another platform, leaping across to the next opening, the basilisk following her trail. How could she move so quickly?

She wove in and out with impossible agility, flashes of the monster cutting across the ravine. It was everywhere at once. Leo started to hack at it, cutting as deeply as his strength would allow. The mountain roared with every strike. Finally, he managed to drive his blade beneath one of the scales. He kept pressing, the flesh shifting beneath his sword. He drove it deeper, cutting through as if he hoped to cleave the snake in two.

The roaring, the shuddering, dribbled into twitching.

He yanked his blade free. Blood gushed from the wound.

Talia appeared beside him.

"Is… is it dead?" he asked.

"Getting there. Don't stop. Come on!"

He raced out of the ravine, down into the forest, not breathing, not thinking, not glancing behind him until she slowed to a stop in a clearing. He panted hard, his chest warm.

She came back.

"I didn't mean it," she spluttered, before he could think of anything to say. "What I said earlier. I didn't mean any of it.

I just... I don't want to see you get hurt. I don't care about freeing the kingdom anymore. I don't care about anything but you. I thought if I could just... I'm sorry. I'm so sorry. I've been an idiot and a fool and I promise I'll explain everything. *Everything.* I have so much to tell you–"

Leo sighed. "Please," he said, half-laughing with relief, "just let me hug you, you silly fool. You can yell at me later. I just want to–"

Something sharp cut into his leg, like a fiery blade. Talia screamed as a weight dropped away from him. He caught a glimpse of a snake slithering off into the dark.

The fiery feeling intensified, spreading through his limb. His knees hit the ground, his head spinning. "Damn..."

Talia slammed to the floor beside him, her eyes wide and fearful, her hands spasming. "I know where there's an antidote."

"Great," said Leo, gritting his teeth, "can you go and grab it?" The rest of him fell to the ground, his eyes rolling. He felt like he was on fire.

"I... I can't..."

"What do you mean?"

"I can't... I can't get it..."

Leo glanced up. Her eyes were brimming with tears. She meant it. For whatever reason, she couldn't get it, and he couldn't move.

Beneath the pain and burning, a new feeling surfaced. A cold, hard dread. "Not... not to put too fine a point on it, but... am I going to die?" The darkness seemed to fold inwards at the thought, clawing at the edge of his vision. All he could see was Talia's face, like a shaft of moonlight in the dark.

His head was heavy.

"No, Leo, *no!*"

Her tears splashed his face. Not a ghost, then. Not if he could feel those. Death would not have been so bad, if it meant an eternity with her.

With some faint remnant of strength, he reached up to thumb them away. He wanted to tell her so many things. Not to be sad. Not to cry. Not to worry. But also that there was a strange kind of gladness. Glad she cared. Glad that she was here. If hers was the last face he saw...

"Talia..."

His palm touched her ice-cold cheek. She let out a sharp gasp, jerking away from his fingers.

No, no, come back.

"You... you touched me."

Damn. He'd forgotten about the rule. "Talia–" he groaned. "I'm... I'm sorry. I didn't mean to–"

Instead of running away, Talia grabbed his outstretched fingers and clung to them, as if she half-doubted they were solid. "It's all right," she breathed, her voice paper-thin. She was white, her face a stark mask of pain. He could tell from her wide eyes just how bad this was.

"I don't want to die," he rasped. His voice felt like someone else's.

"And you're not going to. I get to say when you die, remember? And I'm never going to say that. You never get to die. You hear me?"

"I hear you."

"Good. Keep listening to me. The next part is going to hurt."

"What–"

Before he could make a sound of protest, Talia unlatched her fingers from his, grabbed his thigh, and placed her lips around his wound, sucking hard. It was like being punched repeatedly. He screamed, trying, weak as he was, to push her away. She held firm. She was remarkably strong, her flesh like stone.

She spat his blood – along with some of the venom – onto the ground, and unbuckled his belt. "Stop moving," she said. "I'm trying to save you. I'm *going* to save you. Don't make that hard."

"I... I'll try."

She fastened the belt above his wound and jerked it, tightening it as far as it would go. He felt like his leg was going to explode, but this time he was too weak to move. The only sounds he made were whimpers. It was not over quickly. He thought he might have blacked out briefly, waking up when it was over.

"If the venom doesn't kill me," he said, "I'm fairly sure you will."

Talia managed a weak laugh, as faint as his groans. She touched his arm.

"I'm fetching the antidote," she said shortly. "I'll be back. I'll be back, I promise." She bent down, as swift as a swallow, and pressed her forehead against his. "Don't you dare die while I'm gone. Don't you dare die *ever.*"

He wasn't sure how long he remained conscious after she left. The cramping started shortly afterwards, ripping through his stomach. He managed to turn just in time to vomit, before collapsing into the mud. Panic, pain, fire, all split through him.

This was it, he thought. He was going to die here, alone in the forest. His parents wouldn't even be able to bury him. Not unless Talia–

Gods, she would be furious if he died. He didn't want to put her through that, didn't want her to come back and find him like this, but did he have a choice?

In the absence of her hand, he clung to her words, *don't you dare die.*

Don't die.

Die.

18
The Departures

Talia did not change much in those first ten years. Though saddened by Rogan's death, her voice dulled for a long time afterwards, she remained much the same person that she had been before. Her initial despair had been replaced by a quiet optimism. Yes, none of the first heroes had been for her, but she had plenty of time left. Rogan was gone, but the others remained. She was not alone.

She even managed to eke some joy out of her changed form and new-found indestructibility. She flitted through the forests, observing unseen wonders. She could locate supplies in an instant and save the others hours of work. She made a perfect distraction for enemies. She could visit any part of the wilderness and not worry about a thing harming her.

Sometimes she even liked that nothing changed.

It did get dull, and she vanished often, only joining the bandits for a few hours here and there. Sometimes she forgot to wake, and weeks would roll by. The bandits would ring the bells just to check she hadn't faded away entirely. Ezio rang them more often than anyone else.

One day, she was racing through the woods with Ezio, chasing a deer. The doe escaped, as they suspected it would. They weren't really trying to catch it. They were running for the fun, the pure enjoyment. Sometimes, she felt she still had lungs, lungs that could burst with giddiness if she kicked up enough speed.

Ezio stopped, catching his breath, and they grinned at each other. They were standing very close.

"I wish I could touch you," he said.

Talia sighed. Even now, she still echoed the action. A force of habit. "I wish I could be touched," she said.

"Do you remember what it felt like?"

Talia did not reply. She held out her hand, as if expecting the light to shine straight through it. No shadows danced along the floor of the forest. "Sometimes I think I remember," she told him. "The ghost of a touch. But... no. Nothing... nothing firm."

Ezio held his palm over hers. A misty sensation, if that, skimmed his flesh. "I've... I've been thinking..."

She tilted her head. "Yes?"

"Maybe... maybe I should try waking you."

Talia laughed, but he did not return it. "That's sweet of you," she said. "Really. But you don't have to do that."

"I don't have to," he said. "I *want* to."

Talia's smile turned into a frown. "But... but then you'd have to marry me. You don't want to have to do *that!*"

"I..." Ezio stopped. Talia stared. That single word, that expression, the tightness of his jaw... all spoke louder than his words could express.

"Ez–" she started.

"I... I know you don't see me that way. I know it. That's why I didn't want to say anything. But... but you like me, at least. You haven't liked any of the others that have come through here. Would marriage to me really be so bad?"

"No, no, it wouldn't be bad–"

"So why not try it?"

"It's just..."

"Just what?"

"I... I don't... you're my..."

He sighed. "Things can change, Tal. Things *have*. I have."

"I haven't."

He tore his eyes away from her. "Can I not at least *try?* Would a life with me not be preferable to a life like *this?*" He gestured to her form.

Talia paused.

"What is it?"

"It would be preferable," she said. "It just... it wouldn't be right."

It would also be like giving up, was the thought that she kept hidden away. It had only been ten years. There was still plenty of time for someone else to show up, someone she could see as something other than a brother.

Ezio sighed. "Forget it," he said. "I'm heading back. I'll see you later."

Ashamed of her feelings, or lack thereof, she shimmered back to the castle. She watched her parents sleeping.

If Ezio *could* wake her, they could be back within a few days. She could be with them again. It had been so long, and no amount of summoning them to the lake could make up for a real, new conversation. An embrace. How she longed for sensation...

Maybe she should let Ezio try. What was the worst that could happen?

The worst that could happen is that it works, and he marries you, and you never love him, and he grows to hate you for it.

Didn't Ezio deserve a chance at real love? Didn't everyone?

No one was going to get it in the forest.

She stewed on her thoughts for a long while, maybe days, before returning to the den. Ezio was nowhere to be found.

"He went on a hunting trip a few days ago," they said. "He'll be back eventually."

Ezio did this often, disappearing into the forest for days on end. Talia wished he wouldn't. The woods were growing more dangerous. No matter how skilled a woodsman Ezio was, he was still just one boy.

One man. He was grown now, older than her form appeared. She wondered how old she was. How many weeks, months, years had she been conscious for? Was she nineteen or twenty-seven?

How old would she be when someone finally came?

If someone finally came...

She flitted about the forest, hoping to catch a glimpse of him, still not knowing quite what she was going to say. 'Sure, risk it, let's see what happens'? 'I'm worried you'll grow to hate me if you do this'? 'We both deserve more'?

She could not find him. He did not return the next day, either, by which point she felt she'd searched every inch of the wood.

"Should we be worried?" said Benedict over dinner.

Lorenzo snatched a flower from the vase on the table and clutched it to his heart. "Maybe he finally gave up pining over Talia and decided to leave for pastures new..."

The other men glared, but Talia paid them no heed. She was watching the woods from the window.

"What?" said Lorenzo. "Is it supposed to be a secret, how he feels for her?"

Talia turned towards them. "Tell me honestly," she said, "what would you do? Would you let him try?"

Anton and Benedict both looked down thoughtfully. Lorenzo spun around the room with his flower. "Seize a chance at love wherever it may bloom! Grasp the petals of affection until they burst or wither! Risk it all–"

"Does Ezio deserve the risk?"

Lorenzo shrugged. "If he's willing–"

"I'm not sure the boy knows what he risks," said Anton, stroking his chin. "Talia knows, don't you? She's a little older and wiser than we give her credit for."

"But there is also my kingdom to consider," she said. "Don't they deserve the chance to be free? And... and I miss my parents. So badly. And I love Ezio, I do, just... not like that. And I don't think things will ever change for me. I think they might for him."

Benedict nodded. "Think on it some more. But let him know, whatever you decide."

A part of her wanted to ask him to give her more time, to see if things could change, but she also knew that what she was really waiting for was someone else. Someone that wasn't him. How could she ask him to wait for that–

Something prickled inside her, a sudden, dark feeling, like

someone stepping over her grave.

Ezio hadn't waited. He had gone to the castle alone, to face the thorns, to find her–

She vanished in an instant, appearing by her own bedside. Ezio was crouched against the wall, a narrow gash across his arm.

He'd done it. He'd reached the keep.

"Ezio!" she raced to his side, hands hovering over the damage she could not fix.

"I tried it," he said. "It didn't work."

Talia felt a coldness rise inside her. "I… I didn't want you to do that."

"I know," he said. "I'm sorry." He coughed, clutching at his side. "*Really* sorry."

"Are you injured badly?"

He shook his head. "Bruised ribs, I think. I got off lightly. At first I thought that maybe luck was on my side, that I was meant to reach you… now I think she might have known I couldn't do it. I thought, if I just woke you up, it would prove to you how much I love you. Once you knew that, and you had your parents back, you'd eventually…"

More than ever, Talia wished for her tears. "I do love you, Ez. So much. I will always love you. But… not like that. Not ever."

He pulled himself to his feet, his face contorted in pain but also with anger. "Stars above, what would a man have to do to be worthy of you?"

The coldness turned to liquid. "Not kiss me without my permission, for a start!"

"I thought I was saving you! That you would be…"

"What, grateful? At having my choices wrenched from me yet again? I don't want to marry you, Ezio! I never will!"

He took two difficult steps away from her. "Well, thank you for making that abundantly clear!"

He stumbled towards the door, not looking back. She was pinned in place.

"Sometimes, Talia, I don't think you want to be rescued. I think you'd rather close yourself off and fail than believe in the possibility of happiness. You won't find love like that."

I won't find it anyway, said the dark voice inside her. *It's impossible. A love like that does not exist.*

Ezio's footsteps died away.

She stood staring at her sleeping form for an age. She went into a numb, liquid, shapeless space. She could have been there days or weeks. It was like Rogan's death, that utter sense of loss and confusion. She faded back into her sleeping form, pushing her thoughts away.

Eventually, she half-woke, drifting from her dream, and found the strength to snap back to the bandits' den, appearing in the middle of breakfast.

Lorenzo gave a sharp shriek, upsetting the pan cooking over the fire. "Heavens, girl!"

"Have you seen Ezio?" she asked.

The three faces turned grey.

"He's gone, lass," said Anton. "It's for the best. Packed up a few days ago. Took some coin."

"But... but I didn't say goodbye." She looked up at them. "I didn't say goodbye! I can't let him go after... after..."

Her voice broke. No real throat, no real tears, but the feeling of pain, of desperation, of loss was so overwhelming that even her echo nearly shattered with the force of it.

A word rose out of the darkness. "Did you say... did you say he took some coins?"

"Yeah, he did. I suppose I can't begrudge him a few if–"

Talia tried not to panic. Of course Ezio would need coins for the journey, for a life outside of the forest. But there was something about the secrecy of the act, the slipping away, the quiet shame...

No. No, he wouldn't–

"Talia?" Lorenzo frowned. "Are you all right?"

"I... I have to..." She vanished before she could finish her thought, flitting through the trees, down the route Ezio was likely to have taken. How far could he have gone? He couldn't possibly have reached the edge of the forest already.

She winnowed through the trees, up to the high points, scouring the land in search of him. She was running out of forest.

No, no, no...

She searched all their old stores, every cave and cranny. She went up to the mountains, into the lairs of beasts that could easily have trapped him. She scoured the best hunting stops, the lakes, the rivers and rapids.

Finally, there was only one place left.

The dreaded well.

She had visited it more times than she cared to admit, staring into the blackness, wishing she could snatch back the coin that had wished her into existence. Not all the time, just when the nights got too dark and lonely and she found herself wondering if it was worth it.

She had never known dread like the kind she felt when she saw Ezio beside it, an empty hand outstretched above the waters.

"I traded a centaur for quicker passage out," he said. "I thought you might try to stop me."

"Ezio!" she yelled, staring into the void, as if she hoped to claw back the coin with the sheer force of her mind. "What did you wish for?"

"For you to be happy again," he said. "It'll have a hard time twisting that, since that's all I want."

Talia wanted to cry.

"I... I'm sorry I went without your permission. I'm sorry for the things I said. But you should know... You say you haven't changed. That you won't ever. But I don't think I will, either. I think I'm going to love you until I die."

"For your sake," she said, "I hope that's not true. If... if I could wish for one thing, right now, that's what I'd wish for. For you to know true happiness. For you to find someone who loves you utterly and completely. For you to love them back."

Ezio turned to leave.

"Ezio!" she called out. "I–"

"What?" he said, not turning around. "You love me?"

"I... I *do* love you," she said. "I always will. And... and if it takes a hundred years to free me from this place, I will miss you for every day of them. But I pray you do not miss me. Be happy,

Ez."

Ezio's absence haunted the den. The air was thick with silence. Eventually, they began to fill it, but his bed remained made at all times, as if they hoped he would return.

He never did.

Sometimes, Talia would stay up at night and lie beneath the stars, remembering the carefree days of counting them with him, of making up new constellations and coming up with absurd names for them and silly tales to go along.

She was not awake enough to stop missing him, and the years passed like weeks.

The bandits eventually stopped talking about him, and he sometimes felt more gone than Rogan because of it.

"I almost wish he had a grave," she admitted one day, as Lorenzo lay blooms on the cross that marked Rogan's resting place.

"Do you ever wish he'd managed to wake you?"

Talia paused. "Sometimes, but for different reasons. I just wish I could have kept him here. That's selfish, I know."

"You miss him."

"I'd miss him less if I knew he was happy."

Lorenzo put his hand on her ghostly shoulder. "Let's have faith that he is."

Talia nodded, but she had not told him about the wish.

"Come on," he said. "You can keep me company as I work through the most monotonous of chores…"

For the most part, none of the bandits bemoaned their change in circumstances, their lack of company, or the renewed harshness of life in the forest. Most of them carried on exactly as before. Indeed, so few of them knew much about what life outside the forest was like.

Lorenzo did.

He never said anything. Of course he didn't. But she frequently caught him misty-eyed when doing the laundry, folding his frayed garments carefully away, as though longing for something finer. He spent too many nights staring at the lake, imagining old parties from days gone by. He would not have chosen a life in the forest, if his father had been more understanding. The forest was a different kind of prison for him.

Still, he loved them too much to leave, Talia knew. He had never found acceptance elsewhere. Where could he go?

A few years after Ezio's departure, they were guarding a few knights through the woods. They were a nice bunch. Talia didn't have particularly high hopes for Lance, the chosen one of the group. He was kind, chivalric, unfailingly nice to her, but there was something he held back. He had been selected for the task by his family. She quite liked that about him, that he had limited choices like she did, but she could tell he'd much rather be anywhere else.

One night, as she meditated, pretending to sleep, she heard him conversing with Lorenzo.

"I'm not sure I have what it takes to wake the princess," Lance told him.

Lorenzo tried to sound disinterested. "Is that so?"

"I… I'm not sure we'd be particularly compatible."

"Why would you think that?"

"Because," he said faintly, "she's a girl."

Talia could almost feel Lorenzo's hopeful, frantic heart, beating in the place of her own hollow one.

"And," Lance continued, "she's not you."

Their voices died away, and when Talia chanced to open her eyes, the two of them were kissing.

Halfway through the journey, one of the party was hurt beyond Benedict's means of fixing. That night, after the others were sleeping, Lance stayed up, staring into the fire, trying to decide whether or not they turned back.

"You should leave," Talia said. "You don't want to marry the princess, and you don't want to lose a friend. Turn back and live."

"I have responsibilities–"

"You have a life," she said. "You may not if you continue."

It was all the nudge Lance needed. "Thank you, Talia."

The next morning, the party announced their intention of leaving. Knowing the way back was reasonably safe, Benedict and Anton departed. Talia and Lorenzo escorted them back.

Lorenzo watched as Lance disappeared down the hill.

"Go after him," Talia said. "I beg you. You should go, Lorenzo. At least one of us deserves to be happy."

"I... I can't. We... we barely know each other, and–"

"Seize the flower of love, Lor."

He trembled slightly. "What if it fades?"

"What if it blooms?"

The trembling worsened. "I'm afraid."

"I think fear means it might be real."

"I'm... I'm afraid of leaving you. I... I haven't even said goodbye to Anton and Benedict–"

"You can come back and say goodbye. But if you let him leave now–"

"I know." He swallowed. "I... I don't know what to say."

"Work that out when you catch up to him."

"I don't know what to say to *you*."

Talia could not feel, but there was a pain deep inside her chest. "That you love me. That you're glad we met. That you'll never forget me. That if you live a hundred years, you'll remember me at the end."

"That's beautiful."

"I'm getting used to goodbyes."

And there would be more to come. At least two. Anton and Benedict weren't getting any younger. In a couple of decades, maybe three... she would be all alone. At least this goodbye would spare another, harder one, longer down the line.

"Talia–"

"Go!" she hissed.

Lorenzo started to move, the sunlight stark against his pale skin. He had lived too long in shadow. He turned back only once.

"I'll miss you!" he declared.

He was swallowed up by sunlight.

He never did come back.

They were hopeful, at first, that one day he would, but the years rolled by and he did not return. They hoped that this meant he was happy, that he and Lance were off seeing the world together, or had settled down in some peaceful corner of the world.

The days were quieter without him. Talia missed his inane chatter, his silly conversation. He was the only one of the bandits she could talk to about courtly life. Some nights, the two of them would summon a memory of a ball and dance side-by-side.

Dancing by yourself was not great fun.

She spent less time with the bandits, often appearing only for missions, or when Benedict had something new to teach her, which happened less and less as she knew more and more. She never thought she'd be afraid of running out of things to learn.

Years rolled by. The changes were more obvious when she spent months away, the wrinkles and the grey hair growing exponentially.

The woods grew darker and more dangerous. The thorns stretched for miles, the monsters multiplied, became more vicious, more hungry. They lost more heroes. The number of willing volunteers dwindled. Talia would look at corpses hanging on the brambles, and wonder if she killed them. If she had just died, none of the subsequent deaths would have occurred.

But then, death was not even an option. The counter-curse had been cast when she was a child. It was hard to believe the fairy would have left the kingdom in peace, that she wouldn't have done everything in her power to prevent her curse from being broken.

If she started to blame herself, that would be the end.

And yet every moment of optimism was overshadowed

by the growing gloom and danger. Benedict and Anton were getting too old to defend themselves as easily as they once did.

Three times she told them to go. Three times they refused.

"This is our home," Benedict insisted.

"We don't just stay for you, you know."

"He stays because nowhere else will have his ugly mug."

Anton scowled. "It was nice of Lorenzo to leave you his humour."

Life continued as it had for the past decade or so, dim and monotonous and unchanging. Talia helped in whatever way she could when there was no one to escort, locating best hunting spots and sources for Benedict's herbs.

Until the day Benedict collapsed.

Talia screamed and called for Anton, who arrived as quickly as his old legs would carry him, and, with some difficulty, levered his old friend into his bunk in the cave.

They sat by his side until he woke, Talia occasionally sending Anton to fetch anything she thought would help.

Benedict's watery eyes flickered open. "You both look grim."

"Benedict," said Talia, trying to keep her voice steady, "you're not well."

"No," he said. "I'm not."

"And you haven't been well for a while."

"I hoped... I didn't want to worry anyone, not until I was sure–"

Talia turned away from him, ashamed of her tears.

"It's all right, Talia."

"No, it isn't. It's easy to die, you know. It's living that's the hard part. How dare you make me live without you."

Benedict smiled. "Am I to apologise?"

"Are you sorry?"

"That I'm going first? No, never. That I won't see the curse broken? Certainly."

"It's never going to be broken."

"If you thought that, then why are you still here?"

She bit back tears that could never fall. "To see your stupid face, you fool."

"Take heart, dearest," he said. "I still have faith. He's getting here as fast as he can."

"How... how can you still believe? After everything–"

"Because you're easy to love," he said. "And one day, you'll find someone easy to love yourself."

Benedict's descent was slow. He got weaker day by day, losing colour, losing appetite, losing energy. There were days when he seemed brighter, and other days when he barely roused at all. Talia never left his side, and towards the end, neither did Anton.

Then one night, when his breathing was hard, he turned to the potion he'd had Anton leave for him, just in case.

"I think I might be ready now," he rasped.

Talia swallowed, wishing she could cry, wishing there was some way for the emotion to pour out of her. She wished she could kiss him as he brought the vial to his lips.

"Don't forget what I taught you," he said.

"Don't forget that I love you."

His breathing got easier, and he closed his eyes. He did not open them again.

And then there were two.

After they buried Benedict, she stayed with Anton for a few days, more out of a sense of obligation than anything else. He was as quiet as ever, but his silence seemed to have hardened, the kind of silence that spread to every corner of a room.

"Call for me if anything interesting happens," she said, and faded back to her body.

He called her a week later. Nothing was happening. He was just sitting beside the lake, watching the fireflies dance.

"What's wrong?" she said.

"Nothing," he replied.

"I told you only to call me if–"

"Something interesting was happening, I know." He patted the bank beside him. "Look, Talia– at the way the lights glisten.

Is that not interesting?"

Talia did not move. "You know this isn't what I had in mind."

"Then be more specific with your words." He patted the bank again. "Come. Humour an old man."

Talia sighed, and dropped down to his level. "There's no point in me sitting, you know."

"Here is a better angle."

"If you say so." She kicked the stones beneath her feet, pretending she could feel them. "Are you going to try and convince me that there's still beauty in the world?"

"Why would I try and do that?"

"Benedict would have."

"Benedict is gone," he said sharply. "And yet we remain. It's rather unfortunate that, isn't it?"

Talia said nothing.

"What I would give to trade places with him. All the treasure in the world cannot buy good company. And yet I'm glad I miss him, just as I am glad I knew him. The heart is a strange thing, isn't it?"

Her thoughts expanded, churned inside her, but her voice had vanished clear away.

"It would be so much easier not to care about anything, wouldn't it? Easier to hate. Easier to feel nothing. So why don't we?"

"Because we're human," said Talia faintly. "Silly, breakable, foolish humans... even now. Even after all this time..."

How was it that nothing beat in her chest, and she could still feel it breaking? This angry, raw, pulsing organ, shattering like glass in a fire.

"There we go," said Anton, still staring out at the lake, at the way the lights turned the inky blackness to liquid gold. "I know you don't have lungs, girl, but you still need to breathe."

Anton, for the most part, seemed quite content with his

solitude, and Talia spent most of the next few years asleep, rising only to check on him and escort more hopeless parties through the woods. Every so often, Anton would call her to watch the sunset, or sit beside the fire with him on bitterly cold nights. He rarely ever called her to assist him in any way, although the woods grew darker still.

Sometimes, he would summon a fond memory of the others, and ask her to join him in reminiscing. They did not talk a great deal, only watched and sat together in perfect silence.

It was good to have someone to remember with, but she knew their time together was dribbling through her fingers. Soon she would be remembering alone. She could not clutch time.

One day, she materialised in the Den to find Anton gone. He was not in any of the usual spots, nor was he checking the traps. In fact, they hadn't been checked in days. Where was he?

Before flying into a complete panic, she spied him from the top levels, by the graves of Rogan and Benedict. Only he wasn't visiting them. He was lying between them.

Oh, oh no...

"Anton!" She raced to his side. He was as white as paper and almost as lifeless, his eyes faint and far away. She had seen this look before, too many times. "Why didn't you call me?"

"I knew it could take days," he wheezed. "I didn't... I didn't want you... to wait... all that time."

"I would have done it happily."

"No. You'd have done it miserably. Like you do everything else."

Talia looked down.

"Don't take it personally, girl. It's not your fault you're miserable."

"Isn't it?"

"Of course not. Fate has dealt you a hard hand. You've shouldered it admirably."

"Careful. That was almost a compliment."

"Don't get too used to them." He coughed loudly. "I'm tired."

"Sleep, then," said Talia, her vision blurred. "I'll still be here when you wake."

"What a terrifying thought."

She lay her hand against his chest, shapeless as it was. Something glistened in his clenched fist.

"What's this?" Talia asked.

"The first jewel you ever gave me."

Talia startled.

"I know, turns out I'm a sentimental fool after all."

"Anton..."

"I know, girl. I know. You don't have to say it. You've said it enough."

"What... what else can I say?"

"That you'll keep fighting," he said. "That you won't give up. Be the stubborn little girl you always were."

"I... I'm not a child anymore."

He lifted a hand to her incorporeal cheek. "I pray you get the chance to be one again, with one worth waiting for."

He lost the strength to speak after that, and closed his eyes. Talia stayed by his side as his breathing worsened, and finally slowed altogether.

It was only then, with Anton gone, she knew truly how dark, and how endless, the forest had become.

Anton was gone. The last of her friends, her family.

There was nothing, nothing left for her anymore.

Anton had told her to fight, but what had she to fight against? She was more powerless than the breeze that lifted through the trees.

She would skirt the edge of the forest and pray for the ringing of bells, for Ezio or Lorenzo to return, for words, for a faint semblance of company.

Sometimes she'd hover over the well, above the honeyed darkness, and imagine the wishes she'd make if she had a body to throw coins.

She thought about the one that made her, wondered if she could find it. *Undo me, unravel me, end the darkness, take me home.*

Home, home, home.

Once it had been the castle. Then it was the den; Ezio, Lorenzo, Benedict, Rogan, Anton.

They did not exist anymore, or if they did, they had moved so far away she could not claw back the pieces of her heart they had taken with them.

So home did not exist, either.

It was an emptiness that grew, that gnawed at her every moment she dared to be awake, as deep and dark and unending as the forests, as prominent as the thorns. It could only multiply. How could something so dead and rotten grow? It defied all logic, and yet it did.

The loneliness abated less than a handful of times in the sixty years that followed. The first in a young man who left her the moment she revealed her true identity, angry that he had been tricked, not thinking about why such a judge of character might be necessary. The second time in Edelvard, who seemed only too delighted to learn the truth, making his death a few days later all the more crushing. The third time in a female knight by the name of Aveline, who hunted monsters with her for a few weeks before continuing on her adventures.

Then there was nothing again.

And now there was Leo.

19
A light in the Dark

L eo slid around in the syrupy dark, untethered, lost, burning. He almost missed the pain. The pain was good. The pain let him know he was still alive.

There was a voice, somewhere. Hard, wretched.

Talia.

She was screaming, yelling, cussing. At him or herself, it was hard to tell. He could only catch snatches of it. Suddenly, the voice grew calmer.

"You can do this," she said. "You can save him. He is not going to die."

Something cold was pressed against his lips. "You need to drink," she whispered. "And if you don't, I'll kill you myself."

Are you always so abrasive?

He called her name. She told him she was here.

The darkness folded in once more.

He didn't know what Talia gave him. It was more than just anti-venom. She kept plying him with more, something cold, like liquid ice. It cut through the light, making everything hazy and dark. He drifted in between sleep and waking, feeling everything and nothing. At times he was burning, other times cold and shivery. His limbs ached with such agony that several times he wanted to cry out, but couldn't. But through it all, Talia was there, Talia with her cool hands and gentle voice, whispering to him in the dark. His only conscious images during that time were of her face singing to him, watching over him as he shivered and thrashed and slept and shook. She never left. Not for a moment.

She spoke to him, but he couldn't remember her words. Sometimes he thought he spoke back, too. At one point, she even laughed, stroking his cheek and kissing his fevered brow. He wanted to tell her he liked her like this, liked her anyway, always. Perhaps he did. Perhaps that's why she laughed.

She did not often laugh. At one point, he remembered long afterwards, he asked her to get word to his family if he didn't make it. Let them know that he had tried, where he was, that he hadn't been alone at the end.

She cussed at him through her tears. "I'm doing a really, really good job of keeping you alive right now, you fool! Don't throw that back in my face!" Then her voice grew more gentle, and she whispered in the dark, "You are my last hope, and the only one I wished for. Do not go into the dark. Stay with me."

He felt her cool lips touch his forehead, and in that moment, he felt like he had no choice but to stay with her until it was the world, not him, sinking into shadow. He clung to her like a sailor might cling to a raft, and stared up at her shining eyes like they were the only stars in the sky.

On and on it went, the pain in his limbs fading, the fire in his skin raging on. He was conscious enough to be aware of her feeding him, changing the bandages on his leg, keeping him cool when he wasn't and stoking the fire when he was.

He remembered most her hands on his, against his brow, laced in his fingers. How could a forest guide have a touch so soft and gentle?

"Your hands are cold," he murmured at one point.

Talia startled, as if she'd forgotten he could speak at all. "I'm sorry," she said.

"Don't be. At the moment they're actually rather pleasant."

"Are you hot?"

"Can't you tell?"

Talia swallowed. "No," she said quietly. "I can't. I'm just guessing."

Something wasn't right, was strange about that. Was it him? Was he still half out of it? Perhaps he was the one not making sense. He tried to speak. His mouth felt like sandpaper.

"Hush," said Talia, stroking his brow with those soft, cool fingers. "Rest now. I'll explain everything once you're better. Sleep. Just sleep."

It was dark when he woke. He was inside the cave in the bandits' den, in a makeshift bed. It could have been a day or a week since he was last fully conscious, he wouldn't have known the difference. His limbs were heavy, but his joints felt like jelly, and when he tried to rise, his legs buckled underneath him.

Talia was nowhere in sight, but the faint, shimmering sound of song breezed into the space. She was nearby.

Gingerly, he climbed to his feet, making his way to the mouth of the cave, stumbling like a child learning to walk. He moved towards the noise, towards the lake, and beheld Talia on the shore, singing to the ghost of a woman hovering over the lake, a woman almost as beautiful as she was. They were singing together, their voices joining in perfect harmony.

"Talia," he breathed.

Talia snapped round, the illusion crumbling. "Leo!"

He took another step towards her, but his knees gave way and he spun towards the ground. Talia's arms reached out to grab him. She was cold, desperately cold.

"You shouldn't be up," she said softly.

"How... how long was I–"

"It doesn't matter–"

"Talia," he asked, "please."

She sighed underneath him. "Four days," she said.

"And... and before? With the djinn?"

"Five."

He did a quick count in his head. "Damn. We're running short."

"I know. And... and we won't be able to leave again just yet. You need more time–"

"I'll be fine."

"You won't be," she said darkly. "And I won't be, if something happens to you."

He reached out to touch her cheek. Her skin was like ice, and she didn't move underneath his touch. He grinned faintly. "I knew you liked me."

Talia pursed her lips. "I could change my mind."

Leo lay his head against her chest for a moment, and then rolled off her into a sitting position. He could just about manage it, staring out at the lake.

"Who was she?" he asked. "The woman?"

"My mother. I often come out here to summon her, and remember."

"She's dead?"

"No," said Talia, her gaze silvery. "She's asleep. Asleep like..."

"Oh," he said, with some realisation. "She's in the kingdom."

Talia nodded.

"But... but that's been closed off for a hundred years!"

Talia nodded again. "I have something to tell you." Her voice was quiet. "I... you are allowed to be angry, but... but I'd ask you to remember that my choices were limited, and that I took no pride in deceiving you."

Leo couldn't think of anything to say. "All... all right."

Talia took his hand and placed it against her chest. "Do you feel that?"

Her skin was still ice cold, as smooth and hard as marble. There was something wrong, but he still wasn't sure what he was missing. "I... I don't feel anything."

"Exactly. I don't... I don't have a heartbeat. I don't have a heartbeat because I'm not really here."

For a horrible, horrible moment, he was sure she was a ghost, that solid as she was, she'd died long ago, and this was just an echo designed to torment him, some awful torture of the forest.

Talia went on. "Until a few days ago, I couldn't even touch anything. I am... I am no more than a solid ghost. A solid ghost who can cry, apparently... and who is still alive somewhere."

Relief flooded through him as her eyes glanced outwards, across the lake, to a place unseen. The castle of thorns. She was alive. She wasn't about to be snatched from him like he was nearly snatched from her.

"I was ten years old when I first heard of the curse," she went on. "I fought against it for years. I learnt how to defend myself, I employed bandits to teach me the ways of the forest, I taught myself mental agility to ward off any hypnotic attack that might convince me to prick my finger in the first place. And... then I had a back-up plan. A plan to take the fairy down with me, to tie her to her own curse, and... and to have some say in who came to rescue me. I taught myself how to astral project with the help of a fairy pendant, to cast my consciousness out of my sleeping form. That way, I could aid any would-be rescuer, and ensure no one could wake me up without me deciding they were worthy. It has been one hundred years, and I think I might finally have found that person. That is, of course, if he wants me too."

Leo was silent.

"Say something," she begged. "Please."

"You... you're the princess?"

"Yes."

"It's... it's been you, this whole time?"

She nodded. "I'm so sorry, Leo, but if I'd told you at the start—"

"Oh, thank the Gods."

She blinked. "I'm... I'm sorry?"

Relief shot through him like wildfire. "It's you," he smiled.

"It's always been you. I was worried, these past few days, that... that we were going to do it. That we were going to get there. That I'd actually free her and then... then I'd have to marry her. Marry someone who..."

"Yes?"

"Who wasn't you." He gazed at her, waiting for some kind of similar relief or joy or recognition, but she just looked shocked. "I was terrified of leaving you behind. Of letting you go. I half wanted to abandon the quest altogether, if you were willing."

"You... you aren't angry?"

"You wanted to have some say in who you married. Hard to be angry at that, when I wanted the same thing."

Talia shook her head in disbelief. "I... I should have told you sooner. The moment I..."

"The moment you...?"

"The moment I thought that there was a chance. That you could be the one."

Leo smiled. "No pressure, or anything. For the first time, I'm truly terrified that it's not going to work. Waking you up, I mean."

Talia looked down shyly. "Me too," she said. "Although... I don't know what this means, for my real body. I... I haven't been able to touch a thing in a hundred years."

"Nothing?" Leo frowned, but then a wave of realisation hit him. "Hence the no-touching rule. And the no eating. Of course. But... what's changed?"

Talia's eyes dropped away from his. "I don't know," she said. "I don't know if something's happening to my body back at the castle, if I'm becoming more real because I'm fading there, or if I've just been Talia so long she's becoming more real. Or if this is just a side-effect of the curse nearing completion, or..."

"Or what?"

"I'm not sure." She swallowed. "There's something else," she said. "You can feel me, but I can't... I still can't feel anything. Maybe slight pressure. Nothing else."

"Nothing?" Leo's heart plummeted. He reached across and swept a lock of hair behind her ear. "Not that?"

She shook her head.

"You were touching me before, a lot, when–"

Talia blushed. That was new. "I wanted to touch you. And you didn't seem to mind. I... I didn't know I was so cold. I could stop–"

Leo took her hand and wound his fingers into hers. "If it's all the same to you, I'd rather you didn't."

"If it's all the same to you, I'd rather I didn't either." She gazed at him, and then, very slowly, bent her head towards the wound on his arm. She kissed the skin beside it.

"What was that for?"

"Because I wanted to help you before, and I couldn't. You have no idea how much I wanted to help. With this," she kissed it again, "and this," she kissed his temple, "and this," she kissed his thigh.

Fire shot through him, and he stifled a moan. "Ah, Talia..."

"What is it?"

"You might not feel anything, but I certainly can..."

"Oh," she blushed again, "sorry. I won't do that again."

He really, really wanted her to do that again, wanted her to do it so much he was afraid he would burst. "If I kissed you now," he said, "what would happen?"

"I... I don't know," she said. "It might do nothing, since I'm still not really here, just an echo. Or..."

"Or?"

"It could work. But maybe it might have the opposite effect. Maybe it would try to wrench me from my body completely, try to form a new person, and my old shell would perish. I don't know."

"So... we shouldn't risk it?"

Talia looked away. "Probably not."

Leo grabbed her by the waist, and kissed her cheek, as close and as forcefully as he dared. "It will be one hell of a kiss when we do it," he said, pressing his forehead to hers, "but until then..."

"If this is the dream," Talia whispered, "I don't want to wake up."

"What... what happens when you wake up? To you? To this

form, I mean?"

"It vanishes. Like a dream would."

A cold thought rammed against his mind. "Will you... will you remember all of this?"

"I... I don't know. The words of the counter-curse were that I would *'awake as if no time has passed at all'* but that didn't take into account me astral projecting. I used to wish I wouldn't. Sometimes I wanted to scrub out all the pain and start again. But... but doing so would dishonour my friends' sacrifices. And there is so much of them I long to remember. And so much of..."

"Go on."

"So much of you." She breathed deeply. "I can still count the days I've known you for," she said, "but I don't want to forget a minute of them."

Leo gulped, his throat tight, his heart pounding with the weight of her words and the intensity of her expression. "Not even the bit at the start?"

Talia grinned. *"Especially* not that part."

He tried to focus on something other than the ache deep inside him, but it was difficult to concentrate on anything other than the soft pull of her lips, twisted into a smile just for him.

"Is this... how do you...?" he started.

"What?"

"Is this what you really look like?"

She raised an eyebrow. "Oh, I'm sorry, am I not pretty enough a princess for you?"

"No. No! That's not what I meant. I mean... your clothes, the mud... the dagger at the side I've never felt even when you swiped it at me... You look like a forest guide. It doesn't seem likely that you fell asleep that way."

Talia laughed. "You'd be surprised how much time I spent in my youth looking just like this, but no, this isn't my usual attire." She placed her hand against the pendant on her chest. "It would somewhat give the game away if I was walking around the woods in a gown, so the good fairies gave me a glamour before the curse took effect. Perfect disguise, no?"

"You look every part the perfect guide."

Talia played with the locket. "Would you... would you like to see me without it?"

Leo nodded, his voice failing him. He *did* want to know what she really looked like, desperately, but... he was also afraid of the illusion fading, of finding out she was another person underneath when he'd wedded himself to this image of her. He knew it did not matter, but he did not want this Talia to vanish.

Her body rippled like water, the mud peeling away, the leathery clothes shimmering into a seamless midnight blue gown. Her hair flew free of its braid, brightening in the thin light, a shimmering spool of dark gold silk crowned with flowers. Her skin shone like alabaster, and her eyes... her eyes were just the same. Her entire face looked just the same to him. Still Talia. Still her.

"Gods," he said, "you're beautiful."

Talia's cheeks reddened. She leaned out to run her hands through his hair, her face awfully close. His stomach ached with desire.

"If I haven't already mentioned it," she said, "I find you very attractive. Problematically so, actually. Distractingly attractive."

The ache in his stomach turned downright painful. He felt sick with longing.

"Are you still hot?" Talia asked. "You look hot."

He sucked in his breath. "Maybe."

"I'll fetch you something."

Much as her absence was the reverse of what he wanted, it gave him a little while to compose himself as she collected some water from the campsite and a cool cloth. He did not complain when she mopped his brow and he drank thirstily.

"Seeing as you're awake, and I can touch things again, I ought to go hunting. No doubt you're probably hungry. You've barely eaten anything in the last few days."

Leo wasn't convinced the emptiness inside him could be filled with food, but he shrugged. "I could eat."

"Well, you better. Because we're not even going to *think*

about leaving until your appetite is back to normal. And you can, you know, walk."

"I hear that ability is very useful for trekking through the woods."

She climbed to her feet, and held her hands out for him. "Come on. The sooner I drag your ass back to camp, the sooner I can leave."

"Forgive me, then, if I take my time."

Talia laughed, slipping her arm around him. "Were you always this smooth, and I just never noticed?"

"The words just come easily with you."

"Double-smooth." She clung to him a little tighter, only to lower him gently beside the remnants of the fire a few moments later.

"You're enjoying this, aren't you?" he said.

"I'm enjoying being able to help you," she said. "I will never, ever enjoy you being in pain." She swallowed, sitting beside him with her hands folded tightly in her lap. "Leo, when I... when you fell, and I thought there was nothing I could do... that I was going to have to watch you die... I... I've never known a terror like it. And I've watched a lot of people die. So many. I..."

Leo took her hands.

"I don't even know why I'm telling you any of this."

"You can tell me anything."

She flashed him a watery smile. "And I will," she said. "But first, I hunt!"

She grabbed his bow, slung his quiver around her waist, and shimmered back into her forest guise. "I'll see you in a bit."

She was gone perhaps two hours, giving Leo more than enough time to assess his injury – painful and swollen, but not nearly as bad as he feared – and to process all that he had uncovered.

Talia was the princess. Briar-Rose, the slumbering maiden

he'd been searching for, hardly daring to believe he would be able to care for... and he did. More than he'd ever cared for anyone. More than he ever *would.* How utterly terrifying, to have all your desires and hopes heaped on another person, to know just how surely you'd be crushed if anything ever happened to them.

And something *was* happening to her, something unknown and uncertain. He shared her fears surrounding her growing astral form. They did not know what it meant.

I've never known a terror like it.

He would die before he let something happen to her, but he was also aware of how powerless he was. Especially right now. He'd been so struck by her revelation, it had momentarily distracted him from how weak he still felt. He could barely stand, his legs felt like they could snap from under him, and even though the venom must have left his system by now, he still felt feverish. How long would it take him to recover?

There was a stirring in the bushes and Talia reappeared, clutching a rabbit in her grip. "Behold, the fruits of my labour! Is it not magnificent?"

One look at her grinning face banished his fears, at least for now. "A fine beast," he agreed.

Talia flung it down on the ground. "Not bad, given the fact I haven't hunted in a century."

Leo froze, another realisation falling into place. A century. Talia had been cursed *a century* ago.

"What is it?" she asked.

"How... how old are you?"

"I'm sorry?"

"I mean, I know the curse infamously took effect on your seventeenth birthday, but... that was almost a hundred years ago."

"You're asking if I'm secretly one-hundred-and-seventeen?"

"Yes."

She pursed her lips. "I'm... not sure, precisely. I'm not awake all of the time, you see. I can vanish for months, even years at a time, only appearing when the bells are rung. When the bandits were still around, I spent a great deal of time awake with them. But not all of the time. So... yes, I am older than seventeen, but I'm not centuries old. And I really couldn't give you any estimate. Does that bother you?"

Leo shook his head. "I'd like you, Talia, if you were a thousand years old and covered from head-to-toe in wrinkles. I might not dream of kissing you as much..."

Talia laughed.

"What about your name? I didn't ask earlier, but Talia–"

"Was my maid's name. My *friend's* name. And was a common enough one, a hundred years ago."

"What... what should I call you?"

Talia grinned. "Anything you like, although I have been Talia for a while now. I'm quite used to it. And if we break the curse–"

"*When* we break the curse."

"*When* we break the curse, then, everyone will go back to calling me Briar. You'll be the only one who uses Talia. I... I quite like that."

"Talia it is then." He picked up the rabbit. "I can skin this, if you want to start a fire?"

She bobbed her head. "Don't cut yourself. Don't try to hide how unsteady you are. Plenty of heroes have done similar. I can point out their bodies, if you like."

Leo scowled at her, and slid his knife under the rabbit's skin. "Tell me about the others," he said. "How many have you guided through these woods?"

"Hundreds," she replied.

"Did... did you ever tell any of the others? Who you really were?"

Talia looked down, avoiding his gaze. "Three," she said. "One was very angry. I misjudged him. Another I told the truth to right away."

"Why?"

"Because she was a woman, and I couldn't *quite* see it working out between us."

"What? Really?"

Talia nodded, grinning. "Aveline. Knight of the realm. She

heard a lot of men had failed to wake the famed sleeping beauty, and she wondered if the princess was differently inclined. I assured her I was not."

"What did she say?"

"We talked for hours. I told her the whole story. She decided to come into the forest with me anyway, to replenish the supply caches and re-mark the signs. We had a rather fun time together. I'd love to compose a ballad in her honour."

"And the other?"

The brightness in Talia's face vanished. "Edelvard," she said. "It was difficult, to watch him die. He was the first hope I ever really had... and the last until you. But I... it's not like you. Nothing has ever been like you before. Nothing ever will." She looked up at him then. "Does that make you happy?"

"The latter part, certainly. But... I'm sorry you had to go through that." He yanked the skin free of the rabbit. "What happened to the ones you didn't find...worthy?"

"Other than the ones I told you about, that I abandoned, I just encouraged them to turn back. Took them on a longer route until they gave up."

"What about the ones that were merely mediocre? Like, they were stand-up people but you never felt anything for them?"

"Same thing," she said. "In recent years, I was tempted to let them try, but I knew it wouldn't work, and why would I risk their lives unnecessarily? It has to be someone... someone special."

"How... how would you know that?" he frowned. "If no one's ever reached the castle—"

"One did," she said, her eyes sliding to the flames she'd just provoked. "My... Ezio," she said. "The boy I thought of as my little brother. He... he didn't stay little. And I stayed just the same. He... he fell in love with me. But I never felt the same. He tried to prove his love and went to the castle alone. Thirteen, she wasn't so strong, back then. He made it to my bedchamber, but nothing happened."

"So... not any kiss will do, then?"

She shook her head.

He wanted to ask, *then how do you know I can do it?* But he was equally terrified of her answer. Equally terrified he couldn't. If this Ezio had loved her, and it didn't work for him...

"What happened to him? Ezio?"

"He deserted the forests. To live a life free from me. I do not know what happened to him afterwards."

"Gods, Talia," he whispered. "I'm so sorry."

"For what?"

"For everything that's happened to you."

"It's all right."

"How? How can you possibly say that?"

"Because you're here now," she said softly, and then her face hardened. "Let me gut the rabbit. You're making a huge mess."

They cooked the rabbit together, and Talia looked on hungrily as he ate, encouraging him to eat at much as possible. His stomach seemed to have shrunk and he couldn't manage much, which made Talia fret although she said very little. Her forehead creased, just a fraction. He could tell.

Afterwards, they sat together by the fireside, with her tucked under his arm, against his chest. The warmth of the fire nullified the coldness of her skin. He even fancied she was breathing, some of the time. The flames danced in her eyes. She told him stories, different from the ones they'd shared before. No ancient fables or ballads of long ago. She told him about her childhood. Silly stories about scrapes she'd gotten into, and more serious ones, like discovering the curse on her tenth birthday, hiring the tutors to teach her how to repel Thirteen's magic, and seeking out the bandits by herself.

With every tale, he grew a little more in love with her, this fierce and fearless girl who had battled against her fate till the very end... only she wasn't fearless at all. She'd been afraid. She'd known fears that far outstripped his own, had known tragedies he prayed he never would.

Gods, let me rescue her, he prayed. *Do not let me fail. I cannot live without her, I cannot let her suffer again.*

"Have you fallen asleep?" Talia glanced up at him. "You were very quiet."

"It's late," he said. "We should – I should – sleep." He did not want to burden her with the weight of his affections, did not want them spoken yet, when so much was still uncertain and cloudy. He did not want to tell her how he felt and not be able to kiss her afterwards, or push her into saying something before she was ready. Patience was the only option.

"Of course," she said, helping him to his feet. He leaned heavily against her as she helped him back towards the bed.

"Have you always been this strong?" he said. "Or is it just your form?"

Talia grinned. "I was blessed with strength at birth and have been training since I was a child. You'll have to tell me if I hold you too tightly."

He caught her wrist and pulled her into his lap. Her weight pressed against him, and he could imagine her warmth. She could not hold him tightly enough. He wanted to crawl out of his body and press himself into hers.

"Lie down with me," he whispered.

"I... I'm freezing. Or so you tell me. I can't keep you warm."

"That's what the blanket is for. Unless... you have another objection?"

"No. No other."

She lay down beside him, outside of the blankets, rolling her body against his until their faces were merely inches apart. She dissolved her glamour, hair and gown spooling over the bunk, her grey eyes glistening like pools of rain. Beautiful, unearthly. Still Talia.

"When... when did you realise you liked me?" he asked.

Talia smiled. "To be honest, when we met and you told me you'd spared your knights, and came here in your brother's place to spare him, too. I called you foolish. I thought you noble. But I... I didn't dare to dream. I didn't want to grow fond of you, only to have my heart crushed, one way or another." She paused. "When did you like me?"

"I cannot pin it to a moment," he said. "But I think it was from the first time you sang." He kissed her frozen fingers. "I dreamt of you, you know, in the djinn's trap."

"Me?"

"Well, you and me. Together. In this place. Being... um..."

Talia grinned. "Did we kiss?"

"Quite a lot, actually."

"How did you know it wasn't real?"

"You were too nice."

She laughed.

"Where do you go, at night, if you don't sleep?"

"Away, mostly," she said. "I fold back into a dream. Only... I've been having trouble doing that of late. And I didn't want to leave you, before."

There had been other times when she hadn't left, he realised. Other nights she'd watched over him, when he'd woken thrashing from nightmares, and–

"The night we danced with the nymphs," he said. "You... you seemed like you were sleeping when I woke."

"Meditating," she explained. "Like I'd do if someone needed to keep watch."

"We seemed safe."

Her cheeks reddened. "We were, I just... I rather liked watching you sleep."

"You're blushing."

Talia put her hands on her cheeks. "Strange. I have no heartbeat. I shouldn't be able to. I suppose my real body might be blushing, and this is just a reflection. Without the glamour–"

He tugged one of her hands away and kissed it. "I like it," he said. "And I don't mind that you watched me. It does sound exhausting, though. You should... try and fold away. If you can."

"Perhaps," she said. "Goodnight, Leo."

20

The Depths of the Lake

"**G**ood morning, sleeping beauty."

Leo shifted upwards, rubbing the sleep from his eyes. Talia was grinning beside him, the blanket twisted around them both. "You're... you're still here. Did you stay all night?"

"I did. You're quite sweet to watch." She raised a hand to brush back his hair. Leo didn't think it would ever be possible to get used to her touching him, to feeling her so close beside him, despite the fact she couldn't feel him back.

She got up and went towards the shelves. "Here," she said, handing him a vial. "This is some kind of strength restorative, but you shouldn't take it all at once, you'll burn out. Little and often, Benedict said. I've got some others if you're still feverish, there's one for pain too–"

"Will you think any less of me if I want that one?"

"I could never think less of you for something like that," she said, passing it to him. "Don't be a hero."

"Isn't that exactly what I'm supposed to be?"

"Don't be a foolish one, then. Let me help you."

"You *are* helping me." He took a sip of the first potion, which tasted like barley water and overcooked cabbage, and a little of the second. Talia rebandaged his leg and smeared it with ointment, dulling the pain almost completely. "You said you couldn't touch anything until recently," he said, "but...

you've set up camp before."

Talia shook her head. "I had benign spirits help me. Brownies or nymphs. It looks too strange when I do absolutely nothing. I've never liked travelling with one person, for that reason. Harder to hide that I have no form. Almost impossible."

Leo nodded. "I thought you might be a ghost, at one point." He said. "When I realised you never ate, or slept, and seemed to disappear half the time… and you spoke about these woods as if you'd been here for decades. It didn't matter how solid you looked. I even fancied your mud patches never changed."

"That's because they don't, but I'm amazed you noticed such a thing." She laughed. "When did you decide I *wasn't* a ghost?"

"I didn't. I was just praying you weren't, because if you weren't…"

Talia smiled sadly. "I really wish I'd told you sooner."

"Me too!" he said, claiming her fingers in his. "But I understand why you didn't."

"I still can't believe you aren't angry with me."

"I don't know if you've noticed, but I'm not a very angry person."

"Oh, I've noticed," she said, sliding onto his lap. "I've noticed almost everything about you."

She kissed his cheek, and he felt the familiar swell of desire. Body or not, she must have felt something too. She slipped off and moved towards the stairs. "I'll start on breakfast," she said. "If you want to freshen up…"

A short while later, he hobbled outside to discover Talia throwing herself off logs while something hot simmered in the pan over the fire.

"What are you doing?" he asked.

Talia hit the ground with a resounding thud. He winced, desperately hoping her body, solid as it was, didn't have any bones to break.

"Trying to teleport."

"You can *teleport*?"

"Well, I could," she said, pushing herself off the ground. "How else do you think I met you at the edge of the forest so quickly?"

"Good point." He helped her up. "If you were non-corporeal until recently, how did you manage to run and climb and such?"

"I basically floated," said Talia. "But as I could do those things before I took that form, it didn't look strange. Took some practise to get it right."

"No wonder you always seemed so light-footed."

Talia tugged herself away from him, smiling, and leapt up a nearby tree. "I *am* light-footed," she said, and threw herself down.

"Does the jumping help at all?"

"Even after years of being non-corporeal, instinct is a strange thing. If I fall, I still put my hands out. I still feel the shock of the ground racing up to greet me. I'm trying to shock myself into teleporting."

"It... it doesn't appear to be working."

"Astute observation, Leo."

She climbed up the tree again, higher than before, and dropped from one of the tallest branches. The fall was so high that Leo raced forward, arms open to catch her–

She disappeared a few feet from the ground, reappearing beside him and stumbling, clutching her middle.

"Ouch!" she said.

Leo steadied her. "Did you just say ouch?"

Talia nodded, her face white. "That... was weird. I haven't felt pain in... Since..." She looked back at the tree. "I'm doing it again!"

"If something hurts, the wise thing is *not* to do it again!" said Leo, pulling her back.

"Honestly, after a hundred years of nothing, pain is actually quite pleasant..." She squeezed Leo's fingers, sighing. "Although not as pleasant as other sensations would be..."

"Still nothing?"

"Still nothing."

Leo kissed her forehead. "Soon," he said. "Although, if you could avoid trying to teleport for now, that would be preferable. I don't want to see you in pain."

"You deserve to know what it's like, after what you put me through these past few days." She leaned her head against his chest, as if she were counting the beats of his heart. He wondered if she'd done something similar whilst he was unconscious, and trembled at the thought of having to do the same for her.

"Sorry."

"You don't have to be sorry," she said, slipping her arms around his waist, "you have to be *alive*."

He clutched her to him, wishing more than anything she could feel his arms around her. "No trying to teleport?"

"No trying to teleport." She sighed, and looked across the lake. "I sometimes go back there, you know. Just to check on my parents. To see that *she's* still sleeping..."

"Is she?"

"Inside an impenetrable nest of thorns, yes, but..." She swallowed. "I went back there when the djinn had you, trying to find the fairies. I couldn't. There's a darkness there, stronger than before. And the thorns have grown."

"You're worried."

"Always," she said.

"It... it really won't be long now," he promised her. "We'll make it. We have to. Nothing bad will happen–"

"As long as we're together, right?" She kissed his cheek. "New rules. You still need to listen to me, but you get to ask questions. You're allowed to push me. You're allowed to call me out on things."

He smiled. "What else?"

"You need to tell me when you need to stop. I'm going to be fretting about it with every step. Don't push yourself. Deal?"

"Deal. Is there a third?"

She nodded, linking his fingers in hers and bringing them up to her mouth. She grinned wickedly. "Touch me wherever and whenever you feel like it."

Leo's insides pulsed hotly. "I'm really going to enjoy rescuing you," he said.

They stayed in the cave for another three days, getting his strength up, until he could walk around easily by himself and simple tasks didn't tire him out. There was a bizarre kind of happiness to these days, a simplicity to their routine, an easiness between the two of them that wasn't there before, or was different from *this* easiness. The days seemed all at once too long and over in no time at all. Sure, he was exhausted and aching, but the nightmares didn't plague him when he was plied with potion, and Talia was there. There in a way she hadn't been before, next to his side, tucked against his chest at night and always within arm's reach during the day, save for the few times she went hunting.

She brewed him enough potions to last the rest of the journey, to guard against Thirteen's attacks, and to fortify him as much as possible.

On the last night, having decided that they could delay no longer, they lay together in the firelight, facing one another, Leo's fingers gently stroking her hair. She was back in her true form, and he didn't want to fall asleep and leave her on her own, for he knew she couldn't vanish even if she wanted to and would be awake for hours without him. Sleep was tugging at every inch of his body, and it was all he could do to cling to this moment a little longer.

"I cannot wait to feel you," Talia whispered. "Sometimes, I almost swear I can, like the ghost of a touch, an echo of one. A breeze when I long for a storm."

Leo knew exactly how she felt. Holding her like this was barely skimming the surface of how he wanted to touch her, and knowing she felt nothing back pained him. It was easy to forget, the amount of times she reached for him, as if the very idea set her aflame.

"A part of me thinks it could be enough, you know," she

said. "To live like this. If the fate of at least one kingdom wasn't resting on our shoulders. A part of me thinks I could be content to stay here in the woods with you, feeling or no feeling."

"When do you realise it wouldn't be enough?"

"When I look at you. When your eyes meet mine and I realise how badly I want to kiss you." She traced a finger down the line of his chest. "Amongst other things."

Leo grinned. "Well now I'm *never* going to sleep!"

Talia shifted onto her elbows, and kissed his brow. "You will," she said. "But we can talk a little longer, if you like?"

He did not want this night to end, did not want the bubble to burst. He knew that the next night would not be this simple. No matter how easy Talia tried to make the journey tomorrow, it was going to exhaust him. This night might be their last of simplicity.

"Talk to me," he said. "Tell me everything about you."

He awoke in the night, not sure what it was that pulled him from slumber. Talia was lying beside him, eyes closed, as cold and immobile as a corpse.

"Talia?" he hissed.

She did not reply.

He shook her roughly, whatever good it would do. She couldn't feel a thing. "Talia! *Talia!*"

"The forests are sleeping..." she murmured. "Stars glitter at the bottom of the lake..."

"Are you... are you dreaming?"

Her eyes opened. "Why are you staring at me like that?"

"You were asleep."

"No, I wasn't."

"You couldn't hear me."

"I was meditating."

"Do you mumble while you meditate?"

She sat up. "I was mumbling?"

"Yes, quite a bit."

She stared at him. "Why are you awake?"

"Don't change the subject!"

A sharp chill drifted in through the mouth of the cave. Leo's skin crawled, and his gaze was pulled out over the lake. The surface, usually pristine with stillness, prickled.

"Leo?"

"There's... there's something out there."

He pulled on his boots and reached over to grab his sword, moving stiffly outside. Talia was close behind him.

Something white and round pressed through the surface of the lake. It was a human skull, followed by half a dozen others. Whole skeletons, attached through some fearful magic.

"Run," said Talia. "*Run!*"

She seized his arm, yanking him back up the bank towards the rest of the den. Three other skeletal figures waited for them. Leo pulled out his sword instinctively, cutting through one of them. It did not fall. A ruby did.

A strangled breath escaped Talia. "Anton..."

A rusted blade rose towards them, followed by two more. Leo met them just in time.

"You can't fight them!" said Talia. "There's too many, we need to run!"

She grabbed his hand and dragged him into the woods. The darkness was almost absolute. He could see nothing ahead of him. They both tripped and fell a dozen, a hundred times. The sightless skeletons seemed unperturbed by the absence of light. They were slow, but they did not stumble. Leo's sides were splitting, his lungs burned.

Every time he was forced to stop, they gained.

"Don't stop!" Talia hissed.

"I can't... I can't breathe..."

In a shaft of silvery moonlight, he caught a glimpse of Talia's desperate face, the face that suggested she'd rip out her own lungs and give them to him if she thought it would help. Instead, she seized his sword and went to beat them back, giving him a few seconds to gather his strength again.

They stumbled onwards in the dark until Talia stopped abruptly. "Down here!"

"Down–"

She shoved him into a hole. He fell several feet and landed in an earthy cavern. All light was extinguished in an instant. He heard the sound of Talia scrambling for something, presumably blocking up the entrance. He held his breath as the sounds of the skeletons passed overhead, and vanished entirely.

Talia was silent. For a moment, he worried she'd vanished and left him here alone.

"We should be safe here overnight," she said. "They can't animate in the daylight. We should be safe to leave at dawn…" The horror in her voice was stark. "Her powers are growing. If she can do that, then what else… who else…"

Leo reached forward, finding her in the dark, and grabbed her before the tears could fall. "We'll come back and bury them again," he promised. "When this is all over. We'll let them rest."

She sobbed profusely into his chest. Great, big, gulping sobs, almost like she was drowning. He held her steadily until they subsided and shrivelled away.

"I… I never cried for them," she explained. "I never could. I felt all the grief and had no way of getting it out of me. At most, I've only ever been able to give the appearance of tears in my eyes. They've never been able to fall."

She had been water against a dam, all these years. He leant down and kissed what remained of her tears. They were tasteless, barely there. How could it be, when she was so clearly real and here with him?

"Would you believe me, if I told you it was going to be all right?" he asked her.

"I think I'm rather at the stage where I'd believe anything you told me."

"Then it's going to be all right," he whispered. "Because whatever happens, if we're together, we'll conquer it." He kissed her forehead. "You're the most beautiful person I have ever met," he said, "and I promise you I thought that *before* your costume change."

There was a smile in her voice. "You're the most beautiful person I've ever met," she said. "Inside and out." She raised a hand to stroke his cheek, thumbing the edge of his lips. Leo trembled under her touch. "Are you trembling?"

"Maybe. Slightly. Wait," he said, "can you feel me?"

"Almost," she said.

Leo rolled over, flipping Talia on her back before leaning over her, their faces inches apart. His heart hammered against his ribcage, rising to his throat. Heat pulsed through him.

He brushed his nose against hers. "Can you feel that?"

She shook her head.

He squeezed one of her hands against the earth. "That?"

"Almost," she said, her voice a whisper.

"This?" He kissed her neck.

Talia groaned. "Sadly, no."

Leo exhaled deeply. "If I can kiss your neck, surely I can kiss your lips? What difference does it make?"

"You're just saying that because you want to kiss me."

"No, I'm just saying that because I really, *really* want to kiss you." He rested his forehead against hers. "Amongst other things."

Every touch of hers made his insides quiver. It was almost impossible to resist kissing her. Each twitch of her lips tugged against his, as if begging to be pressed together. He was made to kiss her, to hold her. Maybe this was fate, maybe he was *meant* to kiss her now. Maybe it would work and the curse would be shattered.

Maybe, maybe, maybe...

Are you willing to stake her life on a maybe?

No. There was nothing in this world he would risk her life for.

"Leo?" Talia placed a hand against his chest. "I really, really want to kiss you too."

"Willing-to-stake-your-life-and-the-fate-of-an-entire-kingdom want to kiss?"

"Hmm, not quite." Her grin seemed to emanate. "But close. So very, very close..."

With each word, she placed a kiss against his cheek. He was going to set on fire.

"Is there a lake nearby?" he asked. "Because I want to dive in it."

There was no going to a lake, and nothing more they could do. They curled up together. Leo tried to sleep. A storm brewed overhead; there was a crash of lightning.

"What was with you earlier?" he asked, as rest evaded him. "It was like... like you were dreaming."

"I know," she said. "It was strange. That hasn't happened before."

He paused. "You're worried, aren't you?"

"I don't want to worry you..."

"Talia–"

"Something is happening to my body. I... I was grateful, when it saved you, but... I don't think it was supposed to happen. I think I'm being pulled in two different directions. That's not how this is supposed to work."

Leo's breathing increased rapidly. "You'll be fine," he said. "We're not far away–"

"I know," she said. "I'm sure it's nothing."

21
The Thorn Hedge

I n the morning, Talia went back to the den to salvage their equipment whilst he hunted for food. He'd offered to switch jobs, but it was quite the trek back and she wanted to spare him the exertion while his leg recovered. He wanted to spare her the sight of the bones of her fallen family, but she was insistent.

She returned after a couple of hours, white-faced and bereft of supplies.

"They... they smashed everything," she said. "I sifted through the wreckage but there was... there was nothing..."

No medical supplies. No bow. No notes from Jakob.

"Leo," she said, her voice tight, "the potions."

He swallowed, a cold chill seizing his insides. "It's fine," he said. "We're only a few days away, right? I can handle a few bad dreams."

"If... if you're sure."

He didn't have another choice, and in this moment, after a few days of rest, it didn't feel too much of a struggle. He might feel differently in the morning.

There wasn't much to be had for breakfast. A few berries was all he could find. They trekked onwards, keeping a lookout for anything else. They found some mushrooms around lunchtime, which they roasted on sticks over a fire. Talia caught a few small fish before dinner, wading into a stream until they came crawling into her lap. There were no nymphs here to assist her. The forests were unearthly quiet.

It wasn't much of a meal. A few berries, a couple of fish, a handful of mushrooms... not much energy for a full day's travel.

Not much longer, he told himself, *not much longer.*

He sank into slumber, wrapped in Talia's arms. She wasn't as cold as she used to be, but she wasn't warm either.

The nightmares came thick and heavy. He woke several times gasping, and Talia was not always awake. A part of him liked that, liked not having to subject her to his horrors, not letting her see him in such a state. But another part of him was worried. Worried she'd sink into a sleep she'd never wake from.

Most of his nightmares were about her, now, of a skeleton lying in the tower where she should be.

He did not want to share that with her.

She and the sword had vanished when he woke the next morning. He flew into a blind panic, afraid she'd gone to tackle the fairy herself, but she soon appeared, pulling a bird behind her.

"Catching one of these with a sword is not easy," she said, throwing it at his feet. "Should do for today though, at least."

He was too hungry to be angry with her, but too angry to be thankful. He said nothing as he set to work plucking the bird and she cleaned the sword.

It took forever to cook. This was something he'd rarely appreciated before, how long food took to prepare. But then he'd never known real hunger before now.

It was hard not to devour the beast, knowing he needed to savour it. He hated being grateful that he didn't have to share, that Talia had no need of sustenance.

One night of bad sleep and nothing to dull the pain in his leg was chipping away at him. He didn't like the person he was becoming.

The next night was worse. He had truly forgotten how awful they could be, how his body felt sick with exhaustion the next day.

The look in Talia's eyes was new, though.

"Don't look at me like that!" he snapped across breakfast.

"Oh, what, like I care about you? Like I hate seeing you in pain? Like it doesn't tear me up inside that all this is happening because of me?"

"Yes," he said quietly, "like that."

"You don't get to decide whether or not I like you," she said. "Much like I don't get to decide what happens to you."

Leo sighed, and reached across to grab her hand. "Would you rather I gave up?"

"When I see you like this, yes," she said. "Then I think of what could be, and I tell myself to shelve it."

What could be. How far away that felt, like the faint memory of summer amidst the harshest of winters. The goal was no longer to rescue the princess. It was to rescue Talia, to have her hold him back. To have a future with her.

He had to fight this. He had to.

"Leo," she said softly, "I'm really sorry this is happening to you."

Leo pulled her into his chest. "I'll be all right," he said. "Try not to worry. Soon, this will all seem worth it. We'll look back on these days and laugh."

Talia stroked back his hair, and kissed the shadows under his eyes. "I will never joke about this."

They set off again as soon as he could find the strength. One more good thing about Talia's return to physical form was that she could wield the sword, cutting down swathes of the thorns that occupied most of the woodland now. He had no idea how long it would have taken him otherwise, but he suspected this was saving him days.

"Let me know if you need me to–" he started.

"I will not," Talia said. "And honestly, after all these years, it's oddly therapeutic to be cutting these bastards down. They're a blight on my forest."

"Then swing away," he said, lagging behind her. "I shall not stop you."

That day felt long and endless, although he was thankful for the lack of creatures. A cold darkness emanated from the wall of thorns, and he wondered if even the wildlife was wary of it.

Every so often, they came across the body of an unfortunate adventurer, impaled on the giant thorns.

"Ones who came without me," Talia said. "I've never lost anyone this close before."

"Can... can the thorns move?"

"Sometimes," she said. "But don't worry, I'll protect you."

That did not ease him a great deal, but another part of him worried why the thorns weren't moving now... as if Thirteen were saving her strength for something, or spending it elsewhere.

That night a coldness crept into the thicket Talia had cleared for them, the kind that bit into his bones. He could barely sleep for shivering, at one point giving up entirely and hacking away at some more of the thorns, just for the sensation of warmth.

Then he crawled back into Talia's cold arms.

"I'm not sure this can help you much," she said.

He buried himself in her chest. "I disagree."

Morning brought a welcome relief from the nightmares, but his joints had seized up, and he still felt cold and shivery beneath the watery sun.

"You don't look well."

"I'll be fine. I just need to get moving. Let me use the sword for a bit."

He wondered if the fairy didn't need to expend her energy sending creatures after them, if she knew he'd collapse from exhaustion long before he reached her. She'd been playing a long game, after all.

Not now, not yet, so close.

The exercise warmed him, but it worsened the aching and he soon had to concede. Talia sang as she worked, trying to lighten the mood. He lacked the energy to join her, lacked the energy to do much at all. He'd eaten so little in so long, and he was tired, so tired...

Something crackled behind him.

"What was that?"

Talia stopped. "I heard nothing."

Leo looked about him, expecting something to drop from overhead. Nothing stirred. The imagination of the exhausted, perhaps.

He carried on. There it was again. A low, steady creak. The darkness betrayed no movement, but something, somewhere, was shifting.

He looked ahead to Talia, swinging the sword. Something black slithered around her ankle.

"Talia!"

The thorns snaked around her legs and lynched her off the floor. The sword jerked out of reach. Leo seized it in seconds, swinging it over his head and slicing across the branch. Talia toppled into him, snatching the blade and his hand and pulling him into the bracken. The thorns groaned and tightened as they slid over and under them, racing through the labyrinthine halls of the forest.

Talia was unstoppable, a force of nature equal to that of the wilderness, her swings and dives and jabs expert and precise. She did not falter, did not pause, did not allow him to either.

They hit a wall of rock. No, not rock, smooth stone. The walls of the kingdom.

Talia swung round, cutting through a loose vine.

"Up!" she hissed at Leo, dropping the sword and holding out her hands.

He did not wait to complain or insist she go first. He stood on her hands and allowed himself to be catapulted into the air, clutching the ledge of the wall and hauling himself up.

Talia tossed the sword up next. He caught it and flung it to the other side, holding his hand out to her. She leapt onto a thorn branch, darting upwards as each platform shifted beneath her, dodging and weaving out of the way.

Her hand clasped his, and he pulled her up and onto the walkway.

"Are you all right?" they both asked.

Before either could respond, thunder filled the air, and the skies came crashing down.

"Come on," said Talia, dragging him to his feet. "There's plenty of shelter to take."

She took him into a nearby house, surprisingly well preserved despite the years it had lain dormant. There was barely any dust, no moss growing through the stone. A table was laid out for a dinner that had never happened, not a single chip in a bowl.

"Fairy magic," Talia explained. "Everything slumbers here, even the wildlife."

A dog sat beside a cold fire, beneath the foot of his owners who dozed silently in their chairs. A cook was sprawled out on the kitchen table, still covered in flour, halfway through baking a pie. Her ingredients were still fresh.

The rain lashed against the windows. Leo shivered.

"Come on," said Talia, "upstairs."

She tugged him into one of the bedrooms and immediately started to undress him.

"Uh, ah, what are you doing?"

"You're freezing," she said. "And you're injured."

"No, I'm—" He looked down at his arms. They'd been shredded by the thorns. Talia's skin was as unblemished as ever. Even her clothes didn't look wet. "I... I don't feel anything."

"That's because you're too cold," she said. "Get a fire going. Borrow some clothes from our hosts. I'll be back as soon as I can."

"Talia—"

"I will reinstate rule number one!"

She vanished back into the hallway, leaving Leo to follow her instructions. The minute he sat down, his body seemed to fail him, every pain rushing back in full force. He could barely move. The very air felt heavy. He was only half-conscious when Talia returned and plied him with whatever she'd manage to raid from the local apothecary. Only a fraction of strength dribbled back.

"We... we can't stay," he said, as she cleaned out his cuts. "We're so close now—"

She shook her head. "It's still a long way to the castle, and I don't know what she has in store for us. You can't... you can't fight like this. Please, *please* don't try to. Don't risk it."

"Talia," said Leo softly, catching her arm, "how long do we have left? I'm not entirely clear of the days–"

Talia looked down. "It–"

"How many days?"

"One," she said. "We have one more, not including today. If you can't wake me by sunrise after tomorrow night…"

"Then we need to go–"

Leo tried to get up, but Talia pushed him back to the bed. "No!" she said. "Don't you get it? If you go out there now, like this, you're going to die!"

"What difference would a day make?"

"Everything!" She grabbed his face in her hands. "Don't you get it? Leo, you're everything!"

Leo opened his mouth to say something – anything – but her mouth cut swiftly across his and any thoughts he'd ever had were swept clean away.

It was the strangest kiss of his life, both everything he'd always wanted and also only an echo of it. There was Talia, Talia behind those lips, but no warmth, no breath, no softness, no taste. She was still more real than his paper dream version, and he clung to her regardless, his hands gripped around her waist.

Don't go. Don't stop.

Slowly, Talia pulled away from him. Nothing happened. The rains continued their assault on the roof. She did not fade. Nothing changed.

"Why… why did you do that?" he asked.

"To prove to you that you mean more to me than my life, or my kingdom," she said. "And… and I rather hoped that would work, and then you wouldn't have to go at all, but I suppose it really has to be that body in the castle. The one that pricked her finger…" She slid down beside him. "I would rather fade into nothingness than see you hurt," she whispered. "So please, *please…* just stay."

Leo turned his body to face her. He placed his hand against her cheek, stroked her hair over her shoulder, and kissed her again. Her lips moved slightly under his, but little more. She could not feel him. Her breath was hollow.

"The next time I kiss you," he said, "you will feel it."

"The next time you kiss me, I'll be asleep," she corrected, "but the time after that..." She played with the folds of his borrowed shirt, and kissed his collar bone. "And the time after that..."

She cleaned out each of his wounds, bandaged whatever she had to, and dosed him up with whatever potions she could. Then they went downstairs to raid the cupboards for dinner, promising to repay the family when they managed to wake them.

Leo hadn't eaten so well in weeks, and there was something decidedly pleasant about sitting at a proper table, opposite Talia. He wished she could eat with him.

"Not long," she said, as if reading his thoughts. "There's quite the feast laid out at the castle. I've been dreaming about it for decades."

It seemed strange to loiter about the parlour with the sleeping occupants still present in their chairs, so they cleaned up as best they could, reset the table, and moved themselves back upstairs. Night was still a way off, and the rain had not let up. They stoked the fire and curled up together on the bed, talking of everything and nothing.

"Talia," said Leo, as the darkness folded in around them.

"Hmm? Yes?"

"I'm afraid of falling asleep." He waited for Talia to tease him. She didn't. She clutched him tightly and stroked back his hair.

"I shall sing away the nightmares," she said.

"All night?"

"No vocal chords. I can go on forever."

But she could not go on forever, and both of them knew it.

Eventually, he could fight it no longer. All night, he dreamt of shadows sharp and slippery, of monsters crawling from the corners of the room and a skeletal corpse in a tower. He woke half a dozen times. Every time he did, Talia was there, holding him and whispering to him in the dark.

Sunlight streamed across his pillow when he woke the next morning. Talia was not there. He shifted upwards, scouring the room, but all that was out of place was a stack of papers on the desk he didn't think were there the night before.

He sat up and went towards them.

Dear Briar, the first one read,

If there is a fragment of luck left in the world and we manage to snatch it, by tomorrow morning, you and I shall be one again and there is the possibility that the last hundred years may have passed in the blink of an eye for you. All my memories of the time in the forest may be lost forever. There is a lot I would like to scrub away, but so much more that I would like to remember, to hold next to me until the end of my days. There is so little time left, but here are some things you must know.

There was a collection of notes and letters, some long, some short, some half-finished, as if she'd stumbled onto another thought halfway through finishing one and had to rush it out before it trickled away. They were notes to herself, memories of her time with the bandits, pleas not to forget them... or the person she became.

That seems strange and silly, doesn't it? But that is the thing I am most scared of forgetting. I am afraid of unravelling. I am afraid of not being this version of me.

Sometimes, I am jealous of myself. I am jealous of the girl I was, the girl I may be again. I am jealous of her innocence. I am jealous that all these dark things may be unknown to her. But I do not want to forget myself, no matter how cold or angry or bitter I became in the years that followed my slumber. I became jaded. I became cruel. I forgot how to feel, or felt entirely too much.

But I was still me. The years may have scarred me, but they shaped me too. I may not be as patient or kind as I once was, but I was still me.

Do not forget Talia.

He swallowed, moving on to the one beneath.

Edelvard. After so many disappointments, perhaps it was only natural that I pinned so many hopes on Edelvard. He was so kind, so noble. One of a handful of people to enter this forest with genuinely good intentions. I told him who I really was after just a few days. I did not love him, but I felt that such a thing could happen, if I gave it time.

We did not have time. Edelvard died halfway through the journey. I knew him for less than two weeks, and his memory coloured my interaction with every person I met after. I barely gave them a chance. I was too afraid of the hurt, too afraid that they would be cut down too. I couldn't let myself care for anyone else.

Not until Leo.

Leo, Leo, Leo. The best of them. How could I help but fall for him when he showed up, all alone, intent on minimising the suffering of others? Brave, beautiful, foolish Leo, who protected me when I gave him no reason to. Who found the good in me when I bared it so infrequently.

I am afraid of writing too much about him, because you will need to discover him again. Because hopefully the lifetime that you share will make up for the weeks that you have forgotten. Be nicer to him this time. He truly was worth waiting for. You have no idea how much I want to kiss him right now, to lean across and press my lips to his sleeping mouth. How much I melt away with the very idea! I have never wanted anything more than I want him, and I hope you come to know that longing too, and act on it. He will be gentle. He will give you time if you do not remember. Do not shy away. Do not be so mad that you needed rescuing that you take too long to let him in. His soul is as beautiful as his face. Noble incarnate. If I had ever truly dreamed of the one who would rescue me, they could not have held a candle to him.

I will let you figure out why. But please, I beg you, let him in. Give him a chance. I think he will be very hurt to be forgotten, and I do not want to see him in pain. Not again.

Leo's throat tightened, and he put the letter down. She must have stayed up all night writing them. There were dozens. Maybe hundreds. Each a memory she was terrified of losing, of losing a part of herself. He didn't want her to lose them either. He'd been so focused on just getting here, he hadn't thought about what waking her might mean.

He dabbed his eyes, and went downstairs to find her.

She was nowhere to be seen, but breakfast had been left out for him. For one horrible, sinking moment, he was afraid that she'd deserted him, that she'd gone off to face Thirteen alone. He bolted out into the streets, but he saw her immediately, sitting on a wall, staring up at the castle. A few hours' walk away. So close.

"Morning," she said. "I didn't want to wake you–"

"I read your letters."

"Oh! I... I couldn't find an envelope. I was going to ask you to give them to me if–"

Leo grabbed her in his arms.

"For a moment, I thought you'd gone off on your own."

"For a moment, I considered it."

Leo pulled back, stroking her hair over her shoulder. "What changed your mind?"

"The thought of how mad you'd be. Maybe too mad to kiss me awake."

"I'd never be *that* mad at you," he said. "But you're right, I would have been furious."

"That didn't seem like the best way to start our future together."

Leo's insides trembled at the word 'together'. He took her hands. "We go together, right?"

Talia half-nodded, as though her strength had left her. "Leo," she said, "in case... for whatever reason, if we don't both make it–"

"We are *going* to make it!"

"I just need you to know what I waited a hundred years for you, and... and you were worth it. I'd wait a hundred years again, thrice over. I'd wait a thousand, if it meant just meeting you. That's it," she said shortly. "I just thought you should know."

Leo ate quickly while Talia gathered together a bag of any equipment she thought might come in handy. She plied him with potions, and they set off for the castle hand-in-hand. Leo ought to have felt elated, overjoyed with the idea that in just a few hours, he could be holding her hand and having her hold his back. She could feel him for the first time. Just a little longer...

Instead, he was plagued by an unshakeable feeling of dread. There was only one day left. What would Thirteen do next to stop them?

"You're quiet," said Talia.

"Something about this place is... unsettling," he replied, stepping over a sleeping merchant. "Like a living graveyard."

"I know. It's why I seldom come back here."

They stopped beside a well. Leo drew a draft to refresh himself. The water sloshing about the bucket was the noisiest part of the square.

Something glittered in the base of the well.

"There's something down there!" he said.

Talia shrugged. "A coin, maybe?"

"No, it's too close to the surface. Can you... can you hear that?"

Talia frowned. "Humming?"

He shot the bucket back down and scooped it in, drawing it back up. It was a ball of glowing light, hissing against the sides of a jar. Leo looked at Talia, waiting for her instruction. She shrugged, just as confused as he was.

Leo took off the lid.

"Finally!" the light snorted, wriggling itself free of its prison. "I have been trapped down there *for days.* I thought you would never find me!"

"I'm sorry," said Leo, "but I've not met any sentient floating balls of light before, would you mind giving us your name?"

"It's me! Ariel!"

"Ariel?" Talia said, cupping the tiny form, "but... what happened to you?"

"It's Thirteen," Ariel rushed. "She's found a way to break free of the curse. She ambushed us and drained our power, trapping us in these jars so we couldn't assist you–"

Leo poked her. "You turn into balls of light when your powers are drained?"

"I'm sorry, would you prefer that we died?"

"Ah, no, sorry."

"Anyway, she–" Ariel stopped, tapping Talia's palm. "You have a form again."

"Yes, but–"

"That's not supposed to happen."

"No, and we're not sure how it happened, but we've already tried the kiss and it didn't work, so–"

"*When* did it happen?"

Talia blushed. "When Leo needed me."

"Oh, that's so sweet..." Ariel's light glowed warmly. "But at the same time, worrying. Can you still fade?"

"I'm... not sure. It's hard to. And... I've been falling asleep. In this body."

Ariel was quiet. "We need to wake you up. Quickly."

"Well, we're on our way–"

A voice cut through their conversation, as cool and icy as the north wind. "You shall not get further."

They looked up. Standing a few feet away, flanked by thorny tendrils, was a tall violet figure. Her gaze sucked away all traces of warmth.

Talia picked up the discarded jar and hurled it towards her, but the glass passed straight through her body and shattered on the cobbles below.

"She's... non-corporeal," Leo stammered.

Thirteen grinned. "In a hundred years, you didn't think I would eventually learn how to astral project too? Foolish child..."

Ariel streamed towards her, but a single flick of her wrist and she was sent flying back into the well.

Leo drew his sword. Talia trembled beside him. "Leo–"

"She can't hurt us, right? She can't touch anything–"

Thorns shot through the floor, seizing Leo by his wrists and driving him against a wall.

"Oh, my dear boy, I don't need to touch you."

Talia raced forward, pulling out the sword, but the thorns snatched it from her grip. She seized the binds around Leo and pulled. They did not move. Her eyes were wide with desperation.

Thirteen raised a hand, and one of the thorns jabbed Leo in the side. He let out a quiet scream, trying to swallow it, not wanting to betray the pain. It wasn't deep. It couldn't kill him.

She drove the thorns deeper, and kept driving them until he cried out.

"Stop! *Stop!*" Talia's voice was agony. "Don't hurt him! Please, *please,* just leave him alone! I'll do... I'll do *anything*–"

The fairy's eyes glinted. "Anything?" She smiled. "You know, I believe you will. I believe you mean it even more than your mother did."

"What... what do you want from me?"

"I don't want anything *from* you at all, my dear. I just want your death. I want your mother to see what happens when you try to defy me."

Talia took a deep breath. "She won't see anything," she said. "If you kill us now, if the kingdom doesn't wake... she'll see nothing."

Thirteen raised an eyebrow. "That's true."

"Take me. Let... let me die. Only let the others wake. And let him live."

Leo felt sick, squirming in his bonds. "No," he said. "Talia, you can't."

"I... I don't have a choice..." she said, tearing her eyes from his. "Do we have a deal?"

Thirteen's smile was dark. "Yes. We have a deal."

"No! Don't do this!"

Talia turned back to Leo. She grabbed his face. "It was worth it," she said. "Everything I tried to do. Just to know you. It was worth it. I'd do it again in a heartbeat. I'd do anything for you. I–"

Thirteen clicked her fingers. Talia vanished.

"No!" screamed Leo.

"Oh, hush now, boy. She's still alive. For now, at least. I've just moved her form to within the castle walls. I need to wait a little longer to be free..."

She clapped her hands. A hole opened beneath Leo's feet. Dark waters swirled below. "I wouldn't try to escape, if I were you," she said. "You've already lost."

He plunged down into the dark.

The Tallest Tower

He awoke in the damp, his side splitting. He slid a hand towards his wound. It was sticky with blood, but he wasn't bleeding badly. Most of it had clotted and nothing was broken.

The little fairy nudged his side. "Leo," she hissed, "are you all right?"

"I... I think so. More or less." He looked around him. He was in some kind of disused waterway. "Can we get out of here?"

"Possibly," she said. "The thorns are down here too, though." She moved away, hovering over something beside him. "I managed to get your sword."

"Excellent. Thank you."

"Can you get up?"

Leo climbed shakily to his feet. He was unsteady, but at least his legs didn't appear to have been damaged by the fall. He leant on the sword for support.

"That was terribly romantic, her sacrificing herself like that," Ariel sighed.

"It was romantic," said Leo, taking another step, "it was foolish, it was reckless. When I get her back, I'm going to be very cross with her."

"No, you won't. You'll be too happy to have her back."

"You seem to be enjoying this far too much."

"I love a great romance, what can I say? You mortals seem

to do everything a little more... *epically*, than us fairies. It's probably why we're so fascinated with you."

"I... I can't even see your expression right now, but it's making me uncomfortable."

"Sorry, prince. But you are very dreamy. Briar is a lucky girl."

It was the first time he'd heard someone refer to Talia as Briar. She had known her before.

"What was she like? Talia? Before all of this."

"Margaret knew her best. She was her tutor. By all reports, she wasn't a great deal different from the way she is now. Smart, brave, stubborn, incredibly witty... why do you ask?"

"She's... she's worried she won't remember any of this when she wakes. Can that... can that happen?"

Ariel bobbed her tiny form. "Humans aren't supposed to astral project," she said. "It's not a mortal skill. The pendant alone allows for it. Briar has been Talia a long time. I'd like to believe that that means she cannot be erased, not entirely... but we always knew that was a risk. She was prepared for it."

"She didn't have much of a choice."

Ariel shook her head. "Lie back and surrender to fate, or suffer and have some say in it. Many would have chosen the former."

"Would you?"

"No, I'm all about putting up a fight."

Leo hobbled along.

"As are you." She sighed. "Made for each other..."

They came to a junction. Leo shrugged, picking the better-lit path. They walked on a while in silence, time hurrying past. He wished he could move faster.

Something glinted in the distance, bobbing along the water. A ball of glitter in a jar.

"Ophelia!" Ariel gasped, racing forwards. She tapped furiously on the glass. "Get her out!"

Leo plucked the jar from the water and quickly unstoppered it. The sprite tumbled out.

"Oh, thank the stars! I was so worried–" She buzzed towards Leo. "Are you all right? You look–"

"Awful, I'm sure. But that doesn't matter. Thirteen has Talia and we've only got a few hours until..." His strength failed him for a moment, and he sagged against a wall. Talia's warning stung down the tunnel.

If you face her now, you are going to die!

"Damn..."

The fairies buzzed together, conversing silently. "Let's get out of here," they said. "If we can find Margaret... the three of us combined might be able to restore your strength."

"But I thought Thirteen–"

"She hasn't drained *all* of our magic. We always keep some in reserve. Mortals aren't too hard to fix, anyway. Not when there's breath in them."

"Thank... thank you."

Ariel buzzed around his head. "Don't thank us yet, boy. We're not out of the woods."

They stumbled around in the dark for what must have been hours, illuminated only by the faint glow of the fairies, searching for a way out. Eventually, they located a ladder leading up to a manhole. It was shut fast, but a little fairy magic and a good shove from Leo opened it right up. They tumbled out into a street. It was pitch black. Leo didn't even want to think about what time it was.

I'm coming for you, Talia. I won't be long. Wait for me.

Not that she had any other choice. She'd been waiting for him for a century. If fate was a thing... his statement was truer than he first imagined it. She had been waiting for *him* for a century. Maybe the reason no one else had succeeded was because he hadn't even been born yet, or wasn't ready.

But he was now. He wasn't going to fail her, or himself, at the last hurdle.

Ariel steered him towards an upturned crate and nudged him to sit down. She disappeared with a sharp crack and reappeared a few minutes later, with a plate of cheese, fruit and bread, and a tankard of ale.

"Eat," she commanded.

"But what about–"

"We'll find Margaret. Get your strength up the old fashioned way in the meantime."

Leo did as he was told while the fairies zapped about from house to house, searching for their friend. An eerie silence descended as their search widened, and he found himself alone in the utter dark. He was exhausted, but sleep was far beyond him. Every part of him ached for Talia's company, Talia's voice. Now there was nothing at all to beat back the nightmares, but what could Thirteen send him that was worse than the reality he was trapped in?

There was the sound of something crashing in a building not far away. The fairies returned a few minutes later with their third member.

"Are you all right, ma'am?" Leo asked.

"Am I all right? Am *I* all right? You can barely stand, and you're asking me if a little thing like being reduced to this minute form and having most of my powers drained is bothersome?" Margaret tutted. "I'm beginning to think Briar doesn't deserve you... ladies, huddle please."

They grouped together, a little ways away from him, whispering in hushed voices.

"What are you discussing?"

"How much we can help you," said Margaret. "And what we can spend our magic on without risking our lives and having a little reserved for afterwards. Have something to eat."

"I've already–"

"Eat, boy!"

Leo stuffed his mouth with the remains of his meal, and picked at it for a while as they finished their conversation.

Finally, they drifted back over.

"All right," they said, "getting your strength up is our number one priority, but we have limited magic to work with. We're going to put you in a semi-enchanted sleep–"

"No!" said Leo sharply.

The three fairies shot backwards.

"I can't. There's not time, and... Thirteen, she... she visits me in my sleep–"

Margaret crept closer and buzzed beside his hand. "This will be a dreamless sleep, Leopold, and only for a while, I promise you. We will wake you long before dawn. The castle is not far."

Leo exhaled. "What... what else will you spend your magic on?"

"Lighting the way," said Ophelia. "You can't see anything in this dark."

"And we'll keep the rest back," finished Ariel. "For afterwards, hopefully."

Leo nodded, silently consenting. They hovered over his eyes, and he felt himself falling down, down, down...

"Leo! *Leo!*"

He woke abruptly, light stinging his eyes. For a moment, he was struck by sheer panic; he was sure it was dawn, the light was so bright. But then he realised it was mostly Ariel, hovering too close to him, although the rest of the darkness was lit by a glowing, purplish light.

"It's not dawn," Ariel assured him. "Just a spell we've cast, to help you see."

Leo flexed his hands, his arms, every muscle he possessed. There was a dull ache in all of them, but no pain, no exhaustion. He felt fresher than he had in weeks.

"Come," she said. "Your sword."

He gathered it from beside him and buckled it to him, following Ariel through the streets. She moved at lightning speed. "Where are Margaret and Ophelia–" he started.

"Lighting the rest of the way."

"You don't sound... has something happened?"

Ariel was mute for a moment. "You'll see."

They turned a corner, and in the well-lit gloom Leo could see the castle against the sky, but there was movement along the road that led to it. He focused his gaze.

Spiders, as large and monstrous as the ones he'd encountered in the forest. Ogres, too, by the looks of things. Misshapen wolves, skeletal monstrosities... every dark thing.

"What happened?"

"Thirteen must have realised you'd left the waterways. She's called all that she can to block the way ahead."

"I can't... how am I to–"

"You run," she said. "You head straight for the castle. For the tower. We will cover you."

"But, you're just... you're all so small, and..."

"We have a little magic in reserve, like we said."

"You can't possibly–"

"Leo," said Ariel, with a gentle firmness, "what would you have us do?"

"Not die?" he suggested.

Ariel snorted. "We'll do our best. Are you ready?"

He drew his sword.

"Cut down only what's in your path," she said. "And follow me. Stay focused. Trust in the others."

He swallowed, and Ariel dived into the streets. He fixed his gaze on her tiny form, even as a giant wolf rose up to greet him. He slashed it with his sword, but didn't watch as it toppled away. Out of the corner of his eye, he saw something crash from a roof; a statue pushed by one of the fairies. An ogre lunged at him next. He dodged its mighty swing just as a fairy drove itself into its eye, causing it to miss and hit a nearby house instead. Stone and plaster crashed to the floor. The assault continued as he charged ahead, the ogre's mad swings thudding along the streets. He hoped the people were safe in their houses, that the monsters hadn't gotten in, that the fairies had thought of keeping them safe while they were lighting the way, because there was no way he could stop and save them. No way he could even check.

He had to keep running.

A huge spider blocked his path, its web filling the gap between houses. There was no way to charge through. He would have to face it. But just as he readied himself, he saw the alleyways filling with its brethren. He was penned in. Ariel ran into the large one's eyes, but she had eight to contend with. The others lunged. Leo swung, hacking off legs, lost in a blur of hair and black, beady eyes. It was overwhelming. He couldn't swing fast enough. They were coming from every angle–

An arrow shot out of the darkness, pinning one to the ground, followed by half a dozen others. Leo looked back–

Oakfoot, Acre and Swifthoof were galloping up the streets towards them, cutting down enemies left and right. Oakfoot skidded to a halt in front of Leo, kicking the large spider in the face and sending it reeling towards the web before dispatching it with a quick stab to the back.

He stared at Leo. "Just so Talia is clear," he said, "this is the favour."

Leo nodded, trembling gratefully. Oakfoot held up a hand.

"Get up," he told Leo. "But never tell anyone I let you ride me."

Leo did not waste any time. He took Oakfoot's hand and jumped onto his back. The centaur yanked his blade free of the spider, sliced through the web, and galloped over the body, following Ariel's trail.

Up the winding streets towards the castle they raced, enemies falling behind them, in front of them, because of them. Leo clutched his sword with one hand, the other around Oakfoot's waist, clinging on for dear life and trying not to miss the lack of a saddle. He was nearly thrown loose several times.

A wall of sheer stone swelled in front of them. Oakfoot came to a sliding stop, his hooves shrieking against the cobbles.

"How well can you climb?" he asked Leo.

"Quite well, but–"

"Then go."

He bucked the boy from his back, sending him soaring towards the wall. Leo's hands collided with the thick thorn trellis that bled from above. The thorns were so large they were the size of ladder rungs, easy to avoid being pricked by. He began to climb, struggling to the top of the wall and half-falling down the other side. He landed in a messy pile.

He climbed to his feet, brushing off any loose leaves, checking for injuries. A few grazes. Nothing more.

He looked around him. He was in a courtyard so filled with thorns that the stone underneath was almost invisible, but behind them, so close, was a tower.

The castle. He'd made it.

"Go, Leo!" Ariel hissed.

Something trembled under the thorns. Something huge, long, round. A head rose from the gloom, with milk-white eyes. There was the stench of rotting flesh.

The basilisk, resurrected by Thirteen's dark magic.

"Leo!"

Leo turned. Talia was standing beside a nest of thorns, unglamored, her feet bound. Thirteen's shadowy form stood over her.

"Impressive that you have come so far." The fairy glowered. "But your journey ends here, prince."

The basilisk lunged. Leo dodged, diving into a nearby guard's tower. The serpent struck the stone behind him. The entire building trembled. Leo raced up the stairs and out onto the top level, leaping over the side before the basilisk could rise to greet him, and sliding down its back with his sword. It hit the ground just before he did, but it did not stop. It was no longer alive. It did not have to.

It caught Leo with its tail and sent him sprawling to the floor, its fanged mouth rising over him. Leo raised his blade again as it came crashing down–

There was a flash of gold hair. Something slumped against him.

"*Talia!*"

The basilisk reeled again, but an arrow shot through the roof of its mouth. Oakfoot and a handful of others had breached the gate. Ariel buzzed by Leo's ear.

"Get her out of here!"

Leo swept Talia into his arms and dived into a nearby building. He crashed to his knees, holding her against his chest. A puncture in her stomach pulsed blood.

"You teleported," he said. "Even when... and now you're

bleeding..."

Talia smiled faintly. "Are you... all right?"

"You're asking me if I'm... when you're... you're... what were you *thinking?*"

"That I didn't want to see you dead?"

"You're a fool," he said.

"Maybe," she rasped, "but a fool who..." She folded backwards. "So, now might not be the ideal moment to tell you that I can feel again, but... I can feel again. I can feel everything." She raised a hand to his cheek. It stung with warmth. Then she slumped further into his arms, immobilised by pain.

"Talia!" Leo clutched her to his chest, so fiercely he thought he might break her. He wanted to scream. *Don't go, don't go, don't leave me!*

"I need to fade, don't I?"

Leo nodded, his throat too raw to speak. He held his hand against her wound. Could she even vanish? She looked so human, so human and so perfect...

"If I go," she whispered, "and I don't remember you when I wake up, that'll be like a death, too..."

"You are *not* going to die!"

"But I might not remember... and the others... I can't forget them! I can't forget any of it! And... I'm not the person I used to be. What if you don't like her? What if you don't like who I was?"

Leo swallowed. "You're a giant pain in the ass now," he said, "and I still like you. I will always..."

"I don't want to go!" Talia trembled. "Please, don't make me go..."

"You... you have to..."

"But... but I..."

"I'm coming for you," he told her. "Any minute now. I'll come and find you. I'll wake you up."

Talia smiled faintly. "You promise?"

"I promise."

"Make me remember. Don't let me forget. Not a minute. Not a minute of it."

"I won't."

They were going to have their whole lives together. This wasn't the end. She wasn't really dying. But…

What if he was too late? What if he was killed before he could get to her? What if this injury happened to her real body, too?

What if this was it, if all the time they had together was gone and spent? If all they ever got was a few weeks in the forest and nothing ahead of them remained?

No time at all, but this.

"Talia," he rushed, "I love you."

He clasped only air. She was already gone.

Numb and trying not to think, he stumbled back into the fray.

"Leo!" Ariel appeared by his side. "Where's–"

"She faded," he said. "She's… she's back in the tower–"

The still-moving basilisk reared again, despite being stuck with arrows. Leo darted out of reach, grabbing the sword he'd abandoned when Talia fell, and slashed upwards.

"Get to the tower!" hissed another voice; Margaret. She hovered ahead of him. "Come!"

Thorns still guarded the door to the tower, covering most of the courtyard. The nest at the centre seemed to pulsate with energy. He ignored it at first, hacking away at the wall, but the thorns grew tighter and thicker.

"I can't," he rushed. "There's no way–"

The nest hummed.

"She's there, isn't she?" said Leo. "Thirteen."

Margaret paused. "Yes, but you shouldn't–"

"I can't get through," he said, hacking at the branches guarding the door. "I can't…" He scanned around for another entrance, an unblocked door, a window. Could he climb to Talia's chamber? Would the thorns not wrench him back?

The darkness of the sky was lightening to a purple. He did

not have long. Dawn was close. Too close.

He glanced back at the nest of thorns, and started to run.

"*Leo!*"

Thorn branches rose to greet him, but he cut down each one. He pushed forward, hacking away, ignoring the smaller ones that clawed for his face. He did not know how much Thirteen could do at once. If her efforts were focused on keeping the basilisk mobile and the entrances covered, then maybe, just maybe, she wouldn't be able to thicken the thorns around her sleeping body in time.

"What are you doing?" Her ghostly form rose out of the brambles. "You can't win! Dawn is nearly here!"

Not yet. Not yet, there's still time.

"You have failed, boy. Give up, surrender. I may still let you live."

Leo ignored her.

"You were born for failure. I have seen the truth in your heart. You were born to die here."

Something shimmered ahead of him, a form illuminated by purple light. Thirteen.

"Stop, boy!"

A thorn flung out of the dark and drilled into his shoulder. He did not scream. He cut the end, yanked it out, and moved forward, scrambling over the branches, paying no heed to whatever crammed into his flesh.

I will not stop. I cannot.

He reached Thirteen's sleeping form. The thorn hedge thickened, threatening to swallow him. There was no way out.

His hands clasped around the hilt of a jewelled dagger, still embedded in her middle.

"No!"

He drew it out, and plunged it into her heart.

Thirteen's ghostly form hung above her sleeping body. For a moment, the world stood suspended. Everything was soundless and silent and held like the breath of a newborn.

For a second, he thought he'd failed. This was the quiet before the storm, the moment before death. It hadn't worked. She was too powerful. Even after all these years of half-life, a blade could not kill her.

A sound like a shrill gasp pierced the air. Thirteen's astral form vanished. The thorns withered and died around her, shrivelling into the ground. Only a pale, immobile body remained in front of him.

The basilisk shuddered and slumped to the ground. Other monsters that had breached the wall were scuttling away. Roses bloomed against the stone where thorns had once clutched as light rose into the courtyard.

"Dawn!" said Margaret. "Quickly, Leo!"

He dropped his sword and ran to the door, Margaret's tiny, trembling form ahead of him, illuminating the dark corridors and the sleeping bodies lining the halls. He raced up the stairs blindly, his heart in his throat, paying no attention to the burning or breaking of his lungs until he crashed into the door at the top of the tallest tower.

A quiet fluttering of nerves that had been pressed back by the crushing need to reach her overtook him the moment the door opened. Talia lay on the bed, surrounded by flowers, utterly immobile and as pale as milk. There was barely a breath left in her. The barest, smallest, rising and falling of her chest was the only thing that betrayed life at all.

He knelt beside her, cupping her cheek. The slightest warmth resided there.

No time to be timid.

"Please wake up," he prayed, and lowered his lips to hers.

Wake. Please. Don't leave me here alone. I've come for you, for you... so come back to me.

Something moved underneath him. Her lips pressed back. Her eyes fluttered open.

"Talia," he whispered, just to be sure. If she knew that name, if she recognised it–

Talia smiled. "I love you too."

23
The Curse Broken

He held her in his arms, shaking and trembling, kissing her so fiercely that his lips soon felt numb. All of him felt numb, but in a strange, blissful way, like he'd never known sensation to begin with.

She clung to him, her fingers tight in his clothes, his hair, against his skin. "I can feel you," she whispered, her face glistening with tears. "I can feel you. You're here. You're really here."

"Of course I'm here," he said, pressing himself to her. "I'm here, and I'm not going anywhere."

She pulled his mouth to hers, and he soared and faded inside her kiss. "You feel wonderful," she said. "You *are* wonderful…"

He could taste her tears, and she could probably taste his. It didn't matter. Nothing outside of the room mattered. He would never be pried away from her side. Never, ever…

"I love you," he said. "In case I didn't make that clear."

"I know," she said, grinning through the lines of silver, "I heard you. I don't *think* I'll get tired of hearing it, if you wanted to say it again. I love you, I love you, I–"

He cut her off with a kiss.

"You saved me," she said when they parted.

"I'd *die* for you," he returned. "And you saved me, too."

"A completely selfish thing to do. I've got this awful desire to keep you alive, and beside me, for as long as humanly possible."

Leo grinned. "I'm not going anywhere."

She pulled him further into her arms, and a quiet groan escaped him.

"You're hurt!"

"A slight stab wound to the shoulder," he assured her. "Nothing to worry about."

"You're covered in…"

"Talia," he said, still kissing her, "I'll be fine."

"You certainly will be!" said a voice from the door. A presence glided across the threshold; Margaret, in her full form. She breathed into her hand and sent a glimmering cloud of golden dust floating over the room, making the flowers burst. When the cloud hit Leo, he was struck with the sensation of being plunged into a warm bath, the ache in his shoulder swiftly purged into a dull, tingly feeling.

"There," she said. "A much better state to meet your future in-laws in."

Talia cried, sitting up. "Mother!" she said, racing to her feet. "Father!"

The guards at the door rose from their slumber, and the maid on the bed of cushions pushed herself up, yawning and blinking.

"Briar?" she said. "What–"

Talia flung herself at the maid and cried into her hair. "It's over," she said. "The fairy is gone. But it *has* been a hundred years. This is Leo. He rescued me."

Leo dropped into a bow. "Only after she rescued me, I assure you."

"This is my maid," said Talia. "The one whose name I borrowed."

"Borrowed?" said the maid. "I'm not sure I–"

"I'll explain everything, my dear," said Margaret, "but these two need to go downstairs…"

All around them, the castle bloomed and stirred. Horses in the courtyard stood up and shook themselves, hunting dogs jumped up and wagged their tails. The doves in the roof pulled their little heads from beneath their wings and flew into the sky. Even the fires in the kitchens rose up, broke into flames, and continued cooking the food.

The fairies drifted from room to room, awakening the occupants of the kingdom, while the centaurs beat back any remaining dark forces.

Leo and Talia swept down into the throne room as the rest of the castle woke, as the thorns rolled away, as the dawn broke over the flagstones. Several other fairies arrived to speed up the process, smiling and laughing at them as they glided down the stairs.

Talia broke away from him as her parents rose from their slumber, tumbling into their arms before they were even upright and sobbing profusely. How many years had it been, Leo had asked her once? She had told him she did not know. Not a hundred. But far too many, nonetheless.

"Briar, darling!" her mother wept. "Why so many tears?"

"It's a long story," she sniffed, and then glanced back at Leo. "This is Prince Leopold of Germaine," she said. "He's the one who rescued me. We already know each other and he... he is... well, words don't really describe it, Mama. But we already know each other and I love him beyond all rhyme and reason."

Eleanora glanced back at Leo, smiling through her confusion. "But... but how, dearest?"

"It's a long story," said Leo, bowing. "And we shall tell it to you. It is a pleasure to finally meet you, Your Majesties."

The king rose steadily to his feet, returning Leo's bow before clutching his arm in a firm handshake. "A pleasure to meet you, Prince Leopold. A thousand thank yous for freeing my daughter."

"Oh, she did most of it herself."

The king frowned.

"I did say it was a long story."

"Your Majesties," said a guard, appearing beside them, "there's a party of knights at the gate. Should we let them in? They bear the crest of Germaine."

"Germaine?" Leo knitted his brows. "How could they possibly–"

"Let them in!" insisted the king. "And quickly."

The doors swung open, and in walked a broad-shouldered, dark-haired man, flanked by several weary-looking knights and a surprisingly bright-eyed old man.

Leo stared in disbelief. "Wil?"

The man at the head of the party laughed, and raced forward to clutch his brother. "Leo! Thank the stars. We feared the worst when we reached the kingdom and found it infested. But you seemed to have managed splendidly." He bowed to Talia. "You must be the princess. Not too disappointed in my brother, I hope?"

Talia's smile was radiant. "We shall save disappointment for the years ahead of us."

Wilheim roared. "She has a sense of humour, at least. Maybe she'll be your match after all, Leo."

Leo twined his fingers into Talia's. "Oh, she is."

Wilheim raised an eyebrow. "Am I missing something?"

"Yes, quite a lot, but... what are you doing here?"

"Ingrid and I had a long discussion, and we decided we couldn't let you brave the forest alone, so I set off after you... only to find you'd *dismissed your knights* and gone into the forest completely unescorted."

"Well, not completely..." he said, scratching the back of his neck. "I had a guide... but... how did you get through the woods without one?"

"We had one," said Wilheim. "A very, very slow one..." He gestured to the frail old man, standing behind the knights. Leo recognised him immediately as the one who escorted him to the edge of the forest. His eyes, however, fell past Leo, to the princess standing beside him.

"Hello, Talia," he said. "It has been a very long time indeed."

Talia narrowed her eyes. "Do… do I know you, sir?"

The man laughed. "'Sir'. Sir! Ha. Looks like I finally grew up after all. I can hardly blame you for not recognising me like this. I barely recognise you, either. You look far too clean and proper."

Talia crept towards him, her gaze tightly fixed, as though trying to unravel the layers of wrinkles lining his face. When she met his golden eyes, she gasped.

"It cannot be…" she said. "Ezio?"

With a second startled shriek, she threw her arms around him, screaming and weeping that it couldn't be him.

"You should be dead," she wept. "You should be really, really dead by now!"

"My wish," he said. "I lied. I did not just wish for your happiness. I wished to *see* you happy. My punishment was watching almost everyone go before me."

"Almost?"

"I have a fair brood of great-grandchildren still keeping me busy. Although now I have seen you smile, I suppose my days are numbered…"

"No," said Talia, wiping the smile from her face, "I am miserable, I promise you. I have never been so unhappy."

"I'll try not to be too offended," said Leo, grinning. He bowed to the old man. "Thank you," he said, "for guiding me to her."

"I had a good feeling about you," he returned, winking.

"I can't believe it," Talia said. "You've been alive, all this time, and you never came to see me?"

"I wasn't sure you wanted me to."

"You never grew out of being a fool, I see." She clasped his face, pinching his weathered cheeks. "Never mind. You're here now."

"I'm sorry," said the king, appearing behind them, "but what on earth is going on?"

"It's a long story," they all replied.

The day of Briar-Rose's one-hundred-and-seventeenth birthday was almost as bizarre as her christening. It was filled with fairies, of courtiers young and old, of perfect strangers from far away. There was little talk of curses, but a great deal of strange tales. Talia – or Briar, as she was known to the court – softened the story of her exploits in the woods significantly for her parents, only informing them that she had escorted parties through as an ethereal guide, making it seem like her adventures had been short and minimal. She did not tell them how long she had been gone, let them believe she had been sleeping for most of it. Leo realised that he would be the only one to know the full truth of it, the weight she'd borne for so many years.

The fairies filled in some more of the gaps. At one point, while Ariel was telling a particularly fanciful story about alluding ogres, Wilheim turned to Margaret.

"Forgive me, fairy, but I cannot help but feel we've met before."

"We fairies have a similar aura…"

"I swear, you look just like the one who told father to send one of his sons to the forests."

Margaret got up. "Oh really? Fancy that." She gave him a curt nod and swept away to whisper something in Ariel's ear.

Wilheim turned back to Leo. "Strange. You know who else she reminds me of?"

"Who?"

"Madame Syra. Our old tutor. Remember her?"

Leo shrugged, his gaze falling once more to Talia, her head resting in her mother's lap. With the thought of the future turning his insides to hot jelly, he had no desire to dwell in the past.

The day was both endless and over in a flash. Before long, Leo was escorted to the guest chambers for a much-needed bath. The castle fell into slumber once again.

But Leo could not sleep. Perhaps it was a result of the whatever magic Margaret had bestowed on him, but he was beyond restless and the castle was too comfortable and unnaturally quiet after so long in the forest.

He gave up, and went to the window. The ivy was thick enough to climb, and Talia's balcony was not far above. He could see her, gazing out at the stars, her eyes as alert as his.

He began his ascent. Talia caught on quickly, beaming down at him.

"What are you doing?"

"I am climbing up to your tower, what does it look like?"

"We have doors, you know."

"Yes, tightly guarded ones."

He heaved himself up onto the balcony, tripping over the stone wall and sprawling flat on his face. Talia laughed, stooping over him as he rolled over.

"Hey," he said.

"Hey," she responded, slipping her hands against his cheeks and kissing him.

He slid his arms around her. "I couldn't wait until tomorrow to see you," he said. "I hope you don't mind me dropping in..."

"Not at all. I couldn't sleep. Spent too long doing that." She gazed at him. "I'm still afraid this is all a dream."

"Anything I can do to convince you it's not?"

"Kiss me again."

Leo grinned. "If you insist."

She rippled beneath him, warm and alive. "Please keep going," she whispered. "I had no idea anything could feel this way. I feel like butter, and you're the hot knife..."

"Now you know how *I've* felt this past week..." He ran a hand down her cheek. "How much I've burned with wanting you."

Talia grinned. "I apologise for tormenting you so..."

He kissed her neck, his lips dropping to her exposed skin. "You might have been the one asleep all these years, but I swear I've spent my whole life dreaming of you."

Talia's cheeks reddened. "That was poetic."

"Finally, a use for my expensive education. A way to flatter my future bride."

"Future bride?" Talia raised an eyebrow.

"Well, I, er, that was... isn't that..."

"That is supposed to be the deal, yes. But I still do not recall being asked."

Leo blinked. "You... you want me to ask?"

"Do you want to marry me?" she asked. "And not just because some law demands it? Do you want to marry me, for who I am?"

"Yes," he said softly. "More than anything."

She moved closer to him. "Then ask me what I want."

"Talia," he breathed, winding his body closer to hers, "do you want to marry me?"

"Yes," she said. "I do."

Leo fancied his cheeks were going to ache from so much smiling soon. "Good," he said. "Now that that's settled..."

He kissed her, but she was getting up, tugging him towards her room, her hands pulling his shirt over his head. She sat him down on the bed, slid onto his lap, and traced each one of the scars left silvery by Margaret's magic.

"Do they hurt?" she asked.

He let his fingers glide along her collarbones, placing gentle kisses beneath both of them. "Not anymore," he said.

Talia bent back her head as his lips brushed against her skin. A sigh, a soft moan, trickled out of her.

"A hundred years of feeling nothing," she said, "and I wake up to *this*."

He smiled at her. "Worth waiting for?"

Talia pulled him back, grabbing onto his hair. "Leo," she whispered, "I love you."

"I know," he said. "I love you too. And I don't want to spend another night anywhere but in your arms."

"We'll fight," she said. "We're bound to fight."

He lay her back against the pillows, and pressed his forehead to hers. "It's just as well we're so well matched, then. I reckon I could take you."

Talia didn't respond. She was far too busy kissing him.

Epilogue

With matters of state to attend to, and an entire kingdom to reintegrate into the world, the wedding took longer than either of them would have liked to arrange. The weeks and months that followed were strange, as the two of them were forced to share themselves with others, and Talia, despite her longing to be with Leo, needed time to let her parents get to know her all over again, and to adjust to the wonderful and painful world of sensation.

"Have I mentioned how inconvenient falling is?" she said to him one day. "Everything is so *heavy.*"

There was not a day they did not see each other, and not a night they did not spend secretly in each other's arms, even when Talia travelled with him to Germaine for Wilheim and Ingrid's wedding. The two women got on far, far too well, and Leo joked that perhaps the family couldn't handle both women married into it and he better rethink the entire thing.

The remark earned him a double scowl, and his mother gave him the smallest slice of cake at the feast.

Just before their own wedding, Ezio presented Talia with a gift; a floating white gown of silk and gossamer, embroidered with leaves and flowers and a long, swooping train. A dress from the forest.

"It's perfect," she said. "I never knew you had such a talent for designing dresses."

"I do not," he said. "Lorenzo did."

Talia stared at him, awaiting an explanation.

"I ran into him a few times over the years. We... we both thought about going back, you know. But by this time I had a family, responsibilities... Lorenzo and Lance... they never stopped travelling. I think they saw the entire world together."

"They were happy then?"

"Blissful."

Talia brushed a few stray tears from her cheeks.

"Lorenzo said he had no doubt whatsoever that one day, your prince would come. And he was right." Ezio smiled. "Was he worth waiting for?"

"Yes," said Talia. "He was worth everything."

His grin broadened, breaking through the lines on his weathered face. He looked, for a moment, like the boy she once knew.

"Was your wife?"

"Yes," he said. "She was. And worth all the years without her, too, which is a harder thing to endure." He rose from his seat, and placed a gnarled hand against her shoulder. "I look forward to seeing her again."

Ezio returned to the village shortly after the wedding. They wrote to each other often, but they only saw each other once again, at the christening of her first child. He grumbled that 'Ezio' was a silly name for a prince, told her that she and Leo had better have enough to honour the rest of their friends, while trying not to look too thrilled.

He passed away a few months later, surrounded by his family, never living long enough to meet the rest of their children (Antonia, Benedict, Rogan and Lorena) or see the den restored to its former glory, as a rest for weary travellers or an escape for Leo and Talia, whenever they longed for one.

Before they took the throne, they travelled a great deal, usually in disguise, singing ballads in bawdy taverns and telling tales of heroic deeds, including one of the 'Great Lady Knight, Aveline' that eventually reached the ears of its inspiration, now an old woman who was flattered by the depiction and only too pleased to hear the conclusion of Talia's tale.

Their years together were long and happy, and although the magic faded from the forests, and even the good fairies seemed to vanish as the years went by, Talia and Leo would call their lives together enchanted. So little happened to mar their happiness as their lives continued, even when one of their many grandchildren – named in honour of his grandfather – set off on a quest for adventure and was never seen again. Word reached them that he had found love amongst the fairies, and even though his family missed him, Leo and Talia knew that true love was worth any cost.

"I waited a hundred years for you," Talia would tell him, "and almost all of the time, I still think you were worth it."

Leo would grin, having long forgotten the true horrors of the forest, and told her she was worth the trouble, "most of the time."

And so they lived happily, to the end of their very long days.

The End

If you enjoyed this story, please consider leaving a review, however short, on Amazon/ Goodreads. Reviews are vital to indie authors!

Regardless, I hope you having enjoyed this journey through the woods, and wish you good fortune wherever your own travels take you.

Out Now:

Of Snow and Scarlet: A Little Red Riding Hood Retelling

Acknowledgements

Huge thank you to my betas: Lydia, Elisha, Becky, Lucy, Cat and Elizabeth. Thank you for reading this work first, loving it, and for every comment-- no matter how nit-picky! This book would not be the same without you.

As always, thanks to my sister, for painstakingly listening to every single plot point and providing ever-insightful feedback.

A massive thank you to my editor, Jess, whose eye for detail never ceases to amaze me, and who also loves my work. Sorry not sorry for making you cry.

And, of course, thank you to my readers. I hope to entertain you with many more retellings packed with witty banter, fierce heroines, and gentle love interests, for many years to come!

Other Books by this Author:

The Phoenix Project Trilogy
Book I: Flight
Book II: Resurrection
Book III: Rebirth

In the "Fey Collection" series:
The Rose and the Thorn: A Beauty and the Beast Retelling
A Tale of Ice and Ash: A Snow White Retelling
A Song of Sea and Shore: A Little Mermaid Retelling
Heart of Thorns: A Beauty and the Beast Retelling
Of Snow and Scarlet: A Little Red Riding Hood Retelling

Standalones:
The Barnyard Princess: A Frog Prince Retelling

In the "Faeries of the Underworld" Duology:
Thief of Spring: A Hades and Persephone
Retelling (Part One)
Queen of Night: A Hades and Persephone
Retelling (Part Two)
Heart of Hades: A collection of bonus
scenes (subscribers only)

Coming Soon:
A Rose of Steel: Book One of the
Mechanical Kingdoms Quartet

Afterword

Why are we drawn to fairytale retellings?

I *love f*airytales. I always have. From the simple children's fables to the dark and twisty versions by Angela Carter, I have always had an intense fascination with them. I often find myself longing for a "good" full-length retelling. For me, I think the answer is quite simple: retold fairytales offer that perfect blend between comfort and curiosity. We feel we know what we are getting with fairytales. We can curl up with characters we feel we know, plots that are pleasantly predictable, but also offer us just that right amount of fresh and new. We don't know how *this* retelling will go. We don't know what surprises lie in store. But we are usually quite comfortable knowing that everything will turn out all right in the end.

For me, whenever I retell a fairy tale, there needs to be something wrong with the original, or some element I've not seen in another adaptation. For my Beauty and the Beast retelling, I had to remove the forced imprisonment. For Sleeping Beauty, I had to give the princess some agency. She is the embodiment of the damsel in distress, awaiting her rescue. She has literally no say in any of the things that happen to her. That *had* to go, and so a good portion of Kingdom of Thorns shows Briar actively fighting against her fate.

In a first for me, the rest of the story is told from the perspective of the prince. In the original tale, he literally walks right up to the castle on the day the curse ends and does absolutely nothing to prove his worthiness. Leo, by contrast, has to face several horrors to prove to both himself and us that he is worthy, and a prince worth waiting for.

Sleeping Beauty was not my first choice for a retelling. I was actually working on a version of the Little Mermaid when I got the idea. I'd always liked the *feel* of the tale, and the aesthetic of a beautiful sleeping maiden. But therein lies the problem with the tale; the eponymous protagonist has no agency in her own story and spends most of it unconscious!

The only way to retell it would be if somehow that wasn't the case. The filmed version of "fairytale theatre" from the 1980s goes back and tells a longer version of how the curse came to be cast, but still strips Briar of any autonomy. The oldest version of the tale by Giambattista Bastile "Sun, Moon and Talia" has a 2nd half of the story– with Talia travelling to the home of her "rescuer" and having to thawt his evil wife. There's a reference to that tale both in the chosen alias of the heroine and her mention of a planned sexual assault – in Basile's version, the young lord that finds Talia sleeping has sex with her, an action written as "gathering the fruits of love" but in any modern context is classed as rape. As such, this version of the story places a lot of emphasis on the idea of consent. Briar does not wake for Ezio because she doesn't want to. Is it true love that breaks the spell, or is it ultimately the fact that Talia *chooses* Leo?

That part is ultimately down to you as the reader to decide, but I hope you enjoyed this tale of free will and true love, found even in the darkest of places.

About The Author

Katherine Macdonald

Born in Redditch, England, to a solicitor and an ex-military man, one of Katherine "Kate" Macdonald's earliest memories was of watching her parents disappear behind the pages of a book and wanting to follow them. For her, books were little pocket  dimensions that could be carried about, and the safest way to have a very real adventure.

Rather than rebel during her teenage years, she spent most of them locked up in her room, furiously writing down the hundreds of stories filling her head. Her little sister Kirsty served as her primary audience, and first fan. Without her, she would never have continued to write.

After completing a BA in English and Creative Writing at Lancaster University, she moved to Exeter to train as an English teacher, and then to Kent to start her career.

It was only after surviving a year of parenthood and a full-time job on less than six hours' sleep a night that she finally gained the courage to publish her debut novel,

"The Rose and the Thorn." It's a retelling of Beauty and the Beast inspired by a dream of a girl surrounded by snow in a field of flowers.

At her heart, Macdonald is storyteller, and it is her dream to inspire others in the way that she has been inspired.

You can follow her at @KateMacAuthor, or subscribe to her website at www.katherinemacdonaldauthor.com to be notified of new releases and free review copies!

Printed in Great Britain
by Amazon

83126950R00171